Sherlockian Stories and Studies

Gayle Lange Puhl

Paperback ISBN 978-1-78705-582-7
ePub ISBN 978-1-78705-583-4
PDF ISBN 978-1-78705-584-1

Published by Orange Pip Books
335 Princess Park Manor, Royal Drive,
London, N11 3GX
www.mxpublishing.com

Cover design by Brian Belanger

Stories previously published

by Gayle Lange Puhl

"Like a Folk Tale Character" was published in "Sherlock Holmes is Like," edited by Christopher Redmond, Wildside Press, 2018.

"Colonel Warburton's Madness" was published in "The MX Book of New Sherlock Holmes

Stories Part XI: Some Untold Cases (1880-1891)," edited by David Marcum, MX Publishing, 2018.

"The Case of the Cursed Clock" was published in "The MX Book of New Sherlock Holmes Stories Part VII: Eliminate the Impossible (1880-1891)," edited by David Marcum, MX

Publishing, 2017.

"The Case of the Loud Librarians" was published in "The Grimmer Holmes," edited by Steve Mason, The Crew of the Barque Lone Star, 2018.

"The Blood-Spattered Bridge" was published in "The MX Book of New Sherlock Holmes Stories Part XX 2020 Annual (1891-1897)," edited by David Marcum, MX Publishing, 2020.

"The Case of the Persecuted Poacher" was published in "The MX Book of New Sherlock Holmes Stories Part XIV: 2019 Annual (1891-1897)," edited by David Marcum, MX Publishing, 2019.

"Bringing Holmes the Bacon at Last," was published in "The Serpentine Muse," edited by Susan Z. Diamond and Marilynne McKay, Fall 2013.

"My Correspondence with Vincent Starrett" was published in "The Serpentine Muse," edited by Susan Z. Diamond and Marilynne McKay, Fall 2010.

Royalties from "The MX New Sherlock Holmes Stories" anthology go to the support of the Stepping Stones School, Hindhead, Surrey, U.K.

This collection of my writings is dedicated to my wonderful great-grandchildren.

Table of Contents

Sherlock Holmes Is Like A Folk Tale Character

Through a series of circumstances that surprise even me, I appear to have become an "expert" on Sherlock Holmes and folk tales. A Sherlockian since the mid-1960s, I decided in the late 2000s to begin writing short stories featuring Mr. Sherlock Holmes and his Boswell, Dr. Watson. Needing a template on which to build my original ideas, I chose fairy tales, nursery rhymes, adages, and folk tales.

I resolved on three major requirements: The stories would continue the original Sherlock Holmes and Dr. John Watson adventures in the correct Victorian/early Edwardian time period and with the best rendering of Dr. Watson's writing style that I could deliver; that there would be no magic (fairy dust, talking animals, mythical monsters), only logic; and that there must be a crime for Holmes to investigate.

Those rules made writing the tales interesting. How would you write the story of Cinderella with no fairy godmother? Little Red Riding Hood with no talking wolf? Jack and the Beanstalk with no magic beans?

It was fun. Over the course of jotting down my collected short stories I have, to date, managed to produce twenty-seven tales and counting. Now for this book I have been asked to compare the Great Detective Sherlock Holmes with a folk tale character.

Nursery rhymes and folk tale characters are universal. Such tales, based on stories handed down from the distant past by oral traditions, are known from Russia to Africa, from South America to Iceland, from Asia to Australia. They are supplemented by more modern children's stories, such as "Alice in Wonderland" and "Wind in the Willows." Frequently they are a child's first literature, the first beloved night-time stories offered by parents, and the first moral lessons offered to young impressionable minds.

The themes of most folk tales cover three points. Good and bad morality is first. The good is rewarded and the bad is punished. Little Red Riding Hood disobeys her mother by talking to a stranger. She is then nearly eaten by the wolf, who has gobbled up her grandmother. Her disobedience is redeemed only by the huntsman, who suddenly appears, kills the wolf and frees Red and her grandmother from his stomach. The wolf is punished by being killed by the huntsman's axe.

Each story encourages the upholding of middle-class values. Cinderella is reduced to scrubbing floors and running errands for her horrible step-sisters by her evil stepmother. But she never loses her sweetness and her belief in herself. Her fairy godmother gives her a dress, glass slippers and transportation to the ball. When she arrives it is her own noble nature that allows her to behave as a princess amid all the lights and dazzle, to carry herself with dignity and to impress the prince with her own natural abilities. Contrast that to her two social-climbing stepsisters, who vie vulgarly for the prince's attention and manage to make fools of themselves. When Cinderella is forced to leave the ball at midnight she makes no complaint about the loss of all her gifts and the coach and horses. Back home with her scrub brush, she avoids bringing wrath down on her head by not mentioning her part at the ball. That shows her intelligence. She knows that if her stepmother found out she was the mysterious woman who caught the prince's attention, she would throw Cinderella down into a dungeon or do something worse. When the prince shows up to test the women of the house to see if their feet fit the glass slipper left behind at the ball, she sees her chance. When she is finally quizzed by the prince she pulls out the one bit of incontrovertible proof, the missing mate of the original shoe.

The ugly stepsisters are married off to the butcher and the baker at the castle, and in the original story, the evil stepmother is forced to dance at Cinderella's wedding in a pair of red-hot iron shoes until she collapses and dies. The moral is that everyone has a prince out there and that fulfilment is found in marriage. That was considered a happy ending at the time.

Folk tales are fashioned to teach lessons or demonstrate values important to the culture. With Little Red Riding Hood the message is not to talk to strangers. Cinderella teaches that a sweet, kind girl will meet her Prince Charming and her oppression will end with happiness.

When comparing the Great Detective with folk tale characters there is no lack of choices. In the world of folk tales one can't cross a running stream without stumbling over a talking fish, the third son of a poor miller out to make his fortune, or a shepherdess searching for her lost sheep. The nearby dark woods are populated with dozens of helpful yet vindictive old crones, bands of evil robbers, and dogs with eyes the size of saucers. Overhead, enchanted swans fly toward distant magic castles. One is lucky not to be trampled by the hooves of mighty steeds ridden by questing princes just walking from one poor tailor shop to another.

Then there are the villains. Dragons, ogres, wicked witches with cauldrons, nasty stepmothers, and selfish kings with their own agendas to fulfil are all staples of folk tales. Every time one tries to cross a bridge there is a troll to deal with. Every fourth story has a giant or a big, bad wolf in it.

The victims can be unusual. A prince is enchanted into a frog, a beautiful mermaid trades her fins for a pair of legs, or a wooden puppet desires to be a real boy. Numerous children of both genders, lacking adult supervision, wander into all kinds of danger. Kindly grandmothers and simple townspeople can find themselves caught up in the adventures. It must be hard to breathe with a black pudding attached to one's nose, the result of a careless wish. Some aspects of folk tales are never mentioned but still exist. Crashing giants, falling from the skies, can be a real pain to clean up.

While the hero of a folk tale can vary from a meek little tailor to a simple shepherdess to a third son of the king, there are certain qualities evident in each protagonist. Here are a few.

The hero must have courage. Facing dragons in whatever form they take is not for the meek. A hero can have doubts about his abilities but his confidence must be fortified with strong doses of determination, focus, perseverance and dedication.

The hero must have loyalty. The story of Jack and the Beanstalk had a hero who was a thief and a rogue, but his ultimate goal was to make a better life for his hard-working, widowed mother.

The hero must have honesty. If he made a promise to bring a fresh rose to the princess in the middle of winter, that rose must be obtained. A vow carelessly given or ignored is the surest way to find oneself chained and forgotten in a dungeon or turned to stone on the terrace of an evil sorcerer.

Last but not least, a hero must be responsible. Undertaking a quest only to be distracted by the first pretty wench or keg of beer at the nearest tavern is a blueprint for failure. That lack of character explains why so many first and second sons never return to claim the kingdom/mill/farm/fortune/beautiful princess while the third underrated son succeeds.

Sherlock Holmes bears all those fine qualities. He has courage, with which he faces Professor Moriarty alone at the Falls of Reichenbach in "The Final Problem".

He has loyalty, seeing the trap ahead but allowing the Professor's trick to separate himself from Watson in order to protect the doctor.

He has honesty, telling Watson when they discover Moriarty has eluded the police that the doctor should abandon Holmes at once and return to England. "...(Y)ou will find me a dangerous companion now, Watson. This man's occupation is gone. He is lost if he returns to London. If I read his character right he will devote his whole energies to revenging himself upon me. He said as much in our short interview, and I fancy he meant it. I should certainly recommend you to return to your practice."

He has responsibility, admitting to Watson that "...if I could beat that man, if I could free society of him, I should feel that my own career had reached its summit, and I should be prepared to turn to some more placid line in life."

Which folk tale character, out of the hundreds available, could ever reach such heroic heights as these, to stand as the Great Detective's companion in equality?

I think it is The Third Little Pig.

The timeless story is well known. Three Little Pigs are sent out by their mother to make their way in the world. The First Little Pig builds a house of straw; the second one a house of sticks, and the third a house of bricks. He warns his brothers that a house made of bricks is the best protection against wolves. They laugh at his warning, but he still protects his brothers.

The Big Bad Wolf comes along, well-known for preying on the countryside. He is hungry and knows pigs are delicious. He tells the First Little Pig to "Open the door and let me come in or I'll huff and I'll puff and I'll blow your house in!" The First Little Pig refuses, saying "Not by the hair of my chinny-chin-chin!" The Wolf lets loose and destroys the house of straw. In some versions the First Little Pig runs to the Second Little Pig's house for safety. In many versions he doesn't make it past the Wolf.

The Wolf deals with the Second Little Pig and his house made of sticks in the same fashion. The end result is the same, with the

First and Second Little Pigs either eaten by the Wolf or rooming with their brother in the brick house.

The Third Little Pig, when confronted by the Big Bad Wolf, also refuses to surrender. The huffing and puffing do not work, however. The brick structure holds firm. The Wolf must take another tack.

Three times the wily Wolf makes appointments to meet with the Third Little Pig outside the brick house in order to ambush his prey. Each time the Third Little Pig outsmarts him and remains safe. If his brothers have escaped the Wolf earlier, they remain safe as well.

Out of frustration, the Big Bad Wolf becomes desperate. He climbs to the roof of the Third Little Pig's brick house and attempts to climb down the chimney. The Third Little Pig stokes up the fire, places a large pot of water on the flames, and when the Wolf comes tumbling down and lands in the hot water a lid is slammed down on top of the pot and the Wolf is boiled to death. The Pigs call in the neighbours and have a feast.

Like Sherlock Holmes, the Third Little Pig has courage. He faces up to the Big Bad Wolf when challenged. He is determined to outwit the Wolf after traps are set out to capture him. He never runs away.

The Third Little Pig shows loyalty to his brothers, sheltering them in some stories, revenging them in other versions.

The Third Little Pig is honest. He believes his brothers when they report the Big Bad Wolf's attacks. He admits the danger the Wolf presents to him. He doesn't try to gloss over his situation or wish it all away.

The Third Little Pig is responsible. He builds his house of bricks. He knows he cannot surrender to the Big Bad Wolf and survive. He realizes that it would not be enough to just evade its clutches. He must kill it and end the terrorizing of the neighbourhood for once and all.

There are many heroes in the folk tale world. I chose the Third Little Pig to compare to Sherlock Holmes because he fights the Big Bad Wolf not just to save his own life and the lives of his brothers but to remove a danger to the countryside. He sees the bigger picture and responds for the greater good. Sherlock Holmes, on the cliff beside the Reichenbach, does the same.

Colonel Warburton's Madness

I have written elsewhere of the fact I was twice able to bring to the attention of my friend, Mr. Sherlock Holmes, cases of interest to his extensive study of crime. One I published as "The Adventure of the Engineer's Thumb." The other I hesitated to release to the public because aspects of the story were personal to me. However, under Holmes' encouragement, I have decided to put down the facts at last, in order to clear the name of a courageous and honourable man from the dark clouds that formed about him during his last years.

My friend Sherlock Holmes was away from London on that early spring day of 1888. He had journeyed to Madrid the week before at the behest of a high government official to investigate the disappearance of certain pieces of art from the Palmatoria Muse. The thief had been seen escaping by jumping from a second-story balcony. Soon afterwards, a small fire broke out in one of the galleries. The police were baffled, so Sherlock Holmes was consulted.

Holmes had sent a wire that day that he would return the next morning. I was alone in our sitting room at 221b Baker Street when a young woman was shown up by Mrs. Hudson.

She looked up at me with bright, intelligent blue eyes. She looked to be in her late twenties, below the average height but with a determined air. She was dressed in a walking suit of dark green, with a wisp of a hat on her wavy blonde hair and a package wrapped in brown paper in her neatly gloved hands.

"Doctor Watson? Doctor John H. Watson, who served at the fatal Battle of Maiwand in Afghanistan?"

"I am. But madam, you have the advantage of me."

"I am Miss Katherine Warburton, the daughter of Colonel Jeremiah Warburton."

I ushered her in at once. "My dear, I remember your father well. Please, sit down. The last I heard of the colonel, he had retired and moved to the family home in the Lake District."

She accepted the glass of brandy I offered her from the sideboard. I never claimed to have Holmes' skills at observation and deduction, but the signs of her having been on a long railway journey were evident in the state of her clothes, her obvious fatigue and the ticket she had thrust halfway up the wrist of her left glove. At my remark, she patted the wrapped bundle beside her, and tears welled up in her eyes.

"I come on a sad errand, Doctor Watson. My father devoted his life to Her Majesty's service. He endured many hardships over the decades and never faltered from his duties. But his final posting, to lead the 66th Berkshires during the second war in Afghanistan, broke him.

"He came back to our family estate at Lake Windermere a shell of the man who had left from home leave just three years before. He didn't move into the main house, which he as head of the family was entitled to do. Instead he retreated to a small cottage on the grounds. He refused to accept visitors, withdrew from those who loved him and seldom left his quarters, as he called the tiny cottage. My father was content to continue the arrangement, begun years ago, while his brother administered the estate as he had done during the colonel's long absences.

"The entailment with which the estate had been set up long ago specified that no female could inherit the land or property that it descend to the oldest surviving son. I am given a generous allowance, but everything will eventually go to my oldest cousin. Fenton was a brilliant success at university and has since found fulfilment as headmaster of our local school.

"My father, meanwhile, settled into the life of a recluse. He seemed to tolerate my presence but still at times refused to admit me. He became more solitary. He desired no company. Often, for days and weeks at a time, he would refuse the society of a single human being. The signs of deep melancholia were obvious. This went on for years. The only time he seemed even moderately cheerful was when he spoke of you, Doctor Watson."

"Of me?" I exclaimed. "I think we met only a half-dozen times, and then only briefly before the battle."

"When your story about Mr. Sherlock Holmes came out in the Beeton's Christmas Annual in 1887, he bought a copy and read it over and over. It was the only thing he wanted to take with him and he was heart-broken when that one small kindness was denied."

"What happened to Colonel Warburton?" I asked. I remembered a stocky, bluff commanding officer with a flowing blonde moustache and a head of hair to match, his battle uniform always crisp and neatly ironed.

"His health, both physical and mental, has declined steeply during the past year. Finally, about three weeks ago, I was forced, on the advice of his doctor and my uncle, his brother, to sign the papers to have him committed to a private sanatorium in Carlisle."

I sat stunned. What a sad ending to a long and honourable career! After a minute I looked again at the young woman before me. She was watching me expectantly. There was something else she had to say.

"Miss Warburton, I cannot tell you how much your story upsets me. Is there anything I can do for you or your father?"

She picked up the paper-wrapped package. "I wish you to take his diary, Doctor. He had kept it for nearly thirty years, starting just before his marriage to my mother. He entered notes haphazardly, as his circumstances permitted. He continued his entries after his retirement to the Fortress, as our estate is named. Before his commitment he was making wild and unbelievable accusations about the people around him. I thought that you, being a doctor, could study his record of his own decline and perhaps find out why his illness changed from a deep melancholia to a violent madness that endangered his own life."

"Why don't you give his diary to his own physician?"

"That would be my Uncle Isaiah. According to the quick reading I gave the last pages, he wrote harsh things about Uncle, and I am afraid he would not be impartial to the slurs. Uncle Isaiah has been ill, and I think the knowledge of his brother's accusations would further undermine his health."

"I am sorry to hear of your uncle's troubles, Miss Warburton."

"Yes, he was diagnosed last year. The disease is terminal, and we are very upset. His older son, Fenton, has given up his own educational duties and moved into the Fortress to take some of the burden of running the estate from his shoulders. My other cousin, Farley, Fenton's brother, visits often from Durham, where he is at university. Besides, Father did enjoy your story, Doctor, and I think he would like you to have his writings."

What could I do but agree to take them? Miss Warburton refused any more help and announced she had made arrangements to return to Ambleside in Cumbria the next day. I insisted upon hailing her a cab. Then I returned to our rooms and contemplated the paper-wrapped bundle.

I reflected for a time upon Colonel Warburton's circumstances, the war and upon the concerned daughter who had left his diary with me. Finally, I drew the lamp closer and unwrapped the package.

Sherlock Holmes returned the next day. I had left the loose-leaf diary on my desk. As Holmes roamed about the room, touching items and looking through the windows into Baker Street, he spied the manuscript. He picked up the diary and flipped through the pages with a lazy curiosity.

"This is not your handwriting, Watson," he drawled.

"No," I replied. I told him the story of the diary and the daughter of my former commanding officer. "I have read it. As a military document it is interesting, spanning a recent period of time in British history. However, I found the most fascinating part to be what the colonel experienced after his retirement."

Holmes took the manuscript and settled into his armchair. He thumbed through the pages, giving particular attention to the last twenty. Those pages covered the last years before Col. Warburton's confinement. He read those carefully as I lit my cigar and rang Mrs. Hudson for tea.

It was quite twenty minutes until Mrs. Hudson brought up the tea and Holmes spoke. He accepted a cup from me, and I nodded to the papers now stacked on the table beside him.

"What do you make of it, Holmes?' I asked.

"As a history of a man's mental decline, it has some interest, but I am more drawn to the crime it describes."

"Crime? I saw no sign of crime. The poor man relates from his perspective a slow slide into madness but there was no sign of crime."

"On the contrary, Watson, there is ample evidence of a crime, and a dastardly one at that."

"Please explain."

"You know I have little interest in military matters. Therefore I only skimmed through the accounts of his exploits on the battlefield. My attention was piqued by his description of Maiwand and its aftermath. Although the causes of the battle were later firmly established by a military investigation, Colonel Warburton blamed himself. Guilt crippled him, and shortly after the results became known, he retired. He retreated to the family estate in the Lake District. He refused to move into the Fortress, the main house. Instead he took over an old gamekeeper's cottage and shut himself away from the world."

"Yes, his melancholia was well-developed by then. His symptoms were typical, craving solitude, showing poor eating habits, exhibiting self-neglect, and lack of interest in things he normally would have enjoyed. Then he believed that his mind cracked after the sightings began."

"The sightings?" Holmes reached for his pipe.

"Yes, the delusions. He heard voices, saw spirits in the night, and experienced sleep walking. All signs of a deep mental upset."

"I think the clues he left in his diary do not support the idea that he suffered from delusions, Watson. I think he really experienced all those effects. I think someone close to him used his circumstances to drive him mad."

"That would be diabolical! If true, how can it be proven? To what purpose would such a thing be done?"

"Oh, the motive is obvious. The question is who and how, not why. Persecution like this cannot be allowed to go unpunished. We must go to the Fortress, Watson; consult with Miss Katherine Warburton and investigate. Wire the young lady in care of the stationmaster in Ambleside, tell her we are coming behind her and pack a bag. There is a train in two hours."

As the train pulled out of London and headed north, Holmes spent his time reading the Colonel's diary in more detail. I was happy to be on a case with Sherlock Holmes again. Life had been too quiet while my friend was gone. Now he had asked me to join him to solve the case of Colonel Warburton's madness, and I felt that frisson of excitement that marked our unique relationship rush through my body again.

Half-way through the trip Holmes set aside the diary and began to discourse on the history of British railways, Lake District cuisine and the district's influence on literature.

At Ambleside, up the side of a mountain, we were met by Miss Warburton in a hired trap. The air was crisp with a bite to it, and I was glad we had brought our overcoats. We wound through the pretty little town with its narrow, twisting streets until we alighted at the Lake Windermere pier. There the three of us clambered into a dory manned by a sullen, bearded man in rough fisherman clothing. He took our bags and stowed them away. The man must have had his orders previous to our arrival for he cast off at once and began rowing in a southerly direction.

"There is a road around the lake to the Fortress," said Miss Warburton. "But it is long and one must make allowance for the terrain. I was about to leave in a trap when the postmaster caught me with your telegram. I arranged this because going by boat is much more direct."

Holmes pulled out his pipe and filled it with tobacco from his pouch. He blinked at the sight of the cold lake surface that stretched out for miles before us and the evergreen and oak forest that stood on either side. Hours had passed since we had left London and the sky was darkening. The sun had set before our arrival and twilight was upon us.

Miss Warburton introduced the fisherman as Mr. Bonner, a worker on the Warburton estate. He grunted and stuck to his oars. I asked him how long it would take to reach the Fortress. "It'll take as long as it'll take," he muttered, giving a sharp glance at my city shoes and soft hands. Sherlock Holmes shifted his feet and let his attention fall on Mr. Bonner.

"We are fortunate, Watson, to be under the care of Mr. Bonner, an experienced sailor and former member of the crew of the whaler Bailey's Hope out of Plymouth. I dare say that if we were suddenly attacked by a blessing of narwhals Mr. Bonner would know how to handle them."

Bonner never stopped rowing, but his bearded face turned to my friend and he frowned. "How'd you ken that, Mister? 'Tis true, every word, but I swear I never saw you before in my life, nor your friend, either."

Holmes chuckled. He would never admit it, but he loved dazzling people with his observational techniques. "The foul weather gear you are wearing is heavy duty and designed for Arctic climes. The coat, hat, gloves and boots are necessary for a whaling excursion but very expensive for such berths as the Lake District offers. They are years old, a part of your original ship's kit. The name of the ship is tattooed on your left wrist, which was visible when you extended your hand to take our baggage. As to the narwhals, that earring hanging from your left ear is crafted from a bit of narwhal ivory. Did you carve it yourself, as some sailors do whilst on long voyages?"

Bonner's jaw had slowly dropped as he listened to Holmes, but as the question hung in the air, he snapped it shut and bent again to his rowing. Holmes waited with an amicable air for the man's response, but nothing more was forthcoming.

Sherlock Holmes asked Miss Warburton about the occupants of the Fortress. Beside her uncle and his wife, their sons, Fenton and Farley, had apartments in the big house. Farley was about to take his diploma in engineering at Durham University. There were maids, a kitchen staff, a butler named Morell and several men employed as gardeners and stable workers. It sounded like a large establishment. Miss Warburton admitted that her father had inherited the estate from a rich great-grandfather, who had secured the property in the late 1700s. The Fortress and the 2,000 acres that came with it had been in the family for generations.

Jeramiah Warburton had loved the military since he was a child. He enlisted in the Horse Guards in his twenties and after he became the family patriarch he had seen his brother through medical school, used his money to advance in the Army and married late to Miss Katherine Murphy of the Sligo Murphys. She had died young when her husband was stationed abroad and our client had been raised by her aunt and a succession of governesses.

After nearly an hour our dory approached a pier that extended out from a rocky point crowned with the faded grey stones that supported the Warburton Fortress. Bonner slipped the boat into a covered boathouse and secured the lines. A winding staircase took us up to a path that led to the main house. In the dark of the evening we could pick out the rough limestone walls glowing at the edges of windows lit by the gleam of oil lamps.

Holmes stopped suddenly and turned to Miss Warburton. "Who has had access to your father's cottage since he was removed to the asylum?" She looked at him in wonder. "Why, no one, Mr. Holmes. I locked the door myself, and I have the only key."

"So the cottage is secure?"

"Quite."

Holmes nodded and proceeded to the front door. We were greeted there by the butler, Morell, a silent man who handed off our hats and coats to an equally silent maid. We were greeted in the hall by Dr. Warburton, a stocky yet imposing man with slicked back yellow hair, and his short, round wife. I viewed Dr. Warburton with interest. He leaned on a stick and was too thin, with yellowish, papery skin. It was clear to my trained medical eye that he was well into the final stage of his illness and did not have many months left.

"Katherine, we have been worried about you. How could you go down to London without telling your aunt and me?"

"I left you a note, Uncle Isaiah."

"Highly irregular, my dear. Are these the gentlemen you mentioned you were going to consult?"

"Yes. This is Dr. John H. Watson and his friend Mr. Sherlock Holmes. This is my uncle, Dr. Isaiah Warburton, and my Aunt Susan."

We nodded to the pair, neither of whom extended a hand. Our bags were dispatched to our rooms and, over a cup of tea in the library, Miss Warburton explained that we had accompanied her to the Fortress to examine Colonel Warburton's effects in order to form a theory as to why he became mad.

Dr. Warburton and his wife exchanged a glance. "I know you have been very upset lately, dear Katherine," cooed Mrs. Warburton, "but do you think this course is wise? Dear Jeramiah has been in his new home for nearly a month now, and he seems to be content."

"That place may be the best thing for him but I want to know why he became ill," said our client. "Do not interfere, please, Aunt.

What do you suggest as our first move, Mr. Holmes?"

"The day is nearly spent and we have had a long trip. Let us repair to our rooms and rest. A little sustenance on a tray for each of us would be welcome, since it is past the dinner hour. Could that be arranged, Miss Warburton?"

The daughter of Colonel Warburton nodded. Her aunt, nominal mistress of the Fortress, tightened her lips, but rang the bell. When the butler appeared, Mrs. Warburton gave orders and then her husband escorted us to the curving staircase that led upstairs. Miss Warburton went to her apartment, while Holmes and I were taken to a suite of three rooms on the same floor.

The Warburton mansion was shaped like the letter U, two stories high, with the centre block housing the main rooms and the wings containing several three or four-room suites. Ours consisted of two small bedrooms and a sitting room. The sitting room windows looked over a view of the lake, the water barely visible as the moon rose behind the building.

A maid appeared first, lighting the fires and turning down the narrow beds. Trays of food soon appeared. Mrs. Warburton may have had to obey the requests of the daughter of the house but apparently she did not feel she had to extend the resources of the house to do so. Thin cold sandwiches were good enough for her uninvited guests, along with pickles and more tea. Sherlock Holmes surveyed the spread and laughed.

"Eat hearty, my friend," he chuckled. "If this is what we get for dinner, I cannot predict what our hosts might offer for breakfast. As for me, I am more interested in what is in Col. Warburton's diary than in food."

As I ate what was before me, Holmes sat on the floor and divided up the pages of the manuscript. He set the main stack to one side and spread several pages out in a semi-circle before him. After the sandwiches were gone, I joined him. He took up the first page on his left.

"Here we have mention of the first time he heard a voice. It happened five months ago, during Christmas month. He was alone in his bedroom. He wrote that the voice was hollow and repeated the words 'You know what you did. You know what you did.' He searched the room and found nothing. He then went from room to room and discovered that there was no explanation for the voice. He dismissed it as some kind of flashback from the battle and went to sleep.

"That might have been it but he heard the voice repeat those words twice during the next twenty-four hours, and frequently over the next months, always at night or in the middle of the night. He began to fixate on the words, wondering which of his many faults were being highlighted. He became anxious. He began sitting up late, waiting for the mysterious voice. It was one night while he sat looking out the sitting room window into the darkness that he first saw the floating figure.

"Yes. He was deep into the clutches of his delusions."

Sherlock Holmes picked up another page from the floor. "He saw a white, flapping figure moving under the trees between his cottage and the cliff. There was a waning moon and he saw it through the branches. Col. Warburton described the figure as 'luminous and grey.' It came from the north and vanished into the trees on the south. Soon after it disappeared, he heard the voice again, saying 'You know what you did.' He slammed the shutters shut and hid under his bedclothes until dawn. He didn't sleep all night.

"He got little sleep, according to his diary, after that. The image kept appearing, irregularly, for the next three months. Frequently, the voice was also heard. Sometimes it came soon after the Colonel sighted the white figure. He began to fear that his mind was going. He didn't dare tell his daughter. He thought she would mention it to his brother, and Isaiah would seek to put him away if he thought the Colonel were crazy.

"He wrote that Isaiah was jealous of him because he was the first-born. He believed his brother was plotting against him and that he would snatch the first opportunity given to "depose" him. He knew Isaiah was ill but wouldn't admit to himself how badly off he was."

"Paranoia can be a symptom of melancholia," I remarked.

"He also didn't want to worry his daughter. He loved her very much. He began to have suicidal thoughts." Holmes picked up another piece of paper. "He began to sleep more. He would wake up in places other than his bedroom. Once in the kitchen, once in the front hall. The culmination of these 'sleep walking' episodes came when he found himself in the woods above the cliff outside his cottage. There was a storm that night, and he came to his senses soaking wet and covered with leaves and twigs. He made it back to his rooms without anyone seeing him, but the incident frightened him.

"Finally he started to hide the kitchen knives all over the cottage. Miss Warburton noticed and quietly took them away. She found it increasingly difficult to hide her worries from her father. He could tell that from her behaviour. Finally, one night, he saw the white figure from the window while she was there. He crashed through the glass after it. She screamed for help, and Bonner and Morell chased after him. They caught him on the edge of the cliff and dragged him back to the cottage. He made his last entries in the diary that night under guard. The next day his daughter, on her uncle's advice, signed the papers that put him in the asylum."

I shook my head. "A sad, sad case. He once was an honourable officer, a credit to his regiment. The breakdown of a mind is a terrible thing."

Holmes gathered up the papers and got to his feet. "I think we have done everything we can do tonight, Watson. Tomorrow we shall examine the scene of the crime."

The scene of the crime? I was not convinced there had been a crime. As I lay in my bed that night, I gazed out the window and watched the half-moon suspended in the black sky above. I remembered my old commanding officer, his bright blue eyes snapping in amusement at the banter at the evening mess and the way he sat on his horse as he reviewed the troops. Finally I rose and drew the curtains to shut out the moon. Only then could I sleep.

The next morning began with a bright sunrise. Holmes roused me out and, fuelled by only a cup of coffee, we joined Miss Warburton on the side terrace. The Colonel's cottage was situated only 400 feet away, behind some outbuildings and a line of low shrubs. It was a one-story red brick building with a slate roof. When we stood on its tiny front porch, we could see the line of trees that stood between the cottage and the shore cliff on the left.

Miss Warburton produced a key and unlocked the front door. Before us was a narrow hallway. A row of hooks held a coat and a hat, suitable for colder weather, on our left. Beyond that was an open set of pocket doors that led to a small sitting room, holding a number of books. A cast-iron fireplace stood to the right of the door. An overstuffed high-backed winged armchair was positioned by the window on the far wall. It offered a clear view of the aforementioned line of trees that led up to the cliff's edge. The walls held shelves of books covering the dull dove grey wallpaper. There was a wooden straight chair and two small tables bearing oil lamps. A faded blue rug took pride of place on the wooden floor. The front window looked over the path we had used to approach the house. Thick brick-red curtains hung at every window of the cottage.

To the right of the hallway was another room of the same size, also equipped with pocket doors, set up as a Spartan bedroom. It had a matching fireplace to the left of the entrance and contained little besides an iron bedstead, a chest of drawers, a small rug and a battered military foot locker. The wallpaper in this room was a muted brown. A wash stand stood by the window on the right. That window looked toward the shrubs and sheds that separated the gamekeeper's cottage from the main house. The most notable item in the room was an odd-looking handcrafted Afghan rifle, most likely taken as a souvenir, that hung over the bedroom's front window. Afghan tribesmen were famous for the hand-forged rifles they created in the hills to fight their enemies. Beneath it was placed the foot locker. "Col. J. Warburton" was stencilled on the lid.

In the back were domestic offices, including a modest kitchen, pantries, a coal bin and a back door that led to a walled kitchen garden. It was complete with a garden shed and a pair of apple trees set against the back stone wall.

Holmes lost no time. Pulling out his magnifying glass, he began to examine the contents of the cottage. He took the bedroom first. I kept Miss Warburton out of his way as he systematically covered every item the room contained. She was fascinated to see him at work, opening drawers, examining bedclothes, crawling along the floor into the corners, lifting the lid of Col. Warburton's foot locker and poking about in the contents. He examined the fireplace, looked under the drugget that covered the centre of the room, and even peered through his lens at every inch of the brown wallpaper. He spent extra time on the wall against which the headboard of the bed was placed. I could see no reason why the paper there drew his attention. Finally he left the bedroom and moved on to the sitting-room.

Again he was very thorough. He searched that room thoroughly, opening each book from the many on the shelves, again lifting the rug, poking his long fingers into the armchair's stuffing, and even checking the levels on the oil lamps. Again he paid particular attention to the wallpaper of the room. At one point he picked up a volume from the table closest to the armchair and handed it to me. It was the copy of the 1887 Beeton's Christmas Annual that Miss Warburton had mentioned as her father's favourite reading material.

I cannot describe the feelings that washed over me as I gazed on the cover of my feeble effort to tell of my friend's extraordinary powers of observation and deduction. We had had many adventures together since that first one. Some had gone well and others had ended in stalemate or failure. Yet the case I had titled "A Study in Scarlet" still held a special place in my heart.

To think that my poor attempt at storytelling had comforted my old commanding officer! I tried to imagine him in his chair, holding the little volume and turning the pages as he read it again for the nth time. My heart grew warm as I thought of the old man, beset with fears for his own sanity, losing his worries by following our cab to 3 Lauritson Gardens, or trekking over the wild landscape of the American West in words that I had written down.

Sherlock Holmes had moved away from the armchair to check out more shelves of books. I laid the copy of "Beeton's Christmas Annual" back on the little table with a humble heart. An author is always gratified to hear that his readers think highly of his efforts. In this case I felt unworthy. I moved away from the armchair and went out to the hall, where I paced up and down until Holmes had finished his labours in the sitting-room and moved on to the back of the house.

Here he was no less thorough in his investigation. Holmes peered into the pots and pans stored on the kitchen shelves, sifted through the stove's ashes, tapped the white-washed walls, turned over every lump of coal in the bin and even used his magnifying lens to examine the cracks between the flagstones that formed the floor.

Finally he opened the back door and walked outside. There he briefly searched the little garden shed, paced along the stone walls of the kitchen garden and then circled the cottage. That last manoeuvre took a long time, as he poked and pried at what seemed every exterior brick within his reach.

I was used to his methods, but Miss Warburton grew weary as time passed. I urged her to re-enter the house while I made her some tea. By the time Holmes walked into the sitting room, she was ensconced in her father's armchair with an empty teacup at her side. Holmes brushed off my offer of refreshment for him.

"Perhaps you would like to stay here, Miss Warburton, while Dr. Watson and I continue our investigation," said he. "My next step is to examine the trees that stand between this cottage and the cliff."

"Oh, no, Mr. Holmes," she said brightly, rising to her feet. "Dr. Watson's tea has quite revived me. I am eager to continue."

The three of us crossed the grass and entered the little grove of oaks and beeches. I noticed nothing unusual. Holmes strode along, hands slapping the trunks, shoes shuffling through the grasses, with his eyes darting everywhere, to the left, the right and particularly up at the canopy. At one point he even shinnied up a bole and crept out on a limb to look at something on a budding set of branches that only his eye had seen. Miss Warburton and I remained below, craning our necks and watching as he scrambled from one tree to the next for several minutes. When he dropped to the ground and turned to us he pulled out a handkerchief and wiped his hands.

"This has been a most interesting and fruitful exercise. I think the next step should be a visit with your father."

Miss Warburton looked surprised. She obviously had a number of questions to ask but she had learned by now that it was futile to ask questions of Sherlock Holmes in the midst of his investigation.

We walked back to the Fortress. As we entered the front hall, we were met by Dr. Warburton, his wife, and two young men, obviously also of Warburton stock. The men were putting on their overcoats as the butler, Morell, stood by with an armful of hats and scarves.

"Katherine, where have you been?" asked the older of the two men. Miss Warburton murmured introductions to her cousins, Fenton and Farley Warburton, the doctor's sons. "We were about to go out and find you. There has been most upsetting news from the asylum. Uncle Jeremiah has escaped!"

"Escaped!" exclaimed our client. She went pale to the lips and dropped into a hall chair.

"A telegram was received an hour ago from the institution's superintendent, Mr. Belloes," said Isaiah Warburton. "Jeremiah was discovered missing right before breakfast this morning. The attendants believe he ran away sometime after lights out last night."

"Where is this institution located?" asked Sherlock Holmes.

"In Carlisle to the north," answered the doctor.

"Then he has had plenty of time to make his way back to the Fortress," mused my friend.

Miss Warburton raised her stricken face to all of us. "Why do you think he would come here?" she asked.

"Because here is his home," I answered gently.

"What are we to do? He must not be harmed," Miss Warburton cried.

"Mr. Holmes, what do you think?" asked Dr. Warburton. "He is my older brother, but if he is unstable and offers violence to the women...."

"He must be tracked down and captured," declared Fenton firmly. "Mother and Katherine must stay in the Fortress with the maid servants. Father, you cannot walk far. You must stay with them. I will send Bonner down to the pier to watch for him there. Morell and the gardeners and stablemen can search the outbuildings and the fields, starting at the north edge of the property, closest to Carlisle. Farley and I will contact the local police. Mr. Holmes, you and your friend must guard the Fortress. In his madness, our uncle could be capable of anything. Above all, the women must be protected."

The Warburton men agreed at once. Within a few moments, the available forces had been thus dispatched, and Holmes and I found ourselves alone in the deserted hall. The maids, along with Miss Warburton and her aunt, had found refuge somewhere upstairs in the house. Before he joined them, Dr. Warburton instructed the butler to hand over to Holmes the keys to the Fortress. Out of Miss Warburton's sight, Fenton distributed rifles to his brother and the servants. Two horses were hastily saddled, and the younger Warburtons rode away in the direction of Ambleside.

"Do you have your service revolver with you, Watson?" asked Sherlock Holmes.

"Of course I do," I replied. "But Miss Warburton does not want her father harmed."

"There may not be the luxury of choice available to us, Doctor," replied the detective. "The Fortress is secure enough, but the Warburtons have forgotten something important. Follow me."

Still wearing our outside garments, we slipped through the front door and locked it. Then we silently crossed the distance between the main house and the Colonel's cottage. The door entering off the tiny front porch was easily opened under Holmes' sure touch and we found ourselves standing once more in the little hallway.

"The Colonel, once away from the asylum, is more likely to return here to his cottage. As you said so eloquently to Miss Warburton, here is his home. We must be ready for his arrival. You will find a place of concealment within while I take up watch outside. It is most important that we find the Colonel before any of his family does."

Holmes put his finger to his lips and disappeared outside. I looked around the cottage. There were not many places to hide. The bed sat too low to offer any cover nor were there any to find amid the other bedroom furniture. The back part of the cottage was too exposed for shelter. Finally I closed all the curtains, turned the high-backed wingchair so its back was to the sitting room and seated myself there.

The fair morning sky had turned overcast and in the small rooms, lacking fires and lighted lamps, the corners were full of shadows. The atmosphere grew even more gloomy as the sun passed the meridian and crawled downward. The afternoon slowly advanced. The only sounds were the ticking of the mantle clock and faint noises of Lake Windemere's waters lapping at the bottom of the nearby cliff. I was comfortably seated in the depths of the high-backed wingchair, but the need for absolute silence was nerve-racking. My muscles, motionless and tense with waiting, felt like they were on fire. Involuntarily I remembered that last night before Maiwand, when the entire regiment was ordered to wait silently at arms before dawn broke and the Afghans came screaming down from the hills to begin their bloody slaughter.

It was almost with relief that I finally heard a faint sound from the back of the house. I could see nothing but my hearing was excellent. There was the click of a lock, a door opened, then closed. Faint sounds of scuffling were heard. Footfalls came toward me. They did not come into the sitting room as I expected but instead shifted to the bedroom. I could hear metallic clinking, then the unmistakable sound of a rifle bolt being drawn back. I gripped my revolver and leapt from my hiding spot to confront the intruder.

I only had time to glimpse a muffled figure standing in the hallway. At my sudden appearance the figure turned and I recognized Colonel Warburton's Afghan rifle pointed at me. I raised my weapon, but the rifle muzzle blazed and smoke filled the air. I felt a sharp, hot pain in my right lower leg as my own shot went wild. I fell to the carpet as the mysterious assailant dashed out the front door. Holmes had left it unlocked.

I tried to follow but the pain of my wound made it impossible for me to stand. Blood was spreading across the floor. I grabbed my leg to compress the artery and felt my fibula shift. I fumbled for a handkerchief to stem the bleeding. Outside I could hear yells and footfalls. Time slowed down as I concentrated on my wound until Sherlock Holmes burst through the door, shouting my name.

"Watson! Watson!" Holmes first turned to the bedroom but when I responded with "I'm here, Holmes," he swiftly ran to where I was crouched on the sitting-room carpet.

"Watson! Believe me, if I had had any idea this would happen, I never would have sent you in here!" He dropped to my side and examined my injury. Gentle fingers added another handkerchief to the binding I had applied. He lifted me up to sit on the wooden chair. Holmes' face was white and strained, his eyes anxious. I wanted to reassure him, but for some reason I could not speak. I was growing weak from pain, loss of blood and shock. I did not notice when others entered. Orders were given, and I was carried out of the gamekeeper's cottage and placed into a carriage. Before it left the cottage I lifted my head and saw through the window the man who had shot me. It was Fenton Warburton, securely bound and guarded by a Cumbria policeman.

At the Fortress, where I was carried up to my room, Dr. Warburton examined my injury. The crude Jezail bullet had passed through my lower leg, just above the ankle, leaving a jagged, still bleeding hole. My right fibula was broken, as I had thought in the cottage. The local doctor, a surgeon named Quimby, was called in. Anesthesia was applied. The last thing I remember was Holmes' worried face hovering over me as I counted down to blackness.

When I awoke the next morning Sherlock Holmes was slumped in the chair next to my bed. It was obvious he had never left my side. When he saw I was conscious he gave my hand a warm squeeze. "I shall never forgive myself," he murmured, "for failing to see Fenton Warburton taking the colonel into the cottage after leaving you there." With that he got up and left, sending in the doctor.

I was told by the cheerful surgeon the operation was a success. My right leg was heavily bandaged but the pain was managed. After the breakfast things were cleared away Holmes returned, bringing Miss Warburton, her uncle, his wife and their son Farley. A moment later a knock was heard at my door and a familiar voice asked to enter.

It was Colonel Warburton.

He looked older, of course. It had been several years since we had last seen each other before the battle of Maiwand. He was thinner, his hair was silvered at the temples, and his step was a bit unsteady. Yet his blue eyes were bright and his handshake strong as he greeted me. Except for dark circles under his eyes, there was no sign of melancholia.

My exclamations of surprise were interrupted by Holmes, who bustled about finding chairs for everyone around my bed. When he planted his feet on the hearth rug and pulled out his pipe I knew the time had come for his explanation of the case. Sherlock Holmes would not admit it, but he lived for dramatic moments such as this, when he could expound upon his methods and astonish his audiences with the results.

Sherlock Holmes waved his pipe at the mantelpiece where Colonel Warburton's diary was placed. "I took an interest in this case when Dr. Watson showed me your diary, sir," he said to the Colonel. "There are three ways that a man may be driven to madness. One is chemically, another is by defects of the mind, and the third is deliberately. The entries kept in that diary made it clear to me that neither defects of the mind nor chemicals were responsible for the experiences you had undergone in the past half-year. It was simple for me to pick out the clues that told me you were being persecuted. I determined that the danger had not yet passed and so we made the journey up to Lake Windemere and the Fortress that same day."

He turned to the rest of us. "Miss Warburton allowed us to examine the Colonel's cottage the next morning. The most interesting thing I found was that by the head of the bed in the bedroom and on either side of the sitting-room armchair were odd spots in the walls hidden behind the wallpaper. They were hollow spaces, just the size of a single brick. An examination of the outside of the cottage revealed that at each location the outer bricks had been pried from their places and then replaced. Behind the bricks all insulation had been removed. That allowed someone outside the building to take away the brick and speak into the resulting opening to be heard inside.

"That explained the voices. It also established that there was a plot against Colonel Warburton. Imagination doesn't need to move bricks to be heard.

"The floating figure in the trees was also part of the persecution. Watson and Miss Warburton can tell you that I even went to the extreme of climbing the trunks and balancing on unstable limbs in order to scrutinize the bark of the branches at the top for marks left by a human hand. I found evidence that a wire had been strung between the oaks and beeches in order to convey a lightweight something to the cliff from the other end of the line. That explained the floating figure the Colonel had glimpsed through his window. It was, I surmise, a thin wire framework draped in muslin or a similar fabric. I might also remark that each time the phenomenon occurred it was at night, dark and very late. All the better to disguise the perpetrator.

"Many of the pieces of the puzzle were now in my hands. Motive had been obvious from the beginning. Colonel Warburton was the landowner of a considerable property. He had returned home with no interest in the estate and isolated himself from contact with his family. His brother, next in line, since the entailment didn't allow inheritance by females, was terminally ill and not long to live. I am sorry, Doctor."

Dr. Warburton shook his head. "It is true. Over the past year I have had to turn over much of the running of the estate to Fenton. He has had full access to all estate papers and contracts."

"Therefore he knew best how much the estate is worth," said Holmes. "If he could connive to gain permanent control of its assets, he would prosper far more than working as a headmaster at a local school. Fenton Warburton was an intelligent and ambitious man. Since his own father was dying, he reasoned that only one life stood between him and great wealth. He was also an impatient man. He decided to take steps. If his Uncle Jeremiah was declared to be insane, there would be no question of his ever gaining back control of the estate in the future.

"The reasons for the Colonel's melancholia were well known in the family. From his reading, Fenton found the most effective ways to feed his uncle's fears. The accusing voice in the night, only when he was alone, the spectre fluttering through the trees, even the sleep-walking which was a side effect of the stress the Colonel was under, all served Fenton's purpose.

"He felt triumphant after Colonel Warburton was admitted to

the asylum. His plan had succeeded, and now it would be only a matter of months before everything was his. Fenton was not a good man, and could not be expected to be a good son. With him family considerations did not hold a candle to the possibility of profit. It was his nature.

"Then his cousin, Katherine, left a note and travelled to London in order to consult Dr. Watson, whose good friend was Mr. Sherlock Holmes. The family knew of Colonel Warburton's favourite reading material, the 'Beeton Christmas Annual' which carried Dr. Watson's tale "A Study in Scarlet".

"Fenton, like many intelligent criminals, made the mistake of improving upon perfection. Confinement for attempted self-destruction suddenly were not enough. Colonel Warburton must be proven to be not only a danger to himself but to others. So Fenton devised a new plan. He smuggled his uncle out of the asylum the night we arrived and left him tied up and gagged in an outbuilding close to his cottage. He realized he was taking a chance of discovery but why would anyone look in that storage area without a good reason? Fenton knew the staff at the asylum wouldn't find out until breakfast that their patient was missing. They would then spend some hours searching their own premises before notifying the family.

"In his confession, after he was captured outside the cottage, he told how he watched as Miss Warburton, Dr. Watson and I examined the cottage, the kitchen garden, and the line of trees from which he had previously removed his wire. The telegram arrived from Dr. Belloes, and it was time to raise the alarm.

"He assigned tasks for all the men that would scatter them over the property but not toward the colonel's cottage. Fenton and Farley took the overland route to inform the Cumbrian police, but he faked an injury to his horse before they had gone far. He sent Farley ahead while he turned back to the estate. He spirited Colonel Warburton out of hiding, carried him into the cottage through the back door and left him in the kitchen while he went into the bedroom and loaded the Colonel's old Afghan rifle with Jezail bullets from the footlocker. He planned to fire several shots toward the searchers outside, untie and leave his uncle in the hallway and see that he was blamed for the attack. That would guarantee that Colonel Warburton would never be released from the asylum and he would lose all rights pertaining to the management of the estate.

"Of course, the Colonel would protest his innocence and tell his own story, but who would believe a crazy, homicidal old man?"

"Why shoot Dr. Watson?" asked Miss Warburton.

"Fenton Warburton admitted that the sudden appearance of my friend startled him and his finger slipped on the trigger. He never meant to hit anyone, just to fire the weapon enough times to make us think the Colonel had gone completely mad."

"Well, he failed," said Isaiah Warburton. "I'm sorry, Jeremiah, that I ever urged Katherine to sign those commitment papers."

"You thought you were acting for the best," replied his brother. "Even I was convinced that I had completely lost my senses. I do not blame you for thinking the same. The question is; what do we do now?"

"That is the subject of a private family discussion," said Sherlock Holmes. "If you need the co-operation of Dr. Watson and myself in further dealings against Fenton, Miss Warburton knows our address in London. Meanwhile, as soon as Watson can travel, we shall return to Baker Street."

That is the story of Colonel Warburton's madness and the surprising results of Sherlock Holmes' investigation. Fenton was sentenced to a long term in prison for the attacks on the Colonel and myself. Miss Warburton married Dr. Quimby and they made Colonel

Warburton their special concern. Colonel Warburton became interested in assisting his brother in the management of the estate which helped to lift his melancholia. Dr. Warburton's illness did take him within the year, but his son Farley proved to be an able administrator who became the rock of the family. As for me, for a time, I limped from my wound and even years later damp weather could cause my leg to ache. That was my souvenir from the adventure I always thought of as the Case of the Diary and the Detective.

The Case of the Cursed Clock

Mr. Sherlock Holmes did not believe in the supernatural. His was a rational mind, admirably balanced and logical to the nth degree. To accept the existence of otherworldly interventions in the affairs of men, of supernatural incidents that defied the laws of nature, or to accept the existence of dark and malignant spirits that could cause injury to living people or beasts was abhorrent to such a mind as his. So it was that when a client arrived at our rooms at 221B Baker Street in London to consult with him about a haunting, Sherlock Holmes was at first dismissive of his problem.

It had been a busy year. One of the cases brought to Sherlock Holmes had involved the Royal House of a small European nation. His task was to clear up a question arising from the death of its monarch and complications that endangered the rise to the throne of the true heir. My readers must understand if I elaborate no further, since the case concerned delicate affairs of state.

After that I assisted Holmes in the breaking up of a swindling crime organization in the East End. Only his skills at observation saved a guileless young fellow from the machinations of a clever man intent on fooling him out of his last penny.

It was but a few days into the month of November when a new client appeared. I had risen that morning to find the skies outside our sitting-room windows grey with thick clouds, as they had been for a week. After breakfast I had a full day planned and was just about to take up my hat in order to leave when the doorbell sounded. We heard Mrs. Hudson answer the front door.

"Were you expecting anyone?" I asked Holmes, who had stretched himself out on the sofa with a supply of the morning newspapers to read, his usual morning habit when not actively engaged in a case.

"Not I," he replied. As footsteps mounted the seventeen steps of the staircase to our room, he rose and thrust the stack of newsprint to one side. He smoothed his hair and made himself presentable for whomever was to appear. A moment later the door opened and a man of about fifty years presented himself to our view.

"Mr. Sherlock Holmes?" asked the gentleman. "I certainly hope you can help me. I am quite distracted." Holmes waved him to an armchair. I hung up my coat, took a seat on the sofa and brought out my notebook.

Sherlock Holmes stood in front of the mantle, his hands behind his back, and cast a languid eye over the ruddy-faced, brown-haired fellow. Our visitor was above medium height, with a knobby nose and large ears. His open coat revealed he was clad in a suit of brown tweed and wore black elastic-sided boots. An Albert watch chain was swung across his matching vest whence dangled a couple of pendants. The man handed the detective his card before he sat down and Holmes glanced at it before turning his attention back to his visitor.

"I see here that you are Mr. Richard Orrey, Imports and Exports, with an address in Mousehole, near Penzance in Cornwall." Holmes had given the small port the correct pronunciation of Mow'zel. "Beyond the facts that you were raised in Cornwall, have spent time in the American South, are a widower, have a daughter and keep your own accounts, I know nothing of your circumstances. I think we may understand more after you have explained your problem to Dr. Watson and myself."

The man gave a start and stared at my friend. "How could you know all that?" he exclaimed. "It is all true, but I had not thought that word of my troubles had extended to London."

"I will explain myself, sir. Your name, address and business are on your card, of course. Your accent is Cornish, with a little overlay of American and that tinged with a Southern flavour. That tells me of your origin and where you have spent part of your time. Owning an import and export business, you must have travelled. I would venture to think you have spent time in Louisiana, quite possibly New Orleans.

"You wear a little black pendant with a clear glass front on your watch chain containing a lock of yellow hair curled within. It is a mourning token. It could be for a parent or a sibling, but at your age it is most probably a wife. Beside that pendant is a tiny silver case, an example of those designed to carry strands of hair as keepsakes. It is shaped like a daisy. Flower-shaped watch fobs are more likely to denote girls and I would be willing to wager that your case carries within it a lock of blonde hair. That daisy-shaped pendant is your daughter's. The first is her mother's. But the daisy pendant is a keepsake, not a mourning token. Therefore your daughter still lives.

"As for the writing, the signs of ink smears are visible on the fingers of your right hand. You run an import-export business. It would be very normal for you to be responsible for bills of lading and the payments to your suppliers. You dip your pen nib too deeply when you write."

Mr. Orrey tried to smile. "I see I have come to the right man. Hear me out, Mr. Holmes, and you can judge for yourself as to whether I should be upset about my clock.

"I am a Cornishman, although I had thought that some of my accent had worn smooth during my travels over the years. There have been Orreys in Cornwall for almost as long as there have been people there at all. Over time our estate dwindled until we were left only the house and about fifty acres. My grandfather began the import and export business and it turned out we had a flare for it. I import many different items from the New World to the Old, and have been to some mighty strange places, including South America, Bermuda and, as you said, New Orleans.

"My household at Bluff House consists of my daughter, Dorit; the butler; two maids; a cook; and a yardman who takes care of the horses and also helps in the house when needed.

"During my marriage my wife travelled with me and as a result Dorit was born in Baton Rouge. Dorit is now nineteen years old. My wife, June, however, was never strong after our daughter's birth and died in New Orleans ten years ago.

"After the funeral I settled my daughter with my sister back in Mousehole, in Cornwall, where she lived in the family home. I continued to ply my business alone. But the loneliness was too much, and as Dorit grew older, I resumed taking her with me on my trips during school holidays. Finally, when my sister married last year and followed her soldier husband to India, I returned to the old place again. I wanted to give my girl some semblance of a regular home life. When Dorit became betrothed to young Mr. Winston Looper of Penzance I was very pleased. He is the son of a local jeweller and set to follow in his father's footsteps.

"I have an office in my home. I handle all the ordering and bills and merchandise myself so we are all busy and happy. It is a large house, and I use a few of the rooms and the outbuildings to store my wares before they are transported to my clients.

"A week ago I received a shipment of long-case clocks from the United States for resale. One of them, constructed of hickory and with an unusual gilt dial, was so handsome that I decided that I would put it aside and offer it as my wedding gift to my daughter and her new husband next year, when the wedding is due to take place. Dorit approved of the gift. Accordingly it was set up in the main hall of my house until it would go to the young couple's new home."

"One question," interrupted Sherlock Holmes. "Whence had

this clock been sent to you?"

"From New Orleans, from Abner Wondowner of Jackson Square."

"Is he a regular supplier?"

"I have known him for years. He is a hard man but his goods have always been of the finest quality."

"Very well. Pray continue." Holmes flung himself into his chair and steepled his fingers.

"My butler set up the clock, hanging the weights and setting the time. He is in charge of keeping it wound. Nothing strange was noted for the first few hours. Then the wedding clock began to chime in an odd fashion. Instead of striking as it was set, on the hour and on the half hour, it struck on the quarter hour and then only one chime was heard each time. It was reset by the butler. Yesterday things became worse. The timepiece sounded once every ten minutes, starting at one o'clock, right at lunchtime. I know nothing about the workings of clocks, so I left the re-setting to the butler. He looked at it many times that day. The disruption continued. By five o'clock I called in young Looper, who as a jeweller knows such things for his work. He examined its works. Neither of them found any reason for the clock to continue to chime at odd times. Finally I had young Looper disable the thing."

"How extraordinary!" I exclaimed.

"I do not see how I could help you in this matter," said Sherlock Holmes. "Surely you would be better served with an experienced clockmaker or, better yet, a different clock."

"That is what I thought, Mr. Holmes, until my butler said something. It was that which decided me to come to London and consult you."

Sherlock Holmes' black brows came down over his keen grey eyes. "Indeed. What did he say?"

Mr. Orrey wrung his hands. "He said that the night before he was locking the windows and doors around midnight. He heard a noise in the Great Hall. He went to check the room but all seemed as normal. But when he was turning away to go to his quarters, he saw something near the clock. It was only a glimpse but he insisted upon what he saw."

"What did the butler see?"

Mr. Orrey's face was pale now, and drawn. His eyes fixed on Holmes' face.

"He swore he saw a ghost, Mr. Holmes. A misty spot hovering on the floor in the middle of the room. Then it disappeared into the clock. It was visible in the moonlight which showed briefly through a rift in the clouds."

"Does your butler...by the way, what is his name?"

"Maurice Mulot. He is of French descent and has been serving the family for nearly thirty years."

"Do you have reason to believe he drinks, Mr. Orrey?"

"He has been known to take a glass on occasion, Mr. Holmes, but never while on duty!" Mr. Orrey looked ruffled at the suggestion.

"When was the last time he had his eyes checked?"

"Really, Mr. Holmes! I must protest these attacks upon the reliability of an old servant!"

"Then what do you think is the cause for the clock's behaviour and the ghost?"

Richard Orrey leaned forward toward the detective and, with a trace of a quaver in his voice, replied, "I believe the clock is haunted, Mr. Holmes. I think an old enemy put a curse on it. I saw much in New Orleans during my time there that outsiders would not understand."

"Odd things happen in old houses. Perhaps it was caused by the moonlight, the wind or the ground settling," said Holmes.

"The moon was full that night, quite full. Dorit remarked upon it. But I can't see that has anything to do with Mulot's sighting. It is true that Bluff House stands in an exposed position on a bluff overlooking the shingle of the harbour of Mousehole. The winds that sweep in from the Atlantic Ocean can be strong, but in nearly two hundred years there has never been a single draft reported in the house. The foundation and walls are of Lamora granite and all the windows and doors are sturdy and square, as firm as the day my grandfather accepted the keys. As for the ground settling, tests made when we first moved in proved that in all this time, the place has only settled one-sixteenth of an inch. No, you may dismiss those explanations from your mind, Mr. Holmes."

The detective frowned at his client. He stood up, turned to the mantelpiece and filled his old briar from the tobacco in the Persian slipper. He tamped it down and lit it, all the time concentrating on Mr. Orrey. He paced a bit in front of the hearth and then paused.

"The clock came from New Orleans. You spent a great deal of time in that city. Tell me about it, Mr. Orrey."

"I spent years in the American South. I made many friends and heard stories from them that would astonish you. There are parts of that area that are almost impossible for an outsider to understand. There are several sub-cultures in the South that exist nowhere else. Superstitions, unusual traditions and odd beliefs find their homes there. New Orleans was the scene of my poor wife's death and where she is buried."

"Excuse me, sir, but of what did your wife die?" I asked.

"She died of cholera, Dr. Watson. As I said, she hadn't been strong for years."

Sherlock Holmes eyed Mr. Orrey again. "Did you, personally, ever experience any unusual occurrences during your time in New Orleans, Mr. Orrey?"

"Yes. After my wife died I felt terribly alone, even though Dorit was with me. Abner Wondowner suggested that I visit a medium. In an effort to comfort myself, I attended two seances. I went away unconvinced, although I believed the woman was sincere. Time passed and gradually the sharp pain I felt over my wife's death dulled. I accepted her passing. Then two years ago I had an incident with Abner Wondowner. There was a report he actually hired a voodoo priest to put a curse on me."

"What!" I half-rose from my chair. Even Holmes looked surprised.

"What did you do?" asked Holmes.

"I did the only think I could do, Mr. Holmes. I decided to fight fire with fire. I hired another boker and had him put a worse curse on the man. When the word got around to Wondowner he called off his priest and then I called off mine."

"What were the curses?" I inquired.

"He arranged for my health to take a turn for the worse."

"And you arranged...?"

"For him to lose a lot of money. After he heard that a truce was arranged and both curses were cancelled."

"Yet you still do business with this man?" Holmes asked.

Richard Orrey shrugged. "His products are of high quality and outside of our dispute, there had been no other trouble between us. Business is business, after all."

"What had been the origin of the dispute?"

"He was nearly my own age yet had seen fit to pay court to my daughter. At the time she was barely seventeen."

"Was your daughter receptive to his attentions?"

"No! She found him odious and repulsive. It was her clear desire to have nothing to do with the man. When he was informed of her feelings was when he had me cursed. I suppose he thought with me out of the way he could persuade Dorit to accept him as her protector. But I counter-attacked and his plan failed. Soon after that incident Dorit and I moved back to Cornwall to stay."

Holmes shrugged his shoulders. His next question surprised me.

"So you believe the timepiece is haunted?" Holmes shot me an amused glance. "I would not think that any intelligent spirit would ever chose to haunt a tall-case clock; wouldn't it be a bit confining?"

"You may joke, Mr. Holmes, but I am serious. I saw too many strange things in America to easily dismiss such a notion. Young

Looper thinks there is nothing to it, but my daughter Dorit is quite upset. With her engagement she has found a grown-up dignity. After the clock began malfunctioning, she became agitated. When her fiancé could not fix the problem, she became angry with him. She talks of postponing the wedding or even calling it off completely. Young Looper is very confused. They do love each other, but these unusual happenings have driven a wedge between them.

"I even took the problem of the tall-case clock to our vicar. He did not say that I may be right in my opinion but he did refuse to do any sort of exorcism until the matter had been thoroughly investigated."

"So you wish for Dr. Watson and myself to travel to Mousehole to examine this cursed clock of yours so you may have a ceremony to release the tortured spirit trapped within?"

"Exactly."

Holmes's pipe had gone out during this conversation. We were silent as he struck several matches in order to get the thing to light. Was I mistaken or was his unsteady hand a result of fear? Finally he looked up at our client through a wreath of smoke.

"This problem deserves more investigation, Mr. Orrey. Please leave the name of your hotel with me and return tomorrow morning at this time."

Our client looked rather uncertainly at Holmes but shook hands as my friend led him out of the room. When the detective was certain the man was out of earshot he threw himself down on the sofa and burst into laughter.

I joined in, involuntarily, because my friend displayed such amusement. Finally, when he showed signs of calming down, I ruefully shook my head and said, "Really, Holmes, is that professional? To laugh so at a client's predicament?"

Holmes stopped laughing and eyed me with a smile on his lips. I could see that my impression of fear was totally wrong. Instead he seemed gripped in suppressed hilarity. "You are right, Watson, but I could not contain myself. If I were not hungering for a case, I would have put Mr. Orrey off. I really agreed to look into it because of the engaged daughter, Dorit. No marriage should take place under such uncertainty as is caused by an unreliable time piece.

"Besides, Mr. Orrey was starting to believe in spooks, and such nonsense should be nipped early. I see it as a duty I owe to my fellow man. There is nothing more ridiculous than a credulous Englishman in tweeds."

"You have clearly set forth your credo on the subject of the supernatural. 'No ghosts need apply'."

"Indeed, and it has not changed. What have we, two rational men, to do with apparitions, spectres and such hocus-pocus? I could not allow Mr. Richard Orrey to start down that dark path that ends in trumpets whispering family secrets and bits of cheesecloth insisting they are long-lost relatives. No, better to be hit with a dose of reality now rather than sink into that morass of teleporting fruit and mendacious mediums that awaits such believers."

Holmes retreated to his bedroom. A few minutes later he re-emerged dressed for the street. "I hope to be back sometime later today, Watson. Leave a candle in the window for me."

"But Holmes! Where are you going?"

"Tempus fugit, Watson. As must I." He left.

I found my hat and went out. I spent the rest of the day on my own affairs and did not return to 221B until after dinner. There was no sign of Holmes. I sat reading until the hour grew late with no word. I finally decided it was useless to wait up for him. After my years of experiences with the detective I knew it was equally possible that Holmes was lurking around the seediest dives Whitechapel had to offer or was taking supper with the Queen.

I came down to breakfast the next morning to find my friend sitting in his armchair with a lap full of telegraph forms. He shuffled them into a neat stack and laid them aside.

"Let me pour you some coffee, Watson. I can see that you are anxious to learn of my movements yesterday after Mr. Orrey's visit. My first action was to spend part of yesterday at the telegraph office, sending wires to my agent in New Orleans. In the middle of the correspondence I took time out to visit the British Museum. I researched the practices of voodoo religion as practiced in New Orleans. Then I went back to the telegraph office. I needed to send more wires to Liverpool. It was late when the last reply came in."

My friend just smiled at my questions. That was one of his most irritating traits. I decided to ignore him and have my breakfast. I had just filled my plate when Mr. Orrey arrived. Our client looked as if he had spent the intervening hours not sleeping in a comfortable hotel bed but instead pacing the streets of London. He dropped onto our sofa and looked up at Sherlock Holmes. Mr. Orrey was clearly exhausted. His coat was dirty, his tweed suit was wrinkled, his hair was rumpled and there was a grey cast to his complexion I did not like. Despite the hour I brought him a small brandy. He gulped it down without taking his eyes from my friend's face.

"Have you eaten?" asked Holmes sharply.

Mr. Orrey slowly shook his head. "I don't remember."

Sherlock Holmes piled a plate full of ham and eggs from the platter Mrs. Hudson had brought up earlier. He handed it to our client. The two of us ate in silence. Holmes pressed a cup of coffee on Mr. Orrey and resumed his seat in the armchair. He stretched out his hand and picked up the telegraph forms from where he had left them.

"I have been investigating the origins of your clock, Mr. Orrey. I have a friend in New Orleans and he sent me answers to several questions I asked him by telegraph. Abner Wondowner had that clock made to his design by the Chicago Chiming Clock Company on Canal Street and had it sent to his store in New Orleans. After a few days he shipped it to you along with some other ordinary tall-case clocks. Then he booked a stateroom on the next fast steamer to Liverpool and left New Orleans."

"Abner Wondowner is here in England?"

"He has been here several weeks."

"I had no idea, Mr. Holmes. What do you think he is planning to do?" Mr. Orrey had a sudden thought. "Do you think my daughter Dorit is in danger?"

"I cannot be certain, but I think it a good idea that you and I and Dr. Watson take the first train to Mousehole."

I went upstairs to pack a quick traveling bag. As I came down the steps I noticed that Holmes had also packed a grip, but carried in his other hand a small square case which tinkled faintly as he passed me. I wondered what was in it but from the set of my friend's jaw I was reluctant to inquire.

Within half an hour the three of us were in a first-class carriage rattling across the miles of countryside to Cornwall. Our client sat in one corner and intently watched Holmes' every move. Since my friend spent most of the time silently staring out of the window and puffing on his pipe Mr. Orrey must have had a boring trip. I was silent also. I knew Holmes of old and recognized he was turning over the facts of the case in his mind before he said anything to us. Once when I reached to the window in an effort to open it and dispel some of the tobacco smoke, I was stopped by Holmes' sharp glance and abrupt gesture. He had told me once that a concentrated atmosphere helped him in his thinking. I sat back and made no more moves. Instead I spent the time thinking about the known facts myself.

Mr. Richard Orrey had spent years of his life in New Orleans. His wife was even buried there.

After she died, he attended seances, trying to reach the afterlife. Later he had believed enough in the supernatural to set a curse against an unsuitable suitor for his daughter's hand. He must have a lot of knowledge of spells, voodoo Legbas, charms, amulets, witch doctors and the like, picked up in the normal course of life in the South. Could this tall-case clock really be cursed in order to punish him for past dark deeds he had perpetuated during his life in America? Did it have something to do with the death of his late wife? What was the ghost's origin? Who was Abner Wondowner? Merely a spurned gentleman caller interested in Orrey's daughter or a malignant force bent upon revenge? Why had Orrey continued to do business with the man after the incident of the dual curses?

I shook my head. It was as baffling to me then as when our travel began. Finally the train pulled into Penzance Station. We disembarked and hailed a hack to take us to Mousehole.

This day was overcast as was the day before. We were driven down the Cliff Road to Mousehole, about two and one half miles from Penzance. On the left was a magnificent view of the ocean, massive wave upon wave, breaking and crashing against the enormous rocks that lined the bottom of the high cliff that gave the road its name. I knew that the high water was a sign of a storm out at sea that was soon to hit land. On the right, beyond the row of trees that edged the meadows next to the road, were crooked dry walls that ran back into the countryside. A few stone farmhouses could be seen in the distance, half hidden by the folds of the land. I heard gull cries and saw a few seabirds in the sky. It seemed no time at all until we were rolling up to the handsome house perched on the edge of the bluff overlooking Mount Bay just at the east edge of Mousehole.

Bluff House was a large edifice, made of yellow stone and grounded upon the granite bedrock of the coast. A gravelled approach led to the front porch. Its colonnade ran from one end of the old house to the other. Over its roof loomed two more stories, the windows rimmed with white quoins as were the corners. The landscaping was minimal because the front lawn ended at the cliff's edge only twenty yards beyond the gravelled drive's edge.

The back grounds of the house were more spacious, with small outbuildings and a stone stable in the corner of the property. There was even room for a kitchen garden and a few flowerbeds. Mr. Orrey explained that the rest of his land was located across Cliff Road and was rented to farmers.

Mr. Orrey opened the front door. On the twisting staircase that led upstairs stood a young woman, dressed in a light summer dress, with her blonde hair put up in a simple chignon.

Our client had a question after they had greeted each other and Holmes and I were introduced. "Where is Maurice? Why isn't he here?"

A shadow passed over her delicate features. "He has been taken ill, Dad. Last night his hands broke out in blisters and he developed a fever. I called Dr. Jera and he came out at once. He had no answer for what has caused the blisters but he left a salve. He will be back again this afternoon. Meanwhile I had the cook prepare a light lunch against your return. It's spread out in the dining room."

"If Dr. Jera doesn't object, perhaps Dr. Watson could accompany him when he visits the butler," said Holmes.

Mr. Orrey shrugged his shoulders. "As you wish."

After a hasty meal, Holmes and I were led into the Great Hall where the clock stood. It was a broad, lofty room, well stocked with a mixture of old antique furniture and some more modern additions. Paintings hung from the crown molding and faded but valuable carpets covered the floor. The entire place struck me as imposing yet homey. It was a comfortable room. I liked it at once.

Sherlock Holmes went straight to the tall-case clock. He pulled out his magnifying lens from his pocket and examined the entire timepiece from top to bottom. As he did so he whistled and talked aloud.

"Ahh, this is a handsome clock. Made from hickory as advertised. Hand-carved! A lot of time and thought went into this creation. Look, Watson, at the three-dimensional panels! Scenes of the American South, I'll be bound! Crape myrtle trees, live oak, even palmettos! Look at the fine detail of the Spanish moss dripping down from the oaks. See the animals that inhabit the swamps. Delicate mosquitoes, chunky alligators, half-hidden opossums, raccoons and armadillos. There are even cypress trees. Here is a pack of hunting dogs, with a gang of men behind them carrying rifles and sacks. Here on the base is the image of New Orleans' Jackson Square, with the plaza full of men and women and the steeple of the great cathedral rising behind them. On the sides are street scenes featuring the New Orleans wrought-iron balconies that adorn the old French Quarter buildings. A wonderful example of craftsmanship."

Holmes concentrated on the large dial that rested behind the glass-fronted panel. He looked at the bevelled glass, opened the door which offered access not only the gilt dial but also the chains and hanging weights shaped like graceful herons that propelled the timepiece. He carefully inspected the clock-face itself.

The dial was etched with images of Louisiana's wild flowers picked out in blue and pink against a golden background. Wild orchids and magnolias vied with bougainvillaea and wisteria around the dial. The numerals each corresponded with a different bloom and the end result was most pleasing. After a few minutes, Holmes moved to the small panel on the left side of the clock which, when opened, allowed access to the inner workings of the timepiece. He pulled out a small penknife and poked about for a few moments. He closed the side panel and returned to the dial, chains and the hands of the clock-face. Mr. Orrey and I were startled when he began scraping small flakes of paint off of each!

Holmes carefully placed the flakes into a clean envelope and placed it in his notebook. I looked at him with curiosity. "Why did you do that, Holmes?" I asked.

"You know my methods, Watson. Mr. Orrey, I require that no one else handle that clock until my investigation is complete. Now I think I hear the doctor at the door. It is time to speak to M. Maurice Mulot."

Dr. Jena was an older, short and portly man with a fluffy white beard and a head of hair to match. He had no objection to a second opinion and all of us accompanied him into the sickroom. It was a plainly-furnished room in the servants' quarters. The butler was stretched out on a neatly made iron bedstead. A woman dressed in a maid's uniform was applying wet cloths to his forehead. His bandaged hands lay on the coverlet, and Dr. Jena was silent as he slowly unwrapped them.

I examined the exposed flesh with interest. Large blisters, red and inflamed, weeping noxious liquid, ravaged the fingers and palms of the butler. They looked like burns. Dr. Jena asked Mulot how he came to be injured, but the suffering man had no answer. The doctor cleaned the wounds, applied salve and rebandaged his hands. He checked Mulot for fever and clucked softly at the results. He wrote out a couple of prescriptions and handed them to the maid with verbal instructions about the pain and fever treatments.

Sherlock Holmes bent over the patient. "M. Mulot, can you answer a few question? My name is Sherlock Holmes and I am investigating how you were injured."

The sick man shifted his attention to my friend. "Of course, sir," he murmured.

"Did you touch something hot during the past few days? Is that how you burned your hands?"

"No, sir."

"The dial and workings of the clock are the only new things you have touched?"

"Yes. I set up the clock and adjusted the dial several times."

"How long after you first touched the clock did your symptoms begin?"

"The next day. First there was a redness but it seemed minor. This morning I woke up from the pain and my hands were like this. You are not a doctor, M. Holmes. How can you help me?"

"I do not know yet, M. Mulot. I will do my best, however." Holmes patted the man on the shoulder and left the room.

The four of us regrouped in the hallway, leaving the woman with the patient. Holmes turned to the doctor and me. "What is your diagnosis, doctors?"

I considered the symptoms for several moments. I conferred with Dr. Jena and we agreed. "Those burns on his hands must have come from contact with a flame or touching a heated surface. What is odd is that he has no recollection of doing so."

Holmes nodded. "Mr. Orrey, I think I need to see the other clocks in that shipment."

"Certainly. They are stored in an unused room in the back of the house."

Dr. Jera left. We followed Mr. Orrey to the remaining clocks. They stood upright in a line, the front side of each packing case open. The clocks were packed in excelsior and the excess littered the floor. None of the tall-case clocks displayed the lavish detail and fine carvings that adorned the one that stood in the Great Hall. Holmes brought out his lens again and went carefully over each clock, including the inner works and the illuminated dials. He took samples from each clock as he had from the first timepiece. Finally he put the magnifying glass in his pocket and turned to us.

"It is getting late. Is there a decent inn in Mousehole?"

"There is the Ratonera on High Street, but surely we can make you comfortable here, Mr. Holmes, both you and Dr. Watson."

"I thank you for your offer, Mr. Orrey, but I think under the circumstances it would serve your case better if we stayed at the Ratonera."

As we left by the front door, Dorit was standing there with a paper in her hand. She looked stricken.

Her father went to her. "What is it, my dear?" She handed him the note.

"It came for Dr. Jena. He gave it to me before he left." There were tears in her eyes.

Holmes glanced at it then passed it to me. "This says that Winston Looper has been afflicted with the same malady that struck M. Maurice Mulot. That is the name of your fiancé, is it not, Miss Dickory?"

"Yes! Dad, I must go to him!" She was already pulling on her coat. The sky had darkened and the promised storm clouds were building on the western horizon.

Holmes and I were dropped at the inn. Soon we accepted our room keys from the manager of the Ratonera. I went upstairs while Holmes lingered below. My room was on the floor above Holmes'. When I finished unpacking I went to find him. His door was locked. From behind the panels I could hear the clinking of glass and a pungent smell. "Good night, Watson," he called. "I will see you at breakfast...perhaps."

The storm broke that night. I watched from my bedroom window as black clouds rolled over the bay, streaked in purple and crimson. High winds whipped up the water and drove blinding rain to cascade down from the invisible sky to drench both land and sea. Trees whipped back and forth as if they wanted to fly off the face of the earth. Leaves and trash flew past my window. Thunder rumbled and banged while lightening shot with white crooked fingers across my view. The violence of Nature was powerful beyond expectation. At last, after a number of hours, I finally went to bed. Any noises from Holmes' room were covered by the turmoil of the gale.

Sherlock Holmes wasn't visible when I came downstairs the next morning. The manager said only he had gone out in the middle of the night. I left for Bluff House without breakfast. Mr. Orrey was alone in the dining room. He told me that the butler was a little better; Dr. Jena had already visited him and left, and that Dorit was at the Looper home taking care of Winston who was improving and that he had no idea where Holmes was. He offered me kippers and coffee.

After I ate, I strolled out onto the porch to smoke my first cigarette of the day. The storm was just dying away. There were gaps in the treeline that showed where some trees had been toppled by the wind during the night. Torn leaves and twigs piled up against the foundation and over the gravel drive. Below the house on the shingle a couple of rowboats had been driven up on the rocks and smashed. I saw Holmes leaning over one of the wrecks, pulling on a dark mass half covered by wet sand. As I watched, two constables ran up to him from the Mousehole side. The three men conferred, then Holmes looked up the cliff and saw me standing at its edge. He waved and made his way up the steep path to Bluff House.

"Good morning, my dear Watson," he carolled. He was in a very good mood. There could be only one reason.

"You have solved the case," I said. Holmes did not reply but went straight into the Great Hall where Richard Orrey stood in front of the clock. He turned to us as we entered.

"Mr. Holmes? Any news?"

"Yes. Please take a seat. You too, Watson. I have a tale to tell, and I think you will find it of interest, Mr. Orrey. My researches of the past few days have come to a conclusion and I now have the complete story of your mysterious clock."

Holmes began to pace up and down the room as we settled into arm chairs. His white, nervous fingers were clasped behind his back as was his custom except when he unlocked them to wave them as he made a special point.

"You thought this case began a few days ago, when your tall-case clock began malfunctioning. In reality it started when your wife died. With the help of Abner Wondowner, you were guided to a medium. You visited her twice, then stopped. Wondowner became interested in that world but over time he switched from spiritualism to voodoo, which had many adherents locally. When Abner Wondowner was rejected by your daughter he turned to voodoo to gain his ends. The curse on you was the result.

"When that plan failed, he thought of another. His obsession toward Dorit had not lessened. Wondowner spent time creating the perfect plan. He had this clock made in Chicago and shipped to his warehouse in New Orleans. He had deliberately designed this beautiful timepiece, in contrast to the other clocks he shipped with it, so that you would not sell it, but put it in your own home. You keeping it as a wedding present for your daughter was just a lucky happenstance. He had ordered it built long before Dorit's engagement.

"While he had it in his warehouse in New Orleans, Abner Wondowner applied a toxic substance to the metal dial, the hands and the chains that carried the weights of the timepiece. That is what burned the fingers and hands of your butler, Mulot, and young Looper when they attempted to fix and set the clock. The irregular chiming was built into the works by the factory mechanics under Wondowner's directions so the clock would be handled repeatedly in an effort to correct the problem."

"The devil!"

"Exactly. He had hoped that you would be the one to touch the clock. He didn't foresee that other people would be assigned to that task.

"My agent in New Orleans confirmed his purchase of the acid he added to the paint he used on the clock. My man in Liverpool found the date he had landed in that city and traced his movements. He had slowly travelled through England until he finally arrived in Penzance two weeks ago. He was waiting for the clocks' arrival. Remember, the shipment came by a slower boat.

"The final telegram I received informed me that he had registered at the Ratonea here in Mousehole. I knew his plans were nearly complete. We left for Bluff House at once. I examined the clock and took samples from the hands, the dial and the inner works. Just to be sure I also took samples from the other clocks in the shipment. I had foreseen the need of such testing and had brought a small case of chemicals with me from Baker Street. When we signed in to the Ratonea, I checked the registry to make sure Wondowner was there. He was in the bar. I had a good look at him without his knowledge. While Dr. Watson was settling in to his room, I arranged for the manager to let me know when Wondowner left the hotel.

"In my room I conducted the experiments that confirmed the use of a very strong and dangerous acid on the clock works. None of the other clocks had been altered. The storm was raging and I felt confident that my quarry would not leave the hotel until it abated. I was mistaken, however. About 4:30 a.m. I was told Wondowner had left. He had arranged for his luggage to be shipped directly back to America.

"I followed him into the storm. The winds were still high and the rain was pouring down. The dawn was about to break behind the masses of clouds. Oh, it was a pretty job of shadowing, Watson. He was suspicious and I was hard-put to evade detection. The storm that still enveloped the town around us impeded us both with blinding rain and high winds. I do not know if he ever saw me, but he did run a complicated course all through Mousehole, up streets and down alleys, bent upon shaking off any pursuers. It almost worked, but he didn't know he was being followed by Sherlock Holmes.

"Finally I saw him, his clothes sodden from the rain, creep to the quay and get into one of the rowboats. The waves were still driving into the harbour and rocking every ship and boat in sight. He began rowing in the direction of Bluff House. I saw his plan at once. Since nothing else had worked, he had become desperate. He was going to enter the house under cover of the storm, abduct Dorit, and make his escape in the rowboat. If he could make it to Penzance, he could get a train to Plymouth and leave for New Orleans from there. He didn't know Dorit had gone to nurse her fiancé at his parents' home. It was a mad scheme. I think that by then it was possible that his obsession had overcome his reason and he had gone insane.

"I realized that his original plan had one mighty flaw. It was the storm. No one, not the best sailor in the world, could control that little rowboat in the midst of such a gale. I started to run along the shore toward Bluff House, at the far edge of Mousehole and the bay.

"There were whitecaps on the water. The current pulled his little boat out away from the shore. He did have the wind behind him, so he travelled faster across the water than I could run along the shingle.

"I had to make my way through much debris left by the storm. Enormous trees had fallen over the cliff and landed on the sand. I ran as fast as I could, but when I arrived at the spot below Bluff House a woeful sight greeted me. Among the debris thrown up by the storm I recognized the rowboat Wondowner had stolen. It was smashed up on the rocks right below here.

"What of Wondowner?" asked Richard Orrey.

Sherlock Holmes dropped onto a sofa by the clock. "He is dead. I found his body on the rocks, half covered with sand. One of your neighbours was walking past, assessing the damage, and I sent him for the police. They are down there now, examining the scene."

The three of us were silent for a few minutes. Mr. Orrey sighed. "At least Dorit is safe. But that still leaves the question of the ghost."

Sherlock Holmes went over to our client's desk and scribbled something on a sheet of paper. He carefully folded it and handed it to Mr. Orrey.

"Follow the instructions I have written on this note, Mr. Orrey," said he. "Do not fail to comply in every particular. I will not require that you travel back to London with your results. A wire will find us at home at Baker Street. Good day, Mr. Orrey."

We collected our bags from the Ratonea and took the next train to London.

The doorbell rang barely twenty-four hours later. Holmes stood at the top of the stair ready to snatch the yellow envelope out of Mrs. Hudson's hand as she brought the telegram up. He ignored her squeak of protest and came back into the sitting room where I waited.

He ripped open the missive and read it eagerly. A great smile of satisfaction spread over his face and he handed the paper to me.

I read the telegram with interest. It was addressed from Mousehole, Cornwall and read as follows:

"Have followed your instructions completely. Basil Dotson of enormous help. Last of bodies removed this morning. Timepiece repaired and now in excellent working order. Wedding date set for first of February. Your invitation to follow. Many thanks. R. Orrey."

I looked at Holmes. "What can this strange message mean?" I said.

"It means that Mr. Orrey of Bluff House no longer believes his hickory clock is haunted."

"Who is Basil Dotson?"

"An efficient tradesman of Penzance well known in his field whom I recommended as able to help with Mr. Orrey's problem."

"And this talk of bodies?"

"Every war has its casualties, I am afraid, my dear Watson."

I threw up my hands. "I am totally baffled, Holmes. Whose bodies were removed this morning?"

Holmes dropped into his armchair and reached for his favourite pipe. He tried to look solemn but merriment still danced in his eyes.

"It was elementary, Watson. The tall-case clock had been invaded. I merely arranged for Mr. Orrey to defeat and remove the intruders."

"What are you talking about, Holmes?"

"Mice, Watson. Moon-lit mice. The tall-case clock picked up a stowaway cargo of mice during its travels. Basil Dotson is a vermin exterminator. I plan to write to the British Paranormal Society today to suggest that many cases brought before that committee might have similar causes. Sometimes, Watson, it is the smallest of things, be it mice or microbes, that determines what happens in the world."

The Case of the Loud Librarians

The two women burst out onto the sidewalk, their faces alight with excitement. They were both Americans, young, dressed in long floating summer dresses, with blonde hair framing sparkling eyes and smiles. It was their first time in London, and they had reserved an afternoon to visit Baker Street, the home of their favourite literary characters, Sherlock Holmes and Dr. Watson.

"Did you see the tiles inside the station?"

"See them, Amy? I want them for my bathroom, if I ever buy a house!"

The shorter woman pointed to the left. "Look! There is the statue! C'mon, Sheila!"

They ran up the sun-lit pavement to the out-sized bronze of the Great Detective, who was togged out in Inverness cape and deerstalker, a curved pipe in one hand, as the face stared thoughtfully out over the thick traffic of Marylebone Road.

The women circled it, chattering to each other and taking many selfies. After a few minutes they strolled back to the corner, where the sign "Baker Street" saw them facing right into the famous artery.

Again the road was choked with cars and buses. Finally the lights changed and they made their way to a modest building on the west side of the street. A man dressed in an outdated police uniform and helmet stood next to a painted sign hanging on some iron rails. Beyond it was a door that led into a gift shop. The sign included a profile of Sherlock Holmes and the words "Sherlock Holmes Museum."

ooOoo

"Make a long arm, if you would, Watson," said Sherlock Holmes, "and hand me that book on the shelf next to you."

Watson turned from the window in their shared sitting room and gave Holmes the red-backed volume. Then he went back to his post. It was foggy outside, the facing buildings across Baker Street barely visible, and with the window pane raised just a few inches the sounds of the bustle below were muted.

"What are you working on, Holmes?" he asked casually. The doctor wasn't really interested but it was the middle of the afternoon and nothing had happened all day. No clients, no visits from Lestrade...even Mrs. Hudson's lunch had been sandwiches made from leftovers.

His friend had spent that day, and the two days before it, crouched over his chemical table, working on an obscure experiment that involved a lot of smells and dirty glassware. Each time something went wrong, or his efforts resulted in a visible failure, the detective would sigh, clean up the mess, and begin again.

"Mycroft has asked me to analyse this powder found in the man-made caves under the ancient city of Wanduck near the Khybur Pass. I have ruled out it being an herbicide, a glue, a fertilizer, a clothing dye, or a paint pigment. The next possibility is that it is an additive for gunpowder."

"I need new gloves!" Watson said and stood up hastily. "I think I will go down to Oxford Street and see what Truman's has in stock." He grabbed his hat and was out the door in an instant.

oo0oo

Clutching their museum tickets, purchased at the gift shop, Amy and Sheila climbed the seventeen steps up to the door of the sitting room. Both were having the time of their lives, taking in the vintage wallpaper and counting each step. Suddenly they were conscience of a man on the stair. He was of medium height but very handsome, about thirty years old, with a carefully-groomed moustache. He was dressed in an odd-looking three-piece suit, complete with wing collar, bow tie and a bowler hat. He noticed them too, raised his hat, and politely moved to the side to allow them to pass him.

The stranger smiled in return to their smiles and glanced appreciatively at their thin maxi-dresses and their exposed ankles. The ladies looked at each other and giggled. In an instant they were past him and climbing the last few steps to the sitting room door. They turned to look at him again but he wasn't there.

"Why, where did he go? He was so cute!" exclaimed Sheila.

"I didn't hear the door close," said Amy. "Dressed like that, with the collar and tie, he must work here. Maybe he's a guide."

"Yes, that's possible, but where did he go? The door is the only way out. The stairs go straight to the threshold."

It was true. In the museum reconstruction, the downstairs had been closed off and turned into the gift shop. The stairs had been set up to include seventeen steps to the first floor and offered no access to the gift shop space. The door to the street was the only exit.

"That is odd," Amy murmured. The two librarians went into the sitting room and soon the stranger was forgotten as they oohed and aahed over the contents of Sherlock Holmes's sitting room and bedroom. They climbed the steps to every level of the exhibit, including the surprising bathroom under the eaves, and only while coming down the last length of stairs did they remember the handsome man they had seen there.

He wasn't there now. They re-entered the gift shop and inquired, but the salesgirl, dressed like Mrs. Hudson, knew nothing of a guide dressed in the description they gave. Finally Amy and Sheila let the subject drop and concentrated on buying souvenirs, including matching deerstalkers of real English tweed.

"Oh my gosh, look at the time! We have to catch the Underground to Trafalgar Square and find the Sherlock Holmes Pub and Restaurant!" With that the two young women ran out of the shop and dashed for the Baker Street Station.

oo0oo

Dr. Watson returned to 221B to find the room still intact but Holmes cleaning up from another experiment failure. "So you did not purchase your new gloves, Watson?" Holmes asked.

"No. I met Thurston on the street and we enjoyed a drink at the Stephenson Rest. How did you know?"

"You just took off your old gloves, and you did not bring a package marked Truman's back with you. You came directly in here with no stop at your room. Therefore, no new gloves."

"Amazing, Holmes. Did you take the case of those two ladies I met going out?"

"What two ladies?"

Watson was surprised. "I passed two young ladies on the stairs on my way down. I thought they were coming to see you."

Holmes dumped the last of the broken glass in the wastebasket and looked at Watson. His brows knitted and he looked thoughtful.

"Can you describe them?"

"Two young women, both blonde, wearing thin floral dresses, hems rather high, both with well- turned ankles and unusual shoes."

"No, I have had no visitors today."

"How odd. I could have sworn they were coming to see you."

"Perhaps they changed their minds."

"Yes, that must have been it."

That mystery solved, Sherlock Holmes turned back to his research.

The Case of the Blood-Splattered Bridge

The letter that started us on one of our most dangerous cases was dated 1 November. It arrived the day after, from Kent, in the afternoon post. Sherlock Holmes lifted it from the stack of letters and circulars Mrs. Hudson had delivered a few moments before. He slit the flap with the tiny silver dagger from his desk. The miniature weapon had been a gift from King d'Forrest, a former client who had asked Holmes' assistance with a case involving three lost companions and a malevolent old woman. Holmes perused the missive swiftly, then leaned back in his armchair and read it again. I stirred up the fire with the poker, then settled back into the basket chair with my copy of the Lancet. It had been a slow, late autumn day, cold and overcast, and I had just returned from my surgery. I was in need of some diversion and I had always found reading my favourite medical journal to be relaxing.

Holmes tossed the letter across to me. "What do you make of this, Watson?" he drawled. He picked out a pipe from the several on the table beside him and began to fill it from his pouch.

I tried to emulate my friend's methods. "It is a letter written on inexpensive paper. The message is written in blue ink, with a fine nib, and so closely composed in a cursive style that the meaning is almost lost among the curlicues and flourishes. It is signed Mrs. Tobias Ogden and I think I see mention of..." I squinted at the note, "...a husband and a bridge. Otherwise I can make nothing of it." I handed the letter back.

"Not too badly done, Watson," he smiled. I brightened and laid down my magazine.

"You have grasped the major outline of the letter, but missed all the important details. The style of cursive writing is noteworthy, however," said my friend. "With copperplate written out in this old-fashioned way, the author could not be anyone under the age of sixty. You recall my little monograph on autographs and calligraphies spanning the last three hundred years that was published in *Graphic Studies* last year."

"My dear Mr. Holmes," he read aloud, "please excuse my writing to you directly like this, without an introduction, but I feel my need is great and will not stand delay. My name is Mary Ogden and I am the wife of Tobias Ogden, former coachman of the Duke of Morris. After decades of faithful service, my husband and I were, by the good-will and grace of the Duke, retired to a small corner of his estate in Kent.

"My husband refused a pension, feeling still capable of work, so the Duke set him to see to the care and repair of a small stone arched bridge just outside the village of Livermoore. A bridge, first of wood and later of stone, has spanned the White River at that spot since the Romans were here. There is a road which skirts Livermoore on the way to the city of Moncaster, but using the bridge and crossing the Duke's estate saves several miles, so the bridge is very popular.

"The population of the village is a mixture of estate workers, small shop owners and people who work in the city of Moncaster but prefer country living. The principal features of the place are the church, the village hall, the public house, and the school.

"Two weeks ago, my Tobias and I were woken up every night for seven nights by the sound of thundering hooves pounding over the bridge and the neighing of a horse. When I mentioned it to a woman friend after services at church that next Sunday, she told me of a story going the rounds in Livermoore.

"It seems that an old legend, the Spirit of Dan Rounders, had been revived. He was a soldier, late of Edward the I's army, back in the 1200s. He came back from the first Crusade and wooed a maiden of the village. She rejected him and he went mad. He killed her, her parents, and two neighbours who had been attracted by their cries. He stole the mayor's prize black horse and fled Livermoore by way of the west road going over the bridge. No one knew what became of him after that. The signs that Dan Rounders was abroad were the sound of hooves and the cry of a horse late at night on moonless nights. It had been moonless the week we heard the noises.

"Ben Walker, an estate worker, said he had seen the ghost of Dan Rounder racing through the streets that same night we first heard the disturbance. Two other men said they saw the apparition on different nights. It was the talk of Livermoore.

"Tobias and I don't believe in adding to such gossip, so we agreed to avoid such talk. We had nearly forgotten the story until an incident happened last night.

"We heard the sound of hooves and the horse's cry after midnight. When Tobias went out to inspect the bridge this morning, he found an odd thing. Across the roadway and parapet of the far end of the bridge were large splashes in red. It was extensive and still dripping. We called the constable and the doctor. No accidents or injured persons were reported in the area. The policeman was baffled.

"At the same time, the local town clerk disappeared. The council is checking the town books right now. But what bothers me the most is the source of that blood. I fear that some outlying farmer or poor animal is lying wounded out in the fields and it breaks my heart.

"My husband and I agreed that I should write to you about these things. Please, Mr. Holmes, would you lose no time to come out here and investigate? Thank you.

"Signed Mrs. Tobias Ogden, White River Bridge, Livermoore, Kent."

"What do you think of that, doctor?" Sherlock Holmes peered at me through a thick cloud of tobacco smoke.

"The woman sounds sincere, Holmes," I replied. "Something strange is happening at the White River Bridge. Will you answer her letter?"

"We shall do better than that," said my friend. "If you would be pleased to accompany me, we can leave by the first train to Moncaster, Kent, in the morning. All that blood bothers me too."

So it was that Sherlock Holmes and I found ourselves stepping off the 9:23 to Moncaster on November 3, warmly clad for the country and clutching our grips. We asked about transportation to our destination and were directed to the cab stand. A short trip brought us to the village of Livermoore.

After leaving our bags at the "Four in Hand," which was both an inn and the local public house, Holmes and I walked the few blocks to the Livermoore Police Station. Unfortunately, since it was early November, the beautiful gardens famous in Kent's summer were long past their prime. Blasted plants and bare tree limbs were visible everywhere. Even the scarlet and yellow bushes set along the stone garden walls lining the pavement of the High Street appeared bedraggled and neglected; their branches whipped bare by the autumnal gusts. The sky hung above us, heavy with grey thick clouds, and the cold wind swirled around our coattails.

On the way to the police station, Holmes insisted we take the High Street. We passed gracious old stone and brick buildings, erected very much in picturesque styles, with doors opening directly to the pavement. There was an ironmonger's, a flower shop, a tiny but quaint tea shop, a butcher, a livery stable, a greengrocer's, a notions shop, a dressmaker's establishment, a doctor's office, and two bakeries. The crowd on the pavement was sparse, but there always seemed to be someone around as we strolled along to our destination.

In the street, small puddles had gathered between the cobblestones, evidence of a recent shower.

The Livermoore police station was a thin, narrow edifice, squeezed in between the village hall and another flat-faced building that sold farming supplies. It was constructed of yellow Portland stone, its windows topped with thick grey lintels. We climbed the steps to the entrance, and found the sergeant on duty at a desk in the lobby.

Sherlock Holmes introduced himself to Sergeant Pratt, who received us with an offer of hot coffee. He was a robust man of middle years, nearly as tall as the detective, with close-cropped hair and a ruddy complexion. He ushered us into chairs in his office, down the corridor from the entrance. Another man, his constable, took over the front desk as we walked away.

Sherlock Holmes introduced us. Sergeant Pratt took his card with a sceptical air. "I have heard of you, Mr. Holmes," he said, "but I admit I think the claims made about your exploits may have been exaggerated. Telling a man's travels by the dirt on his shoes and the stains on his sleeve!" He chuckled and smiled at us.

I huffed into my moustache. Holmes smiled at the officer. "My biographer Dr. Watson does have a tendency to romanticize my cases, and I have often taken him to task for it. However, I am willing to put on a demonstration for your benefit. Your shoes, for example, tell me that you bicycle a great deal, no doubt in the course of your official duties. You store the machine in the cloakroom to the right. Your haircut was chosen to disguise the fact you are going bald, as had your father, who was also a Livermoore policeman before you."

Sergeant Pratt stared at my friend in amazement. "How did you know?" he gasped. "It is all true! Both Constable Comstock and I use bicycles in the performance of our duties. Livermoore is a small village and the cost of a carriage must be justified in the expense book."

The detective shook his head. "I have told Watson that I should never explain my methods, that doing so takes away the wonderful effect created and reduces me to the mortal man I really am. My reasoning was simple. Many rural policemen cover their territories by bicycle. Therefore I looked to your shoes for the tell-tale scuff on the inner sole that touches the petal cover. I also see the wrinkles on your pant leg caused by the clip worn to keep the cloth from fouling in the gears. The street outside has several rain puddles and the tyres of your bicycle are plainly visible on the flagstones of your station hallway, turning to the right and disappearing behind the door marked Cloaks. I know it was your bicycle because of the faint splashes of mud upon your cuffs. On the wall behind your head is a group photograph of a line of men posed before the steps of this very building. The style of clothing is that of nearly thirty years ago. The uniformed man receiving a citation from the mayor, distinguished by his badge of office, bears a strong resemblance to yourself. He is bald. Therefore I deduce he is a close relative, even your father, who also served Livermoore in decades past. Was it on the occasion of his retirement?"

Pratt stared at Sherlock Holmes as a man bewildered. "Well, I have never seen the like! It's witchcraft, it is! I am very impressed. You are a man to watch, Mr. Holmes. What brings you to Livermoore and how may I help?"

Holmes explained about Mrs. Ogden and her letter. Before interviewing the woman and her husband, he wanted to learn what the local police thought about the case.

"The whole thing is very strange. Ben Walker has been talking for days about the dark horseman he saw. Two other men, Paul Booker and Jerald Peabody, saw the same thing but at different times. It was always late at night, after midnight; the horse was black, and the rider wore a shapeless hat and a dark cloak. Not a very good description, I am afraid.

"Frankly, if it weren't for the reports of Mr. and Mrs. Ogden, we might be tempted to dismiss the story altogether. Dan Rounder is a local legend around here and usually told to frighten the children. Young men might be up to mischief, but the Ogdens are quite a respectable, settled couple. They were adamant about what they heard and, of course, there was the blood."

"Ah, yes, the blood," said my friend. "What can you tell me about that?"

"There was a lot of it, several quarts, I'd say. It was found the morning after the last reports of the sighting of Dan Rounder by Peabody and Booker. They staggered into the bar of the "Four in Hand" just at closing time, downed several drinks, and told everyone there that they had just seen the apparition gallop out of town on the west road, which went over the bridge. The village had been on edge about the sightings for a few weeks, so no one was eager to rush out and see what happened to the ghost. The next morning Tobias Ogden walked into town with the report of the blood.

"I had Constable Comstock fetch Doctor Mainstead, and we went out to the bridge, followed by half of the population of Livermoore. Comstock was tasked with keeping back the crowd while the doctor and I examined the scene.

"We found much blood, but no sign of a body. A complete search was made of the fields for over a mile beyond the bridge, but nothing was found except for a few tufts of grass torn up along the road's verge and tossed aside. There doesn't seem to be anything else we can do. There have been no reports of sightings or sounds of the spirit of Dan Rounder since."

"No unusual activities in the village lately? No uptick in break-ins or such?"

"Well, the town clerk didn't show up for work that morning. Claude Penn is his name. He was seen the night before, but in the morning the only sign of him was a note slipped under his landlady's door saying he'd decided to emigrate to America and she should hold his things until he sent for them. Had three days left on his rent, too."

"What did the village think of that?" I asked.

"I tell you, the first thing the mayor did was have someone come in and go over the books! They are at it now, at the hall, but word is they won't be done for several days. It is hard to believe such a thing about Claude Penn, though. He was always such a mousey sort of man."

"What did he look like?" I asked.

"Short, just shy of forty, with a round, bespectacled face, blond hair worn a little long, always with a book in his pocket. Very easy not to notice." Pratt felt the coffee pot, but it was cold.

Sherlock Holmes rose to his feet and I followed him. He thanked the sergeant for his help and asked how to get to the Ogdens' home by the White River Bridge. As he drew on his gloves and turned to the door, he inquired casually, "Was Mr. Penn a good horseman, then?"

Sergeant Pratt could not hold back his laughter. "Why, Claude Penn lived here five years and nobody ever saw him near a horse, much less astride one. I believe the man was afraid of them. Didn't get along with dogs, either. Tolerated the landlady's cat, she said, but wouldn't let it in his room."

With another chuckle, the sergeant closed the door of the police station behind us.

Ten minutes' walk from the outskirts of Livermoore brought us in sight of the hump-backed bridge and its cottage off to the side of the road. The White River burbled along on the left, the cold water steaming slightly in the chill air. The sizable bridge was ahead, spanning the water as it flowed to the right, and the Ogdens' cottage stood about fifty feet to the river's side. The cottage was built of stone and the dry vines on its walls only hinted at the glorious garden that must have surrounded the cottage earlier in the year. Dried dead leaves piled up in the corners and skittered across the brown grasses. Far away in a field a man was bent over some twisted branches, digging with a grubbing fork. A knock at the door brought both Ogdens to us. Tobias Ogden was a tall, dignified man with grey hair and knotted fingers dressed in rough trousers and a dark workman's shirt. His wife's hair was white and tightly curled. She was not quite as tall as her husband, but was rounder, garbed in a simple blue dress covered with a white apron. They invited us in and soon tea and biscuits were served on the gingham tablecloth of the kitchen.

Mrs. Ogden retold the story contained in her letter. Her husband, who seemed content to let his wife take the lead in the conversation, said little, but corroborated everything she said. After a few minutes Sherlock Holmes expressed a desire to see the bridge itself. We were soon standing on the flagstones of its arch and Holmes whipped out his magnifying lens. The old couple watched from their window for a while, then left us to ourselves.

I expected him to begin with the dried substance splashed over the roadway and the stone sides of the span. Instead he started at the other end, toward the village, with a close examination of the dirt road. He fell to his knees, crawled over the path and over the grass lining both sides, and only after he had finished with that did he approach the bridge.

Again he examined every inch of his subject. I stood silently to one side as he crawled, climbed, scrambled, and laid flat upon his face to run his lens over the hump-backed bridge. He even extended his search to the roadbed beyond, sifting through the mud and gravel of the road. Finally, he concentrated on the blood that covered the rough stones of the bridge's sides.

The liquid was dried now. Holmes removed his gloves, ran his hand over it, picked at it with his fingernail, and even licked his thumb and rubbed it on one of the spots. Each time he would check the results with his lens. Finally, after what seemed to be hours, he rose to his feet, thrust his magnifying glass into his pocket and pulled on his warm gloves.

"The day is advancing, Watson, and I have finished here. Let us return to the "Four in Hand" and seek out some lunch. I have a busy afternoon planned, and you shall be a great help. Wave goodbye to our clients and let us be gone, doctor."

An hour later, with a good ploughman's lunch, supplied by the bar of the "Four in Hand" inside us, Sherlock Holmes and I found ourselves on the doorstep of Claude Penn's rooming house. A farm wagon rattled by. Holmes had gotten Penn's address before we left the station. It was a stolid brick building, with starched lace curtains at the windows and a pot of aspidistra in the parlour window that shouted "Respectable!" louder than the curtains.

Holmes took off his hat and nudged me to do the same. At his knock the door was opened by a worn little housemaid. Upon Holmes' inquiry for Mrs. Clements, we were ushered into a front room so spotless the very furniture appeared to squeak in protest. Colourful wallpaper framed a cast iron fireplace stoked with a small coal fire.

After a few moments the landlady came in. Mrs. Clements was one of those High Church-attending, middle-aged women who gave the air of having come up in the world through her own determined efforts and was now resolved to hold her independence and her respectability in equal measure. Her manner changed from distant but pleasant regard to a barely disguised eagerness to gossip when she learned we were not interested in renting rooms from her but in the doings of her absent tenant. A mention of Sergeant Pratt appeared to encourage her cooperation.

"Well, I'm not one to pry," she said archly. The maid brought in tea, and she poured three cups with a regal air that went oddly with the parrot-printed wallpaper and the aspidistra. "I believe in giving my guests their privacy, but there are certain...uh, things, that a boarding house owner finds out over the course of time. After all, Claude Penn has lived here for five years.

"Mail? Oh, he gets letters occasionally, not just tradesmen's bills, you understand, but real letters. At least, he did for the first four years. From Birmingham, where he came from. From family, if one could trust the names and addresses on the back flaps. Not that I ever pried, you understand, but there they would be, visible on the paper. But then I noticed the letters stopped. He did get one last one, heavy paper and a strange-sounding name on the back flap. He went away for a couple of weeks after that, last December, but never said a word about his traveling when he got back, for much as I hinted and gave him plenty of chances. He is close, is Claude Penn.

"He works as a clerk at the village hall. There were never any bad reports about him that I heard, but that's not to say there might not have been some strange goings on. Always dressed well. Why, two new suits in five years! I don't know how he could wear them out, just sitting at a desk all day. He did start sending his shirts out to launder a few months ago. He said I didn't do them well enough for him! Tried one washerwoman, but she ruined them and he had to go out and buy new ones. Ha! Ha! Sometimes I wondered how he could afford it. Well, they are checking the village books, so we may have an answer to that pretty soon. Keeps himself to himself, but that could mean he has something to hide. You can't trust the quiet ones, you know. Go along nicely for years and then murder their wife and children with an axe and run off with the barmaid.

"Married? Not that I ever knew. I only rent to respectable single people, men on the third floor and women on the second. The only time they mix is during meals and in the big parlour after dinner. No, I never noticed Mr. Penn giving any extra attention to any other woman in the house. I have three ladies with me just now, Mrs. Bailey and Mrs. Hind, both elderly widows, and Miss Bradley-Knowles, who was the sister of Sir Arthur Bradley-Knowles, the former MP of our district. She kept house for him but when he died, she heard about my establishment and was glad to get a suite here, second floor front. Always pays her rent on time and doesn't niggle over extras, either."

With a little difficulty Sherlock Holmes got her off the fascinating subject of the estimable Miss Bradley-Knowles and back to her missing boarder, Claude Penn.

"Pastimes? No, he reads a lot, the room is full of books, and he takes walks, but there was never...well, there is that one thing..."

"Yes?" Holmes said encouragingly.

"Last year, in February, a bunch of young people decided to form a sort of amateur theatrical group. Not a lot to do in Livermoore in the winter, I suppose, and he was urged to join it, although he was probably fifteen years older than them, if he was a day. He got them a place to rehearse in the village hall and wrangled the use of the main room for the shows, so I guess they wanted him in for that. He got a part in the cast, too. They did *Merry Wives of Windsor* last fall and he was one of the husbands, I don't remember which one. Miss Bradley-Knowles wasn't quite sure the town clerk being in a play was respectable but she enjoyed it enough when we went to see one performance.

"He told me he was going to be in the next play too. I asked him why he was staying out late so many nights."

"What was the name of that play?" asked Sherlock Holmes.

"It is an old one, something I remember from the days when my husband was still alive. *Murder in the Red Barn* it was. He got the part of the old father. Came down one evening all decked out with a bald cap and false whiskers. Looked quite the sight, but that was what he had to wear, I guess. It certainly gave us something to talk about after he left to meet the others."

"Do you know who else is in this group?"

"Silly bunch of youngsters if you ask me. Alice Bowditch, whose husband should have known better than to let her make a spectacle of herself, and her best friend, Rosie Windom, who was always a little wild, and those boys from the "Four in Hand." Ben Walker and the Peabody lad and three or four others. I suppose Claude Penn is a sort of steadying influence on them, he being so much older."

Holmes asked her if we could examine her tenant's room and she consented after a show of reluctance. Holmes reminded her that we were working with the police and that helped her decide. Mumbling that his rent week was about to expire anyway, she led the way up the stairs to his door on the third floor. Unwillingly she left us there, after unlocking it, and we waited until we heard her footsteps descend the steps all the way to the first floor before entering.

There was nothing remarkable about his furnished room except for the table situated in one corner. A large mirror hung over it and the surface was littered with grease paint, false hair, and other tools of the theatre. A plain chair sat before the mirror and a row of hooks on the wall next to it held costumes and hats that went with the position of elderly father in the play *Murder in the Red Barn*.

Sherlock Holmes went over the entire room, of course, but paid particular attention to the table's contents. He found the script, much marked with notes, and sat in the chair to read it.

That took some time and finally I had to strike a match to light a candle against the darkness of the November afternoon. Holmes started out of his concentration as I did so and rose, laying the sheaf of paper on the table. He glanced out the window at the dusky street.

"Watson, I had no idea it was getting so late. Let us get back to the pub. It is nearly time for tea and you must be hungry."

I was hungry and followed him willingly. To my surprise, however, after leaving Mrs. Clement's boarding house, he turned not left to the "Four in Hand," but right to the road leading to White River Bridge. He ignored my inquiry so I just followed, surmising that something in Claude Penn's room had given him a clue which I had missed, and he was now pursuing it at the cost of my dinner.

The sun behind the clouds had set before we left Mrs. Clement's and we had no lantern. We passed only a few people on our way. The Livermoore street lamps were sufficient to our purposes until we got beyond the village limits, but then we had only the half-light of a waxing moon to guide us. Around us was silence, broken only by the sound of dried leaves rustling in the never-ending breeze and our boots crunching on the gravel of the road. After a brisk walk we came through the darkness to the bridge to see candle-glow from the Ogdens' kitchen gleaming to one side. Holmes did not go to knock on the front door, but headed for the span instead.

My friend stepped to the far end where the spilled blood still clung to the rock walls of the parapet. He motioned for me to hold open an envelope he handed me from his pocket and knelt to scrape some flakes of red into it with a penknife from his pocket. This took several minutes. We were crouched together at this task when I felt a sudden, hard blow between my shoulder blades. I staggered forward and dropped the envelope. A second later I saw Holmes jerk sideways and fall to the ground. In an instant the two of us were grappling with a crowd of unknown men armed with clubs or staves.

We were unprepared and unarmed. It proved to be an uneven fight. I believe I got in a few good blows, but the struggle ended with both Holmes and I being lifted up and dumped over the side into the river. We landed with a splash and floated under the arch and downstream.

What moonlight there was glittered on the rushing water and cast ragged black shadows from the skeletonized shrubbery lining the river banks. The water was shockingly cold and struggled to drag me down into its dark depths by my soaked wool coat and thick country boots. I fought to keep my head above water as I flailed about, searching for Sherlock Holmes.

I choked on the freezing water as it forced itself down my throat and splashed over my head. I despaired of finding Holmes as the minutes passed and my energy was sapped away by the cold water and my exertions. It seemed like I was trapped in an increasingly vain attempt to survive. A realization of my own mortality seized my spirit and I began to panic. With my last desperate surge of strength I flung out an arm and touched a yielding surface. I grabbed at it but my freezing hand slipped.

Instantly I felt Holmes' strong fingers grip my coat sleeve and draw me close to him. Kicking and splashing, gasping words of encouragement in my ear, my friend struggled to reach the river's edge. Sputtering and dripping wet, he grabbed roots of bushes growing there and we helped each other climb out, digging our heels into the muddy bank and snatching at any dead vegetation we could reach. The attack had happened so swiftly that we had not had a chance to cry out. Now, as we stood shivering on the bank, we could hear footsteps and see in the moonlight a huddle of figures running back towards Livermoore.

Holmes made a motion as if to follow them, but I, mindful of pneumonia, held his sleeve and started for the nearby Ogden cottage. Luckily we had emerged on the correct side of the water. Two astonished people opened the door to our frenzied knocking, and in a few moments we were sitting in matching rockers close to the Ogdens' kitchen fire, being plied with blankets, hot drinks, and cries of dismay.

After listening to our story, Tobias Ogden disappeared to alert Sergeant Pratt. Mrs. Ogden wrapped us in wool blankets and dried what clothing of ours she could by the fire. She kept our coffee cups full, even adding a splash of something from a jug stored in one of the cupboards. I supervised as she brought out some hot water and clean gauze and dressed the cuts and bruises we had acquired during the fight and our attempted drowning.

The policeman and his constable, a short fireplug of a man, showed up in a carriage with Mr. Ogden not long after we had dragged ourselves from the river. They listened impassively as Holmes recited the facts. In the middle of it, Pratt dispatched Constable Comstock to retrieve the envelope I had dropped on the bridge. Constable Comstock returned with the envelope, dirty and trampled from being underfoot during the fight. Apparently the mysterious men had not thought it important enough to destroy or carry away after our dunking. Holmes checked the contents and put it in the pocket of his coat. Constable Comstock also handed Holmes the little pen knife with which he had been scraping at the stones when we were attacked.

Pratt's face was grave at the end of my friend's tale and he shook his head solemnly.

"This has gone far beyond a joke now, Mr. Holmes. The legend of Dan Rounder and a mysterious horse galloping through village streets at midnight is one thing, but a physical attack on peaceful men is another."

"I don't think our attackers viewed us as peaceful, Sergeant," said Holmes. "I think we have been watched ever since we arrived in Livermoore, and by tonight our rowdy friends decided we were posing a threat to them. This attack was a message for us to drop our investigation and leave the village."

"Shall you?"

"Of course not! There are too many unanswered questions. Who were the men who attacked us tonight? Are they the same people responsible for the blood splashed on the bridge? Where did they get such a quantity? How does Dan Rounder's story come into it? What happened to Claude Penn? Is he connected with our attacks, and how? Is there money missing from the village accounts? If so, who took it and where did it go? No, Sergeant. I am more determined than ever to clear up these mysteries before I see London town again. I think this object will help me."

He opened his hand and handed a tiny item to the sergeant. I was seated too far away to see what it was, but Pratt turned it over in his hand and gave it back to the detective.

"Well, it is more than we had before, Mr. Holmes."

"I see our stockings are dry now, and our shirts nearly so. We must not impose upon the Ogdens' hospitality any longer. It is getting late, and Doctor Watson has missed his dinner."

At that, Mrs. Ogden protested that it would be a shame for her to let us leave with empty stomachs. We told her it wasn't necessary but in ten minutes a nice little supper was laid out, featuring cheeses, cold ham, and homemade bread. More coffee was brewed and the entire company tucked in. I admit I was grateful and did my best to uphold the honour of London in my appreciation of the county cooking Kent and Mrs. Ogden could supply.

Sergeant Pratt and Constable Comstock dropped us off at the local inn before midnight. As we made our soggy way through the lobby to the staircase leading to our rooms, a man with black eyes and a scraggly beard thrust his head through the door that led to the "Four in Hand" public bar. He watched us enter with a grimace on his face and called back into the bar, "Looks like someone went for a swim!"

A voice answered "Who would be that stupid in this weather/"

The answer came. "London people!"

Sherlock Holmes gave him a piercing glance.

With that the man disappeared into the bar. There was a burst of laughter and I heard some ribald comments from the crowd within. We proceeded to our rooms, and Holmes bade me goodbye until the morning. I warned him to keep his bandages clean and told him I would redress them in the morning.

I came down for breakfast to find my friend picking at a plate of eggs and country ham. He had ordered for me and I ate mine hungrily. Holmes was silent until I had finished and redressed his wounds. I had attended to myself earlier. The cuts and scrapes we had received were healing nicely. As I lingered over my coffee, he told me he had contracted a slight cold from our adventure the night before.

"Then you must go straight to bed!" I exclaimed. "You do look flushed and tired. You must rest. I will order you a brandy at once."

Holmes waved a hand. "I will rest today, Doctor," he said. "But I prefer to sit quietly downstairs, not in my room. The fireplace does not draw well and the wind rattles the window. They stock the London papers here, and the bar will supply all I need in the matter of hot drinks and food. I promise you I will remain still and not excite myself. Meanwhile, I want you to go to the village hall and ask the mayor about Claude Penn. You know, work history, impressions of the man, perhaps get a report on the checking of the financial books. Then talk to his tailor and his laundress. Find out everything you can about the man, including his financial history if possible."

I was flattered to find Holmes was relying on me to discover so much about the missing clerk, but I was concerned about leaving him alone so long. He scoffed at my worries and waved me out the "Four in Hand" door. I left him sitting at a small table in an alcove of the public bar, well-supplied with newspapers, cigarettes, and a hot toddy.

I had escaped the chill that had sickened Sherlock Holmes, and I was glad he could spend his day indoors by the fire. The weather had grown more windy and the temperature had dropped by several degrees, so I clutched my overcoat to me as I hurried down the cobblestone street toward the police station. At Holmes' suggestion, I was calling on Sergeant Pratt to add his official influence to my errand.

For the rest of the morning Sergeant Pratt and I spoke to others who knew Claude Penn in Livermoore. That included the mayor, the auditors, and several of Penn's fellow office workers. No irregularities had been found in the books yet. The mayor, one Garrison Whitney, spoke favourably about Penn, but under the current circumstances would admit to no final conclusion as to his character. The clerk was regarded as friendly and efficient among his fellow workers. He came across as a loner who was always ready for a night out or a frolic but never volunteered, always waiting to be asked.

We proceeded to the Livermoore haberdashery and talked to the young woman who sold him his socks and handkerchiefs. She giggled a bit about his choices, declaring he "was a bit of a dandy" and always fussed about his ties and gloves, requiring "the best in the shop." Her employer, the tailor, confirmed that in the past five years he had ordered two new suits but emphasized that he always paid his bill promptly and in full, unlike others in town he could name. In fact, there was a handsome broadcloth suit waiting to be finished for him right now in the shop, and what was the man to do now that he was missing?

We left the tailor to his problem and sought out the laundress, Mrs. Beech, in a little cottage on the edge of town. She was a late middle-aged, big, red-faced woman, out back in her yard, surrounded by her bubbling laundry cauldrons, clothes lines, and flapping sheets and hand towels, assisted by her equally red-faced daughter. A couple of young urchins, future laundresses both, tumbled about at her feet as she lifted her head from the steam and the linen to answer our questions.

She was proud of her work. Did the gentleman desire some washing done? No? The London gentleman doesn't need to give her anything but, thank you sir, much appreciated. She was glad to answer questions, especially as Sergeant Pratt said it would help the police. She and all her family were honest people, to be sure. Yes, she did Mr. Penn's shirts and small clothes. Yes, he engaged her last winter, right after Twelfth Night. No, she had not worked for him before that. Who had recommended her? Why, she didn't know. He just showed up one morning with a bundle of things. Who else did she work for? Why, the mayor himself sent his washing to her. Also the doctor, the priest, all the tablecloths and sheets of the "Four in Hand", and half the shopkeepers in town. Who had done Mr. Penn's shirts before? That was her rival, Mrs. Newton, in Hastings Lane, a silly old woman more likely to lose buttons and tear the cloth than do a good job. Her only virtue was she was cheap. Didn't care how much she charged because the old biddy drank it all anyways. Oh, thank you again, sir, and maybe she would take her daughter and the babies out for a treat on Sunday.

Our trip to Mrs. Newton, in Hastings Lane, was wasted time. Sergeant Pratt and I found her passed out by drink at her kitchen table. She made no coherent sense to anything we asked her, and we finally gave up and left her to her bottle.

On High Street Sergeant Pratt and I called on the president of the Livermoore bank, Mr. Hawkins. On behalf of police business, he brought out Claude Penn's accounts. What I discovered seemed to put a whole new complexion on the case.

Sergeant Pratt left me as we passed the police station and I hurried to tell my news to Holmes at the "Four in Hand." I found Holmes, much improved, sitting by the fire in his bedroom upstairs, newspaper stuffed into the cracks around his rattling window.

He had ordered sandwiches and hot tea against my return, and I sat down to eat my lunch as I reported on my investigations. Holmes listened with interest, asking questions at intervals, and I finally came to my last bit of information.

"Last December Claude Penn's uncle, his mother's brother, died and left him a tidy inheritance. The chief feature was a brewery, along with several rental properties, including two shops and four flats in the city of Birmingham. There were no other relatives. Penn travelled up to the city for the funeral and to consult with the lawyers. That was the trip he refused to tell his landlady about.

"He received checks from the Birmingham lawyers and opened an account at the Livermoore bank in January. There has been a lot of activity in his account. According to the records, he has been using most of his new-found wealth to support the theatre company. That included an order of cheap jewellery for the *Merry Wives of Windsor* play. Strangely enough, two months later, there was a charge to the same Moncaster jewellery shop for a real silver and garnet pendant and later for a woman's gold ring."

"You have done very well, Watson," said Sherlock Holmes. I glowed in the warmth of his rare praise. "I, too, have spent a fruitful day. Sequestered in the bar of the "Four in Hand," I made a study of the local inhabitants. I even managed to be told the legend of Dan Rounder and his ghostly horse several times. By a generous dispersion of shillings and pence, alcohol has assisted in my enquiries, and I believe I now have all the threads of this case into my hands."

"You have solved it?"

"Yes. If you have finished your food, Watson, would you be so kind as to go and ask Sergeant Pratt and Constable Comstock to be here tonight at eight?"

"Both of them?"

"Yes. Our strength may well lie in numbers."

My errand soon completed, I rejoined Holmes and insisted he lie down to rest. I took my own advice and came down at six o'clock to find him again sitting up and eager for our guests to arrive. I recognized the signs. Having solved the case using his unique powers, he was now impatient for the final act, the confronting and apprehension of the plotters and the clearing up of any such questions that may remain. He refused to reply to my comments but concentrated on a small collection of bowls and jars on the table of his room. A small spirit lamp was extinguished as I entered and Holmes sat brooding over the results of his experiment until the arrival of the local constabulary.

Sergeant Pratt entered first, a telegram clutched in one hand. Constable Comstock slipped in behind him and stood silently by the door. Pratt advanced and thrust the opened telegram toward Holmes.

"This changes the case, Mr. Holmes. Now it is murder most

likely, and someone shall swing for it."

Sherlock Holmes read the message and handed it to me. It was sent by the Chief Constable of Kent, advising Sergeant Pratt that a drowned man had been found miles down the White River, and asking for assistance in identifying the body. The description of the man fitted the Livermoore village clerk. One detail mentioned was that the poor victim's skull had been cracked before death.

The village clock outside the window chimed eight. Sherlock Holmes arose. "It is time."

He led us down the stairs and into the public bar of the "Four in Hand." Three or four men stood at the bar and a large group of diners was seated at one side. A door on the back wall gave entry into a private room. Apparently it had been hired for the evening for a "Reserved" sign hung by a tack from the panel. Holmes strode purposefully to it and opened the door. He entered, the policemen and I right behind him, and interrupted the party within. A bearded man, vaguely familiar to me, was sitting at a table with several others. He was laughing when we entered, but at the sight of Holmes and Sergeant Pratt the smile vanished from his lips and he motioned the others with him to hush.

He was the same man who had taunted Holmes and me for coming back to the inn wet from our adventure the night before. I realized that he was Ben Walker, the man who had made the first report of the return of the Spirit of Dan Rounders and his ghostly black horse. He was dressed in a rough tweed suit and gaiters, such as groundskeepers wear, his black hair flopping into his grey eyes, and his thin nose slicing his blotched face in half. With a twisted mouth and disfiguring whiskers he looked far gone to drink, even at this hour. The others at his table were nearly as intoxicated. Mugs and glasses crowded the table before them. It was obvious that they had been sitting there for some time.

I now noticed that two of the group were women. They both sat with another man between them on a sofa set against one wall, near to the fire. Sergeant Pratt addressed each person with familiarity, pointing them out to Sherlock Holmes as I stood with Constable Comstock against the door. It was the only exit.

I was right to think Ben Walker was the man with the beard. His companions included Jerald Peabody and Paul Booker, who also had reported the appearance of the Spirit of Dan Rounder. Another man, Peter Glass, scowled at us. On the sofa Bernard Bowditch sat between his wife, Alice, and Rosie Windom. We had intruded into what appeared to be a meeting of the core of the Livermoore theatre company.

Sherlock Holmes stepped forward. "I have been investigating the blood-stained bridge outside of town," he began. Walker and the other men seated at the table looked at each other and hissed a few words to the others. Holmes paid them no heed.

"As a result of that I have also been looking into the disappearance of the village clerk, Claude Penn." Paul Booker opened his mouth, but a fierce glare from Walker made him shut it.

"I am going to tell you what happened that night and any of you can correct me where I have gone wrong," purred Holmes. The people all shifted in their chairs and Mr. Bowditch spoke up. He ignored Sherlock Holmes and addressed Pratt.

"I don't understand, Sergeant. What has the disappearance of Claude Penn have to do with either me or my wife?"

"Mr. Holmes is going to tell us a story, sir," replied Pratt. "Surely listening to a story is a harmless enough activity. If anyone objects they could leave, but that would only insure further investigation of that person in the future."

Alice Bowditch whispered in her husband's ear, and he lapsed into silence.

"Claude Penn was the village clerk of Livermoore. He lived a quiet life, more from circumstances than from choice, for he was shy. Last December he learned that his uncle in Birmingham had died and left him a considerable fortune. He didn't tell his landlady and made only a few changes in his habits, but somehow word got out about his money. Suddenly, he was invited to join a merry group of younger people to form a local theatre troupe. He agreed and soon found himself not only one of the cast but also the chief financier of the theatre activities.

"He found the attention agreeable but as time went on things slowly turned sour. Expenses were more than he thought necessary. Rosie Windom encouraged his attentions at first, but as he grew more serious, she began to draw back. He noticed that Ben Walker seemed to be against their relationship. He started to think Walker was poisoning Miss Windom's mind against him just as Walker was demanding more and more money for sets, props, and costumes.

"Perhaps Claude Penn decided the costs of the theatre were too high for him to sustain. Perhaps the cooling relationship with Miss Windom had something to do with his thinking. He had given her a silver and garnet pendant which she had accepted, but when he offered her marriage and showed her the ring she turned him down. Is that the pendant Mr. Penn gave you, Miss Windom, the one you are wearing around your neck right now?"

Rosie Windom raised her hand to clutch the glittery ornament resting on her bosom. Mutely she nodded, her eyes fixed on Sherlock Holmes as would a snake on the flute wielded by an Indian charmer.

"After he was refused by Miss Windom, Claude Penn told Ben Walker that he planned to withdraw all support from the theatre company. He even planned to move to Birmingham to better attend to his affairs there. Walker convinced him to support one more play, the aptly named *Murder in the Red Barn*. It is a melodrama about a young woman who is murdered by her perfidious lover, who hides her body in an old barn. The case is only solved when her mother dreams that the girl appeared before her and directed her mother to her burial place.

"Penn still questioned every bill for the production. That was a threat to Walker, who had been padding the expense accounts from the beginning and keeping the excess for himself. He devised a plan.

"He would frighten Claude Penn so badly that the man would leave the village and never return. He would be so scared that he wouldn't even return to question the money lost in the theatre business. Walker convinced two of his friends, Mr. Booker and Mr. Peabody, to help spread a rumour that Dan Rounder and his ghostly horse had been seen in Livermoore. After weeks of increasing tension, Walker and his friends kidnapped Penn on the night of 31 October and brought him to the White River Bridge. There they beat him, tossed a bucket of fake blood as called for in the play over him, and threw him into the water."

Walker, Peabody, Booker and Glass began to object loudly. They struggled to rise from the table, but I drew my revolver and showed it to them. Lulled by our bucolic surroundings, I had neglected to have it with me before the attack at the bridge. Now I carried it everywhere. Constable Comstock stepped forward, his truncheon at the ready. The commotion faded away as the men recognized their dilemma.

"When Dr. Watson and I showed up, my name was recognized and we were put under continuous watch. Soon it was obvious that we were on the trail of the blood splashed on the stone bridge and the disappearance of Claude Penn. These men thought they had successfully driven Claude Penn away.

"They decided to use the same methods on Dr. Watson and me. The night was dark, they sneaked up on us from behind, and attacked so suddenly that we could not defend ourselves. Throwing us over the parapet was the same method they had used for Penn. They felt secure that we would fold our tents and steal away after such treatment. Fortunately, we were able to escape the river's grip and seek help."

Ben Walker sneered at Sherlock Holmes. "A very exciting tale, Mr. London Detective, but you can't prove it. You admit you never got a good look at your attackers."

"No, but I was able to cut this button off a coat while I was being beaten. I believe it belongs to you, Mr. Peabody." Holmes stretched out his hand and opened it to reveal a brass button, embossed with a pine tree. Our eyes shifted from the button to the man's brown coat. A bit of thread hung from the place where there was a missing button. All the other buttons on his coat were embossed with a matching pine tree.

"Earlier today Sergeant Pratt received a telegram from the Chief Constable of Kent announcing that a drowned body had been recovered miles down the White River from Livermoore. It has been identified as Claude Penn. It was discovered that someone had cracked his skull before he went into the water. He is dead."

Peabody's eyes shifted from the dangling thread of his coat to Holmes' open palm where the embossed button lay to Ben Walker's twisted, angry face. His own visage was drained of blood. He leaped to his feet, almost crashing his chair into the fireplace, and yelled, "Penn is dead? Penn is dead?"

"Yes," Sherlock Holmes replied.

Peabody raised a shaking finger to Ben Walker. "He made me do it! We were only going to scare him! It's all Ben Walker's fault!

He said it was only going to be a bit of fun! He carried the heaviest stick!"

"Shut up, you fool, or we will all hang!"

Ben Walker lurched across the table at Peabody. The policemen were ready. In a few minutes everyone was secured, including Bowditch and the two women. The confessions came quickly. Holmes was proven correct in every detail. Rosie Windom sobbed her heart out, telling how Walker had pressured her to lead Penn on, then to cut him off after he proposed to her, and Walker, with violence, had made her refuse him. Soon after Penn had announced he was leaving Livermoore. The other men blamed Walker as the mastermind of the whole scheme of beating and scaring the clerk and denied any knowledge of the money Walker had stolen from the victim.

Ben Walker, once restrained, slumped in his chair, mumbling threats against everyone including Holmes. Bernard and Alice Bowditch escaped the accusations. Everyone agreed that those two were not involved in the scam or the attack. They had really joined only to indulge in play-acting. Ben Walker admitted that Rosie Windom had only been a pawn in his plan. Those three were allowed to go free.

With the help of the innkeeper, who had sufficient reasons to stay on Sergeant Pratt's good side, our villains were transported to the police station and the Chief Constable was notified.

The next morning Sherlock Holmes and I met the Sergeant at the station as we prepared to board the train to London. Although he had spent the night taking statements from everyone involved, Sergeant Pratt still had a few questions for my friend.

Pratt held open the door and leaned into our compartment from the platform as we settled our bags and found seats.

"Mr. Holmes, grabbing that button was quick thinking. How could you have solved the case without it? That was excellent luck."

"Luck had nothing to do with it, Sergeant Pratt. It was all observation and logical thinking. I knew when I first examined the blood on the bridge that it was fake, made from a formula popular in the theatre. I have some experience in that line. Connecting the blood with the Livermoore theatrical company was simple. It was only after I learned about Penn's inheritance that I thought there could be a very good reason why so much blood had been spilled on the bridge. When we went back there I was looking for the real blood the fake blood had been thrown over to hide. Where is the best place to hide a leaf? In a forest. So it was with the blood of Claude Penn's head wound. I later isolated the human cells from the dyed syrup in my room at the "Four in Hand.""

"Since I noticed we had been followed ever since we arrived in Livermoore, I was half prepared for the attack. Cutting off the button with the penknife in my hand was but the work of a moment. I also took note of several points of interest in the garb and faces of the gang, but that knowledge proved unnecessary once Peabody broke down. However, I would take prompt action in securing that heavy stick Peabody mentioned. Check it for hair and blood."

"I already have," said Pratt. "It was hidden in a woodpile behind Walker's house. There was a tweed thread caught in a splinter that matches Walker's sleeve."

"I gathered the last bits of information I needed while apparently nursing my cold in the bar at the 'Four in Hand'," said Holmes. "Sorry, Watson, but I am afraid my cold would have never responded to your nostrums, seeing as it was quite imaginary."

"I am not surprised," I said wryly. It was not the first time I had been duped by my friend about his state of health for the sake of a case.

Sherlock Holmes continued. "Then it was just a matter of allowing my suspects to gather so arresting them would be convenient for you and Constable Comstock. If you ever get to London, sir, please drop by for a drink. I would like to introduce you to some gentlemen we know at Scotland Yard."

With those parting words Holmes pulled shut the first-class carriage door, the whistle blew, and our train slowly steamed out of the station.

The Case of the Persecuted Poacher

It was high summer, and Sherlock Holmes and I had just finished a gruelling case over the course of twelve days. We tracked down the culprit of the arson of the Wholen Bucket factory and the slaughter of the company's mascot, a fallow deer named Eliza. Pet of the company's founder, Sir Henry Wholen, the animal's body had been found in the smoking ashes of the fire set to ravage the production floor. A bizarre tale of rage and revenge had unfolded as Holmes investigated the crime. Sir Henry said at the police station as the arsonist was thrust into a cell that he had never seen such clever work in his life, and frankly, I could not determine if he was referring to the criminal or to Holmes.

When we arrived back in Baker Street Mrs. Hudson stopped Holmes at the door as I trudged up the seventeen steps to our sitting room. She seemed to be upset with him. I was exhausted. As I lay slumped down in my armchair in front of the empty fireplace, I could hear footsteps sounding from the lumber room overhead. A few minutes later Holmes astonished me by coming in with rods and reels and other fishing equipment in his arms, dumping it all on the carpet at my feet.

"What is this, Holmes?" I exclaimed.

My friend was smiling but behind his eyes I could see concern. He, too, had extended himself physically in the handling of the last mystery. A slight clumsiness, a certain fumbling of his pipe and matches were the only signs he gave of his exhaustion. Otherwise his stern, cold exterior remained intact. I knew how he worked to present such a front to the world, even to me, and I worried that one day the control would slip and the man I knew would break down. Now he had some scheme in mind, and I realized I would have to humour him for his own sake.

"This time I must play the physician, Watson. Do you think that I have not noticed the effort you put in these past two weeks as we searched for the Wholen Bucket arsonist? You have become a shadow of your normal self. Mrs. Hudson has taken me to task about your health. I cannot not have her worrying me about your welfare every time I bring you back from one of these little escapades."

"You are sending me away!"

"No, my friend. I am proposing a little trip for the two of us to the banks of some chalk stream, where the fish linger in rocky pools and the cool shadows of the overhanging trees play among the burbling pools of clear water. A week of us catching our own suppers and trekking over verdant hills back to a comfortable inn should restore the sparkle to your eyes and the vigor to your step."

This behaviour was very out of character for Sherlock Holmes. I looked into his eyes closely. I realized that he was fighting the very demons that both of us feared, that could be calmed only by the use of the contents of a morocco case and small bottle of liquid that resided in a locked drawer in his desk. I needed to help him from reaching for the key that could plunge him into the desperate existence I had worked so hard to rescue him from years ago. I knew what part I had to play in this drama, but I also knew I could not allow Holmes and his pride to know that I knew.

"I could say the same about your step, Holmes, but I am too tired to argue. Where shall we go?"

"All that can be determined in the morning. I have asked Mrs. Hudson to prepare a nourishing supper for us both. After a good night's sleep arrangements will be made. Leave it all to me."

I came down to breakfast the next morning still very tired. A cup of hot coffee and a good breakfast did little to revive me, and I was ready for a nap. Holmes had been busy, however. He was dressed for travel and had already picked through and set in order the rods and other fishing gear he had brought down the night before. Now he was consulting railway timetables and looking up inns from a collection of guidebooks he kept in his bedroom.

I awoke from a doze in my chair to find him standing at our sitting-room door, murmuring instructions to a uniformed commissionaire from the messenger office down the street. Money exchanged hands, and Holmes turned to find me upright and blinking, fumbling with the teapot.

"A fresh pot of tea, Mrs. Hudson!" he called down the stairwell. "That tea is cold, Watson," he said, taking the teapot out of my hands. "I have completed the arrangements and when Willard returns with our tickets we can leave. I have already packed both your bag and mine. Ah, Mrs. Hudson is ahead of me. Here is the tea and some biscuits. Let us refresh ourselves. Our train leaves from Euston Station at noon."

"Where are we going?" I asked.

"A charming place called Shottery, one mile from Stratford-upon-Avon, the birthplace of William Shakespeare. I have booked rooms at a local guest house and there are several trout streams within walking distance."

This all sounded wonderful, I had to admit. Holmes seemed invigorated and bustled about the room, putting the finishing touches on our luggage and even consented to drink a cup of tea. I went upstairs and changed into my country tweeds. As a last-minute thought, almost a reflex action, I slipped my service revolver into my pocket. When our tickets arrived Mrs. Hudson slipped a package of sandwiches into my hand as we entered the cab to the station. Once there it was the work of a moment to find our carriage. The train left London for Warwickshire soon after.

Soon the crowded streets and polluted skies of that great city were left behind. Our view out the windows gradually changed to green fields and tidy little farms. Halfway through the journey I unwrapped the sandwiches, and Holmes and I had lunch, assisted by the flask from Holmes' pocket.

We departed our first-class carriage at the station. Holmes had arranged for us to be met by a hired trap, driven by a local man. It was only a mile to Shottery and with our bags and fishing tackle in the back, it was a pleasant drive through country lanes shaded by over-arching trees. There were many spots of green dotting the landscape, both at the fields' borders and lining the roads we travelled. The sky was cloudless and a bright sun laid dappled light over lanes and fields alike. We passed thatched houses, some half-timbered and others brick, accented by banks of flowering shrubs and neat stone walls. Off in the distance but not too far ran a twisty little stream, reflecting the light with multiple sparkles off the water.

The driver drew up to a sturdy brick building with the sign Green Bush hanging over the door. It was a riot of what the Americans called "Steamboat Gothic." There were turrets, balconies, multiple stories, steep roof lines, ornate stained glass windows, and a wide veranda that twisted around the entire ground floor like a wide ribbon. A section of it had been glassed in. On every level elaborate gimcrack wooden trim was hung and draped, gleaming white against the rosy red brick of the structure. The sweep-up to the front door was crushed gravel and as we descended from the trap the large oak double doors opened onto the porch. A rotund man, about forty, obviously the owner, came out and shook both Holmes and myself by the hand. He was my height and along with his girth, he was notable for his snapping black eyes, flashing out from over red, bulbous cheeks. A young boy scurried past us and carried our bags and fishing tackle into the house.

I surveyed the front of the guest house. "What an unusual building, Mr. Flagg."

He smiled at us both. "I'm a lucky man, sir," he responded. "My wife brought this into the marriage. It has proven to be a nice little property with the added advantage of letting us meet interesting people like yourselves, gentlemen."

We turned from the welcoming smiles of our host, Mr. Hyram Flagg, to the view from the Green Bush veranda. The clumped and gleaming spires and roofs of Stratford-upon-Avon shone bright in the distance, nearly hidden by the greenery of tree and shrub. To the south was the flash of the rails of the train line that had carried us here and to the north rising ground displayed trees and dry stone walls encasing fields of barley and wheat.

As we turned to enter the guesthouse, Mr. Flagg cleared his throat. "If you gentlemen find the charms of fishing and hiking starting to fade, I could recommend some other activities," he said confidentially. "We have no theatre in town, but the shows and opportunities offered by the 'As You Like It Club' have entertained many gentlemen from London in times past." His sly grin and wink left no doubt as to the landlord's meaning.

I was not shocked by his words, but I felt a wave of revulsion. I was well aware of the existence of such "houses" in London. I had been introduced to one when I was a young medical student by a trio of enthusiastic fellows from my college. After a few trips as an observer, my common sense and my newly found knowledge of certain diseases that could be found in those places decided me to swear off such "amusements." Suddenly the green innocence of the countryside was tainted. Sherlock Holmes brushed past the man with a set face, and I hastened to follow him into the lobby.

Inside the Green Bush the ceiling and the wainscoting echoed the outside decor. Doors led away to other rooms and an ornate set of stairs twisted up to the upper floors. We followed our luggage upstairs to a comfortable suite consisting of a tidy sitting room and two small bedrooms. There was a community bathroom down the hall.

The sitting room was furnished with a fireplace, filled with potted flowers, comfortable armchairs, a table with four wooden chairs around it and a gas lamp hung from the ceiling. The view out of the sitting room window matched that of the one we saw from the front porch. Outside the pane of glass we could see the window opened to a tiny balcony hung with more "wooden lace," the hallmark of the Green Bush.

I suggested a nap was in order after our train ride. Holmes agreed and we retired to our respective bedrooms. Within fifteen minutes I was asleep. When I awoke, the afternoon was long advanced and Holmes had left the rooms. I took the opportunity to do a hasty search of his luggage. I was dismayed to find the morocco case tucked into a corner of his bag, along with the little bottle. The bottle was full, its contents as yet untouched. I heard a footstep in the hall and rushed back to the sitting room, where I dropped into a chair and picked up a newspaper lying on the table. A moment later Holmes, followed by the young boy from our arrival carrying a tea tray, entered the room. My friend dismissed the boy and handed me a cup from the tray.

"Have some tea, my dear, Watson," he said. "I think we have enough time for a walk before dinner. Mr. Flagg informs me that there are several trout streams within two miles of this inn, and his other guests have given good accounts of the fishing. Mrs. Flagg is in charge of the dining room and posted a toothsome menu on the notice board downstairs."

"That sounds fine, Holmes." I replied, and in a little while we were out of the Green Bush and strolling down Shottery's High Street.

Shottery was a tiny village decorated mainly in a half-timbered style. It's most famous claim to fame was as the home of Anne

Hathaway who married William Shakespeare of nearby Stratford-upon- Avon. We passed her home on our walk, tucked off the road with a thatched roof and plastered sides. Surrounded by flowers and a few trees, it was a charming sight in the summer afternoon.

We strolled down the High Street. It was remarkable for the number of businesses named out of the works of the Bard. At the edge of town were a few buildings that appeared smaller and more shabby than the rest of the neat little community. I noticed a public house with the sign "The Rose and Thorn" hanging over its door. Next came some shops carrying second-hand clothing and a boarded-up restaurant. Beyond was a pleasant path that wound through a field or two before returning us to our guesthouse.

We returned with good appetites. The dining room was situated just off the lobby. It was half-full and we had no trouble finding a table for two in a corner. Our fellow guests appeared to consist of middle aged couples and groups of young people on walking trips. There was one table of fishermen. Holmes preferred not to mingle. Instead, he amused me all through dinner by murmuring his observations and deductions of our fellow travellers' occupations and points of origin by what he saw as they ate at their own tables. Mrs. Flagg, a plump, pleasant woman, directed the waitresses while the young boy who had carried in our bags cleared the plates and brought glasses of water. After a satisfying meal of roast beef and mashed potatoes, we returned to our rooms and turned in for the night. Holmes made arrangements with Mrs. Flagg before we went upstairs to have an early breakfast served to us in the morning. He also asked that a picnic hamper be prepared for our lunch the next day.

By noon of the next day Holmes and I were casting our lines into a quiet corner of a secluded stream nearly two miles from Shottery. I had watched Holmes' manner carefully when we got up that morning and again checked the bottle when he was in the bathroom. There were no signs it had been touched. Reassured, I had given myself up to enjoyment of the day, including our walk through the countryside and our successful haul of fish. A fat trout lay in Holmes' creel atop a bed of fresh green grass. I had reeled in another trout and was setting my eye and hook on a promising bit of cover under a fallen tree in an eddy when Holmes called for a break. I took in my line as Holmes uncovered the picnic basket from the cool shade of a nearby tree and pulled two bottles of beer out of the water below it.

We had just repacked the sandwich wrappings and the empty bottles back into the basket when our solitude was interrupted by the appearance of the young boy from our guest house. He obviously had run all the way through the fields and was panting for breath as he handed Holmes a note.

"It is from our landlord, Watson," said Holmes. "He tells us there has been a tragedy on the grounds of Drinkwater Hall, the estate of Sir William Singer, the local lord of the manor. Sir William has learned of our presence here and asks that we attend him at his home. He fears that this matter is beyond the resources of the Stratford police."

"What can have happened, Holmes?" I asked.

The young boy piped up. "It's murder, sir. I heard Strom talking to Mr. Flagg. Old Woods, Sir William's gamekeeper, was murdered."

"Who is Strom, son?"

"Sir William's butler, sir. Mr. Flagg said it was urgent. Shall I carry your fishing tackle and the basket, sir?"

"Yes, take them back to the Green Bush. First direct us to Drinkwater Hall." Holmes was poised to leave, his formerly languid manner gone. I was sorry for the death of an unknown man, but inwardly I rejoiced at the bright look in my friend's eye, the snap in his voice, and the energy with which he moved. With a case of possible murder at hand he no longer needed the stimulation contained in the little bottle secreted in his bag. All thoughts of fishing evaporated. The boy went off one way to return our belongings to the guest house, and I followed Sherlock Holmes to Drinkwater Hall.

It was a large Portland stone building, complete with a west tower and a crenelated roof line. A porch, adorned with stone pillars and a crest carved in the keystone over the front door, offered entry. I discovered later that the estate was nearly 2,000 acres, although it had formerly encompassed nearly 20,000 acres when it was first founded by Sir Titus Singer back in the 1400s. We had followed the stream as instructed and then walked up the gravel lane that stopped at the wide steps of the entrance. Beyond the stately home the brook continued in a curve around the side of the mansion. To the right was a rose garden and a grove of ancient trees. A wide swath of gravel apron surrounded the building. Manicured grass and tasteful shrubbery completed the look. An ancient stone bridge arched over the stream and linked the road from the Hall to the rest of the world.

Sherlock Holmes knocked on the massive front door. A tall, thin man, with slicked hair smoothed back over his ears, who was obviously the butler responded. He took our names and led us down a wide hall to what appeared to be a sitting room. We were announced and the door closed behind us. We were face-to-face with Sir William Singer and his wife, Lady Singer.

I had expected a man and woman to match the grandeur of the building, a pair august and austere, aristocratic, with faces out of a medieval tapestry. Instead, Sir William and his wife sat on an overstuffed couch together. She held some needlework and Sir William fingered an old book. I was suddenly reminded of the elderly couple who kept the sweet shop and post office in my hometown when I was a young boy. Lady Singer was dressed in a lavender afternoon dress and Sir William wore an elaborately quilted dressing gown with slippers on his feet. Both smiled up at us, their faces maps of wrinkles and their hands dotted with age spots. Their white hair and their mannerisms told the story of a long relationship. It was obvious that Sir William was an invalid, with a Bath chair parked outside in the hall. Lady Singer's mild eyes strayed often to her husband, her hand always ready to smooth his robe or tuck back a bit of wayward hair.

I recognized Sir William as the hero of Odessa Harbour in the Crimean War. As a Navy officer he had assisted in the defence of the HMS Furious when it was shelled by Russian forces just outside the Dardanelles. Although wounded he had continued at his post and had also dragged three injured men to safety during the battle. Later he was knighted by the Queen and retired to Drinkwater Hall where his family had resided for generations. I did quick calculations in my head. Sir William had to be nearly 100 years old and his wife just a bit younger.

Much of the estate had been sold off in the eighteenth century. The Singers had no children but lived a quiet life, cared for by the faithful Strom who managed a small group of servants.

"Welcome, Mr. Holmes, welcome," said the knight, "and Dr. Watson. You must excuse me for not rising. Age and my past have conspired to anchor me to my seat. I really fear my dancing days are behind me."

Sherlock Holmes smiled at Sir William's words as he greeted the knight and his lady. I followed his actions as Lady Singer waved us to chairs and rang a little bell on the low table before her. A moment later Strom entered, a loaded tea tray in his hands. He placed it on the table and left.

"We are just having our lunch," said Lady Singer. "We dine lightly at our age but you are welcome to join us."

Both Holmes and I accepted a cup of tea. The tray was removed after a few minutes and Sir William got serious.

"You must understand why I called you here, Mr. Holmes. Your talents are well-known in this neighbourhood, thanks to Dr. Watson, and news travels quickly in a small community. Early this morning, about seven o'clock, one of my men found Donald Woods' body on the bank under the ash trees. Woods is...was...my gamekeeper. He has been with us for more than fifty years, coming to Drinkwater with his widowed father as a lad of ten when the father took up the position of gamekeeper. The estate has grown so small the gamekeeper's position is less important than back in the day, but my people are loyal to me and I to them. I kept him on and he was very useful on the estate.

"I'm told his head was bashed in and a bloody tree limb lay next to his body. I called the police and I understand they are still down there. I asked for Scotland Yard's help. The Commissioner's grandfather was at school with me. An Inspector O'Reilly was sent at once. He has questioned me and my wife. Unfortunately, we had little to tell him. Woods was last seen after supper last night by Strom, walking across the lawn to his quarters near the stables. He was known as a sober man, hard-working, who has not taken a vacation in years. His family, a sister and brother-in-law, live in Lancaster. Woods never married. Strom said he was tight with a dollar, which is better than being free with his money."

"What do you wish of me, Sir William?" Holmes inquired.

The old man stirred in his seat. "I used to be athletic, sir. I played rugby when I was a youth, and cricket. I travelled the world in service to my country. But now I cannot do such things and I need someone to go where I cannot go and do what I cannot do. Investigate this murder, Mr. Holmes, and report back to me. Find the killer of my employee. Do not allow me to leave this sphere with this uncertainty hanging over my head. My people are my family, Mr.

Holmes, and it is my job to take care of my family." He looked at Holmes with a steady eye, his military bearing giving him a dignity one would not expect from a man sitting on a couch.

"I would be glad to look into this for you, sir," said my friend. "Since Inspector O'Reilly has done the groundwork, I shall start with him. Excuse us, Sir William." We bowed ourselves out, found Strom waiting in the hallway, and were directed to the Scotland Yard man.

We found him at the scene of the crime, a quarter mile beyond the mansion beside the banks of the stream. The body was about to be taken up and moved to the local morgue. Inspector O'Reilly stood by the wagon, a short, slender man, nattily dressed in a city suit quite out of place in that rural landscape. His brown hair was thinning on top and a pair of round silver spectacles rode on his stubby nose. A sturdy sergeant, tall, broad, and silent, stood by his side. Inspector O'Reilly thrust out a hand.

"How do you do, Mr. Holmes? I am proud to meet you. You are almost a legend at the Yard. Inspector Lestrade speaks of you often, and of you, Dr. Watson. I was glad to hear that Sir William was going to ask for your advice. I have no hesitation in saying that I am baffled. No footprints on this hard ground, no witnesses, and the rough bark of that club yields no finger-marks. All I can say with certainty is that Donald Woods is dead, his skull beaten in by that branch, recently ripped from the young ash tree over there. Splinters of wood were found embedded in his scalp and strands of hair and blood cling to the discarded weapon. Here, see for yourself."

The Inspector led us over to a sheet-draped figure lying on the grass near the trout stream. He pulled back the cloth to disclose the battered head and upper torso of a man. Sir William had said that he was over fifty and his white hair, now clotted with dried blood, confirmed that fact. Holmes asked for the sheet to be removed. Wood was huddled on his left side with his right hand thrown over his body and his left arm wedged beneath his side. The victim was dressed in worn tweeds, brown gaiters, and stout boots. Blood had dried on the features and the skull was battered and broken. Sherlock Holmes knelt down and with his lens gave the body a thorough examination. He paid particular attention to the hands, boots and the head wound. When he had finished he turned to the murder weapon. It was a thin, leafy limb with a thick base, the raw wood coated with blood and gore where it had been beaten against the gamekeeper's head.

"Watson," he murmured, and I also examined the body. As I rose to my feet I saw him at the ash tree, running his magnifying glass over the gash where fresh wood showed where the branch had been torn from the trunk.

"You are correct, Inspector. The ground is too hard to take foot marks. Yet here there are signs of a slight scuffle and there in the grass are splashes of blood flung out by the attack. What did you find, Doctor?"

"Put simply, the right side of Wood's skull has been beaten repeatedly with that branch. Here are the ash splinters Inspector O'Reilly mentioned and I see several strands of hair matching the victim's stuck in the blood of the limb. Hit on the right side of the head, I would conclude that the killer was a left-handed man."

"Thank you, Watson. I am always interested in your observations. However, by the splashes of blood on the grass here and here, and by the way his body fell, I believe the victim was attacked from behind by a right-handed person. Inspector O'Reilly, I would now like to see Wood's quarters."

Dismayed by Holmes' comment about my analysis of the case, I followed the two men and the constable to a tiny cottage set back in the trees on the other side of Sir William's mansion. It was a weathered building, plastered and with a shingled roof, surrounded by pheasant pens and rabbit hutches. Inside there were no signs of a woman's touch. The few bits of furniture were old and utilitarian. The rooms were cluttered with discarded clothing and old boots. Apparently Woods took all his meals at the servant's hall at the mansion. The only signs of organization were the neatly-kept guns and well-oiled traps of various sizes hung in up the second bedroom. Holmes poked around Woods" desk. He sifted through the old clothing and counted the number of bottles in the trash. He was inside for over an hour but emerged with a long face. He walked around the pens and checked the fences and cages but found nothing of interest.

Sherlock Holmes bid goodbye to the Inspector and we began our walk back to the Green Bush. He was silent as we left Drinkwater Hall behind us. Therefore I was surprised when after we had walked nearly a mile he paused on the path, leaned against a handy tree and pulled out his pipe and tobacco pouch. He chuckled.

"What is so amusing, Holmes?" I demanded.

"How did you find the gamekeeper's cottage, Watson?" he asked.

"It was a disorganized mess, Holmes. Hardly fit for human habitation at all."

"Yet there was one room where order and cleanliness reigned. One room where the tools of a man's trade were kept in excellent condition, ready to serve their purpose at a moment's notice."

"The second bedroom!"

"Exactly. Did you notice the small desk in the corner of that room?"

"Well, yes, but it was the display of guns and traps that drew my eye."

"Fortunately I have trained myself to look for the gold among the dross to which others are attracted. I searched that desk and found the ledgers and journals which make up a gamekeeper's working records. Several books held accounts, breeding records, reports of the migration of various animals and birds across the estate. I also found these few pages, torn from a book, pressed in the back pages of one of the account books. The inspector glanced at them, decided they were unimportant and allowed me to take them away."

Sherlock Holmes drew three sheets of what appeared to be notepaper from his pocket and handed them to me. I found three typeset pages. They were torn and dirty, much folded and refolded, and with tears and holes on each sheet. There were hand-scrawled dates on each and the contents referred to hawthorn trees. I looked at Holmes in confusion.

"What do these papers have to do with Woods' death, Holmes?"

"That is what I plan to devote my evening to discovering, Watson. Let us go on our way. The sun is low, and I am sure a good dinner awaits us at the Green Bush."

There seemed to be more excitement than usual as we entered the lobby of our lodging-place. Several guests were clustered around the admitting desk listening to Mr. Flagg, our host. He turned to us as we entered, his dark eyes glittering, and motioned Sherlock Holmes to approach.

"Here is Mr. Holmes now. He is sure to know. After all, Sir William sent for him himself. Mr. Holmes, is it true? Has Donald Woods been found murdered on Sir William's own doorstep?"

My friend was displeased at being so publicly questioned, so his normal stiff demeanour became even more reserved. "Donald Woods was found dead, Mr. Flagg, but not on the doorstep of Drinkwater Hall. You understand that, being called in to consult with

Scotland Yard, I am not at liberty to comment on the case."

"Of course not, of course not," said Mr. Flagg with a twisted smile, "but I am a betting man, Mr. Holmes, and I am willing to wager that it was that Tom Tittlemouse who had something to do with it."

"Who is he?" I asked.

"He is the local poacher, Dr. Watson, and as slippery a character as you are ever likely to meet. He came of good family, but his folks died when he was young and he took to the woods soon after. He lives here and there, said to have some shelters set up in the lands around Shottery and Stratford-upon-Avon, and lives on the rabbits he can trap and the fish that he pulls out of other men's waters. He's had a running feud with Woods." His face was eager and wide-eyed as he waited for Holmes' response.

At this point Holmes was handed a note by the ubiquitous young lad who had carried home our fishing gear. He glanced at it and then coldly announced to the whole lobby, "I am sorry, but I never comment on a case in which I am involved. Come, Watson, I see the dining room is open, and I am hungry."

We took the table we had eaten at the previous night and the crowd, seeing that they would learn no more from the renowned detective, went off to find their own dinners. The two trout we had caught that morning were presented to us ala almandine, and I dug into my share. Holmes, for all his protestation of hunger, merely picked at his. Although strawberry shortcake was offered as the pudding, Holmes refused it and led me back up to our suite as soon as possible.

Night had fully fallen. Outside the windows of our suite a sliver of moon hung behind the trees and darkness enveloped the view like a fog of black.

As soon as we stepped through the door he handed me the note he had received in the lobby.

"Anonymous source identifies Thomas Tittlemouse, well-known poacher and troublemaker, as attacker in Woods' murder case. Please meet with me at 10 tomorrow morning at Drinkwater Hall to discuss plans on questioning same. O'Reilly."

"Well, that seems to wrap it all up, don't you think, Holmes? This poacher tangles with Donald Woods, probably about some game Woods caught him making off with, and Tittlemouse clubs him down, then disappears."

"It is precisely because I can think, Watson, that I find this easy explanation suspect. Who is the anonymous source? Are a few rabbits or a couple of fish enough to serve as a motive for murder? What about those odd pages we found in Woods' desk? They must be important because Woods kept them so carefully. One was dated yesterday. No, there is more to be found than what information has been presented to us and the police. For a beginning, what about these pages concerning hawthorns?"

Holmes took the chair by the table and turned up the hanging gas lamp. I sat in the chair opposite him, my back to the window. He removed the pages from his notebook and examined them carefully with his magnifying glass.

"Nothing," he muttered. "Nothing! Confounded pages! The left sides show that all three have been ripped from a small book, the size to carry in one's pocket. Very handy for consultation in the field. Consecutive pages! My, my."

He ran his lens over each sheet, front and back. He held them up to the light. To my great surprise Holmes first smelled each page, then licked them one by one on both sides. At my expression of amazement he glanced at me, then smiled.

"A good detective must have many tools easy at hand and ready to use under unusual circumstances, Watson. I do not always have access to my supply of chemicals or the laboratory at St. Bart's. Invisible inks have their own odours and tastes, as do poisons and other liquids. It behooves a detective to have extensive knowledge of such things. I once wrote a small monograph on the subject."

He stood and carefully held the sheets to the gas flame one after another. "Not lemon juice or milk, then," he said. He sat down and spread the three sheets out on the desk.

"Dated in pencil yesterday, two days before that and one week ago. Standard information on Crataegus, or hawthorn. Flowers, fruit, habitat, useful in hedges, found all over the Northern Hemisphere , and so on. Yet these must be important! Why, why? I am baffled, Watson. Sherlock Holmes baffled by three torn, filthy pages about hawthorns!" He slid back in his chair and stared at the mysterious papers with a disgusted look on his face.

I had seldom seen my friend so frustrated before. I put it down to the exhaustion from which we were both suffering from our hard work on the Wholen Bucket case.

I picked up one of the pages from the desk and stared at it, hopelessly looking to see some fact the great detective had missed. Could I aspire to do such an impossible feat? Could I, in my ordinary, blundering way, find a clue that Sherlock Holmes had missed, despite all the knowledge and experience he had accumulated in his career?

"These papers remind me of Mr. Poe's story about the 'Purloined Letter'," I mused. "The letter in question turned out to be so dirty and torn that it was dismissed as unimportant and therefore invisible to those searching for an important document."

Sherlock Holmes slowly straightened in his chair. He turned to me and said, "Watson! Again you have pointed the way to light when all around me was darkness. I am really very, very grateful!"

I was flattered but bewildered. "I don't understand, Holmes. What did I say?"

Holmes had taken back the page I was holding and was arranging it with the other papers on his desk. He again lifted each up to the light of the gas lamp. "The rips, smears, and holes disguise the true purpose of these pages. It is hard to see, but on certain letters on each line are tiny pin-pricks. Write these down, Watson."

I scrambled for my notebook and pen as Sherlock Holmes began reciting letters from the page dated one week before. As he continued with the other pages a message slowly became clear.

"Warning keep your nose out of my business or you will regret it.

"Stop talking you will pay.

"Meet me at bend in stream tonight midnight your place will make it worth your time."

"The bend in the stream was where Woods' body was found! Holmes, these warnings are most sinister!"

"Yes, the messages demonstrate a clear escalation of threats against the gamekeeper over the space of a week. One can deduce that Woods had some knowledge the murderer wanted kept secret. Woods was either talking about something illegal he knew about or he was planning to talk to the police or his employer, Sir William about whatever it was."

"The last message sounds like the murderer wanted to pay Woods off in return for his silence."

"Yes," said Holmes. "Or it could be a way of luring Woods to a place where he could be attacked without witnesses."

My friend fell silent, still stretched out in his chair, hands resting on the table top, eyelids drooping, and his face aimed toward the balcony window behind me. I also sat quietly, so as to not disturb his thoughts, until I began to wonder at his immobility. When I opened my mouth to speak about it, he motioned toward me with a slight movement of one finger, and rose from his chair. He turned down the gaslight and sighed.

"It is late, Watson, and time all honest men were asleep. We will return to this problem in the morning. Good night to you."

He slipped his hand into his pocket as he turned away to his bedroom door. I was instantly on the alert. It was a simple little gesture he had used before, in a dangerous situation on another case, and I understood his meaning. I too rose and walked to my own room, but once inside I removed my coat, waited a few minutes, then dosed my own light. I secured my revolver and stood behind the bedroom door. I held it open a crack and listened carefully.

At first there were no sounds in the sitting room or from Holmes' room beyond it. But after five minutes or so, I heard a slight scrabbling on the tiny balcony that hung outside our sitting room. I heard the window sash being raised and a few faint noises like someone was crawling in through the opening. There were soft footsteps, a match flared and then I heard Sherlock Holmes' voice commanding the intruder to raise his hands.

Instantly I flung open the door and strode in, my weapon at the ready. Holmes had entered before me and was pressing the stem of his pipe into the back of a shabbily dressed man standing by the table with his hands up. In one hand a wooden match was still glowing. Holmes took it from the man's fingers and used it to light the lamp. I showed our visitor my very real revolver and searched him for weapons. Outside of a well-worn hunting knife in a sheath at his belt he was unarmed. I tossed the knife on the table and Holmes motioned him to one of the wooden chairs.

As he took his seat I looked him over carefully. He was thin but wiry, his hands and face well-browned by exposure to the elements. He wore his brown hair long and shaggy and he was dressed in a ragged old coat and crudely-patched trousers. His worn grey shirt had no collar, there were cracks and scrapes on his thick-soled shoes, and the battered old hat he twisted in his hands was simply unspeakable. His nose appeared odd, as if it had been flattened some years ago, and his eyes were green, sharp and betrayed an intelligent gleam as he stared back at us.

Sherlock Holmes picked up the knife and examined it swiftly, the lens from his magnifying glass reflecting the flaring gaslight. When he was finished he flung it at the table where it stuck upright and quivering, the blade tip buried into the wood.

"To what do we owe the honour of this visit, Mr. Tittlemouse?" he said, in a surprisingly mild voice.

"I've come to consult you," the brown man said. He blinked at the sound of his name but did not ask how Holmes knew.

"On what matter?"

"Why, on the murder of Donald Woods, sir."

"For which, I have been informed, the police suspect you."

"That is just it, Mr. Holmes, I didn't do it!"

The flood gates opened. "I had nothing to do with it. I didn't like Donald Woods, it's true, I thought him a hard, tough old man, but

I didn't kill him. Him with his 'Sir William said this' and 'Sir William said that' was enough to drive a man to drink, but he was doing his job, I guess. It made a bit of fun to outsmart him and get away with the fat rabbit or pheasant on occasion and he never knew how many fish saw my dinner plate and not Sir William's. No, it was not me that did for Donald Woods. Yet I am the hunted man, while the real murderer gets away."

"Where were you last night?"

"I cooked my dinner next to the Avon, on the west side of the river. I can show you the campsite. After that I walked about a bit and spent an hour at the public house 'The Rose and Thorn.' I was asleep before eleven."

"Can you bring any witnesses to support your story?"

"Yes, a number of people at the 'Rose.'

"After the 'Rose'?"

"Well, none after that."

"You wish to consult me?"

"Aye. Everyone knows you two are here and that old Sir William called you in, along with that London copper. But I need you more. For them it's the answer to a question, for myself it's the rope. I heard you pride yourself for standing up for justice and wouldn't let an innocent man go to the gallows. Prove me innocent, Mr. Holmes."

"You realize that it is most difficult to prove a negative, Mr. Tittlemouse. To clear you I would have to find the real killer. Sir William has already engaged me to do that. I cannot have two clients. Sir William is my client."

Tittlemouse shifted his shrewd eyes from Holmes to me and back again. "I know that, sir. I want you to know that I didn't do it. But I have a suggestion. Have Dr. Watson here," and he gave me an amused glance, "hang out with one of the hostesses at the 'As You Like It Club.' He might come out with a few bits of information a gentleman like yourself would never be told."

Holmes' lips turned up a bit at the corners at this suggestion and I felt my face getting red. The impudence of the man! "Holmes," I said sternly, "this man is a murder suspect. Shall I send for Inspector O'Reilly?"

The poacher was halfway to the window, his blade in his sheath, before I finished my sentence. Holmes raised his hand. "I don't believe our business is concluded, Mr. Tittlemouse. As I said, I already have a client. However, I also don't believe you attacked Donald Woods. Therefore I can treat you as a source of information rather than a suspect."

"How can you decide that, Holmes? He sneaked in here and he is armed!" I cried.

"With a knife, Watson, not a tree branch. If an attacker possesses a knife, would he choose to use another weapon, one that takes time and effort to prepare for use? There were no signs of blade work on either the young ash tree or the limb ripped from it. The dead man had not been stabbed. I believe our friend here. Are there any other leads you can give us, Mr. Tittlemouse?"

"Not now, Mr. Holmes. I'll keep my ear to the ground. Goodbye, Dr. Watson. Ask for Muriel. She's a real chatterbox." With a wave and another grin, Tittlemouse was out the window and enveloped by the darkness of the night before I could stand up.

Sherlock Holmes explained to me that earlier over my shoulder he had seen faint movement on the balcony outside which had prompted him to set the trap that caught our intruder. Finally I was allowed to take to my bed just a few hours before dawn.

The next morning we met with Inspector O'Reilly on the steps outside Drinkwater Hall. Holmes informed the Scotland Yard man the details of his interview with Thomas Tittlemouse the evening before. Inspector O'Reilly showed Holmes the smudged note accusing Tittlemouse that had been shoved under the door at the local police station. Sherlock Holmes examined it with his lens but aside from the note being written in block letters with a dull pencil on a scrap of paper torn from the back of an old envelope with no other markings he could find nothing. Leaving the huge constable to guard the steps to the mansion, we went in and were shown by Strom to Sir William Singer. He was in the sitting room. The old knight was alone and explained his wife was upstairs with a headache. He was able to tell us little more about his gamekeeper Donald Woods. At last, Sherlock Holmes asked him who were Woods' friends.

"As far as I knew, Strom was the man closest to Woods," said Sir William. "I would suggest that you talk to him next."

Holmes decided not to do that in the presence of the butler's employer. We found Strom in his sitting room in the back of the house. The tall, thin man sat impassively as the questioning began.

"How long have you worked for Sir William?"

"I was first hired nearly twenty-five years ago as Sir William's steward. He had managed his estate before that, but his health finally demanded he get help. After a few years the old butler, Zale, died and he asked me to take over the butler's duties. As you can see, the estate is not that extensive or that active so I agreed."

"How large is the staff you manage?"

"The inside staff consists of myself, the cook/housekeeper, Mrs. Smith; Rosie and Maggie, two housemaids that come in from town daily; Maggie's younger sister, June, who acts as scullery maid; Brenton and Andrews, two men that serve in the mansion and do work outside; a stable man named Timothy and his young son who helps him; Woods as gamekeeper, and old Blake who is head groundskeeper. Blake suffers from arthritis and rarely leaves his armchair these days, but he has a great memory, knows every inch of the estate, and instructs Brenton and Andrews about work that needs to be done."

Inspector O'Reilly made note of the names. "I will arrange interviews for all those people later today," he murmured.

Sherlock Holmes concentrated on Strom. "Donald Woods was here when you first arrived."

"That is correct."

"What sort of man was he?"

Bertram Strom fiddled with the salt and pepper-pots on the table before him. "Dour. He was faithful to his duties but seemed to have little joy in his life. As steward I worked closely with him. He was village-educated, knew a great deal about the animals, birds, and fish in the area, and could name every tree on the estate. But he never married, seemingly talked to no one but old Blake and me, and had no family around here. He idolized Sir William and his wife, always speaking of them with great reverence and respect." Strom kept his eyes focused on the landscape outside the window, as if he were trying to recall details of a man's life that were already fading from his memory.

"Did he attend church?"

"No. Most of the help are members of the Church of England

and attend services with Sir William and Lady Singer every Sunday. Woods would disappear Saturday nights and not be seen again until Monday mornings at breakfast in the servants' hall."

"Interesting. Did he mention where he went Saturday nights?"

"Never. His demeanour was such that it was not the sort of question that anyone felt comfortable asking him."

"Do you have any ideas about places Woods would visit on his time off?" asked Sherlock Holmes.

"None."

"Tell of the last day you saw him."

"That would have been Saturday. Today is Monday. He ate breakfast at the servants' hall. I asked him what he planned on for the day, and he told me he was going to check some rabbit warrens near the stream a mile up from the mansion. Later that evening he ate supper with us, and I watched as he walked out the servants' entrance and made his way toward his house. That is the last time any of us saw him alive."

"Mr. Strom, I want you to gather all the servants and bring them to the kitchen. Inspector O'Reilly, with your permission, I would like to sit in while you question them."

"Of course, Mr. Holmes." The butler nodded and left the room.

"I will come with you, Holmes," I said.

"That is not necessary, friend Watson. The constable can take notes. I have another task for you. I want you to investigate how Woods spent his time off from work. Canvass both Stratford-upon-Avon and Shottery. No shop is too humble, no church is too grand.

Question everyone. At the railway station inquire as to anyone who has arrived and departed in the last 48 hours."

Sir William's carriage took me to the railway station, then returned to Drinkwater Hall. I tracked down the official in charge, a short, peppery man in his fifties, ex-military, and punctilious to his duties.

I established my credentials and, it being between trains, he took me back to his private office and offered me tea.

"Helping Sir William and Scotland Yard with Donald Woods' death, eh? Well, sir, I am glad to be of assistance. Passengers in and out of this station for the last two days? Why, man, that's impossible without a detailed description! This is the summer season! Hundreds pass through every week. Some are day-trippers, some come for a month, others for a few days, like Mr. Holmes and yourself."

"Well, can you at least tell me if Donald Woods was a customer of yours? Was he ever in the habit of taking the train to another town or city on Saturdays or Sundays?"

The stationmaster was thoughtful. He had seen Woods many times over the years, particularly when he came to the station to pick up shipments relating to his job on the Drinkwater estate. He could not remember the gamekeeper buying a ticket to another destination in all those years, much less every Saturday or Sunday.

I thanked him for his time and stood on the platform for a few minutes, smoking a cigarette. I was perplexed. If the murderer came on the railway from another location, it was impossible to trace him through the station. Each passenger carried a ticket, but those were frequently discarded after the passenger left the carriages. No ticket carried a name, only a number, and since the tickets were usually paid for in cash, there was no way to track the purchases. Woods, the stationmaster insisted, had never left the area by rail. How then, indeed, had he spent his hours away from Drinkwater Hall? Did the answer lay in the people and buildings on the High Street before me? I was in Stratford. Could the answer be in Shottery?

Clearly I had a long day before me. Rather than march into every shop, restaurant, and public house available and announce my purpose, I decided to be more subtle. I would pose as a customer and deftly extract information from the clerks and serving staff of each establishment. I could see no flaw in this plan so I started with the small restaurant next to the station.

The small eating place proved of no help. No one knew a Donald Wood or had ever served him. The results remained the same all down the High Street. I methodically stepped into each place and asked about the weather, their goods, and finally about the Drinkwater Hall gamekeeper. Despite purchases of cups of tea, sweets, tobacco, and even measures of lace, a pamphlet on the beauties of the River Avon, and other things useless to me, although some might be utilized by Mrs. Hudson, I learned nothing. I was perplexed. Sherlock Holmes made it look so easy. He could walk into any public house in the land and leave with enough facts to write a history of the locals, including their great-grandparents and every dog and cat in the area. I would leave with only the taste of the local beer in my mouth.

Perhaps my plan would work better in Shottery. It was a pleasant stroll through leafy paths to that village so close to Stratford-upon-Avon. On the High Street I realized how hungry I had become and stopped in the first restaurant I saw. It was called the "Falstaff Arms" and advertised a hot lunch and friendly service.

The house stew was hot and even tasty. The service was friendly, personified by the perky red-headed waitress who brought me my meal and coffee. Since it was after the normal luncheon hour the dining room was empty except for her and I. She gave me a smile when I remarked on her appearance and expressed surprise on her employment in such a small town. Surely she was made for more than dishes and scrubbing flagstone floors?

"Thank you, sir, but I am quite happy here. My father is the owner, and my betrothed is a young farmer from just outside of town. Oh, but I do see all sorts of people, sir. Lots of people come here interested in William Shakespeare or Anne Hathaway. I imagine you are yourself, sir."

She laid a serving of warm sliced home-made bread next to my plate. She was so young and pretty. Her answer to my next question caught me by surprise.

"Why, yes, sir, I did see Mr. Woods frequently. I was sorry to hear of the murder. My Harold doesn't like me to speak of it, sir, being that I am a respectable girl and engaged, but Mr. Woods used to come in here every Sunday night and get his dinner, rather late. He didn't drink much here, but I believe he always had his fill and more before he showed up. He would try to give me a squeeze or snatch a kiss, but I am a respectable girl, sir, and he never succeeded."

"What did your young man think of that?"

"Oh, he was not very pleased, sir, as you might imagine. The last time I told him about it he offered to punch Mr. Woods' eye if he ever met him on the street."

"When was that, may I ask?"

"Let's see, it must have been a week ago, sir. Yes, a week ago exactly. I wasn't working here this past Sunday because my aunt had invited me to go to Cambridge on Saturday to select my wedding dress as her gift to me. She married a professor at St. John's College and has always been fond of me, sir."

"How did your fiancé spend his time then?"

"Oh, he had plenty to do on the farm, sir. When we got engaged, he told me, 'Kate, you must understand, on a farm there are always plenty of chores. What with the animals and the sowing and the harvest and the upkeep on the buildings and fences there is always plenty of work." I laughed and said 'Oh, Harold, I'm not afraid of hard work. I've work in the 'Falstaff' since I was a little girl and learned everything about running a house from my mother. You'll be getting a willing helpmeet when we are married, Harold Prince!'"

"Was anyone helping him?"

"Yes. The hired boy, Richard Blue, was with him, fixing the stone wall and working with the animals. Some of the cows got out and into the corn and they had to chase them back and repair the damage. Harold said they worked all afternoon and into the night."

I sipped my newly filled coffee cup and sat in thought. It sounded as if while Harold were upset about Donald Woods annoying his girlfriend, he wasn't upset enough to kill him. Plus, he had spent the entire day doing hard physical work on the farm. Would he have been energetic enough after all that to trek out to Drinkwater Hall and beat the gamekeeper to death with a tree branch? As a farmer he would know of the hawthorn tree and all its uses. Kate was an attractive young woman. Had she told me the entire story about Donald Woods and herself? Had she told Harold?

Another customer walked in the door. Kate turned to show him to a table and I managed to ask one last question. "Did Donald Woods ever talk about how he spent his free time away from Drinkwater Hall?"

"No, I'm sorry. I think he must have had a lady friend, though. He did mention someone named Honoria."

With that she was gone. I finished my coffee and went out to continue my mission.

I started down Shottery's High Street, using the same plan I had used in Stratford-upon-Avon. Again I accumulated a varied collection of items, including more tobacco, a card of buttons, a packet of tacks, and two different booklets about Anne Hathaway's cottage. By the late afternoon I had worked my way down to the edge of town and stood before the door of the "Rose and Thorn."

I was reaching for the handle when a strong, thin hand grabbed my wrist and restrained me. I looked up in astonishment to find Sherlock Holmes at my side, pulling me back. He spun me around, matched me across the cobblestone street and into an alley that led away from the shabby public house.

I started to protest such treatment but Holmes shushed me and hurried me onward until we were well away from the town and strolling down a path through a meadow in the direction of the Green Bush. I recognized the place as the path we had taken after exploring Shottery the first evening we had arrived.

"I think we have missed tea," he said. "But we shall have plenty of time to get ready for dinner."

"Holmes! You startled me!"

He smiled and pulled out his pipe. We were walking down the gravel path, rich pasturage around us and some dull-eyed sheep staring at us from a small knoll close by. Wisps of raw wool, pulled from their coats, fluttered on a few prickly plants near the path. Overhead the sky sported some low clouds and the light was slowly fading as the sun neared the horizon.

"What have you discovered, Watson, during your little walk?" asked Holmes.

Little walk, indeed! I had tramped up and down the High Street of two towns in a vain effort to discover how Donald Woods spent his day off work. I decided to give Holmes a full report, putting in every little detail I could remember, including the conversation with the waitress Kate at the "Falstaff Arms," and every mention she made about her fiancé Harold. I would overwhelm him with each boring fact available.

Unfortunately for my feelings, he didn't appear bored at all. He listened quietly to my report and even asked a few questions about Harold. By the time we approached the porch of the Green Bush I was torn between irritation at his calm attitude and flattery at the close attention he was giving me.

"How was your day, Holmes?" I finally asked, a touch sarcastically.

"Interviewing the servants was not very productive, I fear. I did discover one lead with promise. I must admit your efforts have been most useful to our case. Now I suggest we get an early dinner and a little rest. We have a big night before us."

"Whatever do you mean, Holmes?'

"Later, Watson. It will all keep until after dark."

Sherlock Holmes had the bad habit, as I saw it, of never explaining his plans during the course of solving a case. I knew it was futile to continue asking questions. My feet hurt from all the walking I had done and actually an early dinner was attractive. There was baked chicken for dinner and strawberry shortcake.

It was not to happen that night. We got a pleasant surprise after we returned to the guest house. Mr. Flagg handed over an envelope bearing the monogram of Sir William Singer. He watched with snappy little black eyes as Holmes opened it. We had been invited to dinner at Drinkwater Hall that evening. The carriage would be sent. Holmes sent back his compliments and accepted for both of us.

We were the only guests. The meal was expertly served by Strom. When Sir William asked about the case, Holmes replied that he never spoke during the progression of his cases, only at the conclusion. He did entertain Sir William and Lady Singer with stories of previous cases, including the Bobby Shafto disappearance and the Doctor Faustus's Dancing School scandal. Sir William and Lady Singer loved listening to Holmes' stories.

After dinner our hosts took us on a tour of the Main Gallery. It was a long handsome hall, with a parquet floor and lofty ceilings. Hung along the walls were tier after tier of family portraits and paintings of royalty and nobility dating back generations. They were all done by the fashionable artists of their times. Finally we stopped before a detailed oil of Sir William painted in his younger years wearing his military uniform and medals. When I commented on how life-like it was, Sir William grinned broadly and said, "You compliment my wife, Dr. Watson."

"You painted this portrait, Lady Singer? It is wonderful," said I.

"I had a talented governess who taught me well. I have sketchbook after sketchbook filled with little studies in charcoal and watercolours. I went through a phase of oil painting many years ago. I suggested that Sir William pose for me as my gift to him for our anniversary. He agreed and then insisted that it be hung in the Gallery. I have always wondered if I should have chosen a darker background colour..."

"Nonsense! It is perfect just the way it is," said Sir William. He leaned out of his Bath chair and reached for her hand. They smiled at each other and I felt a pang that such a perfect decades-long love should still exist in such a troubled world as ours.

Our night was not over. We arrived back at the Green Bush in Sir William's carriage by eleven o'clock. Instead of going to bed, Holmes told me to change to my fishing clothes while he did the same. Then he led me away from our guest house along the path that led to Shottery. The sky was clear and there was enough starlight to get along without a lantern. Sherlock Holmes had excellent eyesight and guided me through the darkness. It was just before midnight when we both approached the front door of a closed "Rose and Thorn." It was locked and the building appeared deserted.

The street was empty, the windows of the public house black behind the limp and dirty curtains. Faint streetlamps glowed from down at the cross street. Sherlock Holmes stood poised on the steps, his impassive face held high, as if he were sniffing the air. He left the front and started to circle the building. It was a one-story brick detached construction with windows at shoulder height. On the sides were other windows low to the foundation, nearly covered with rank weeds. No light emanated from them and upon closer inspection I could see there were dark curtains hung behind the glass.

The alley behind the "Rose and Thorn" was narrow. The blank backs of old buildings looked down on us. It was obvious that most of them were either warehouses or abandoned. A back door was secured tightly. Holmes knelt at the lock and pulled out a set of pick locks from his coat.

Suddenly I heard footsteps coming up the street. A light flashed down the gap between the pub and the building to our right. We froze. A man's voice called out and was answered by another from our left. After a few minutes it was clear that the two men, old friends, were not going to move from the front steps of the "Rose and Thorn." From their conversation it was easy to deduce that one had a bottle. They sat on the steps to share the contents.

To continue on our mission was futile. We could be discovered at any minute. Holmes motioned silently and we picked our way down the alley toward the path that led back to the Green Bush.

Less than half an hour later we were back in our suite. Without explaining anything, Holmes retired to his room. I also went directly to my room. I thought about ordering a pan of hot water for my feet but the house was silent, all the occupants having gone to bed. I was reluctant to awaken anyone so I went to bed myself.

By breakfast I had several questions and I was not in a mood to be denied answers.

I attacked my morning egg while Holmes spread marmalade on his toast. He munched away calmly as I gathered my courage to question him.

"Holmes," said I, "I think I deserve some explanation for last night."

"Do you, Watson?"

"Yes. To begin, I hope all the work I put in going door to door gathering information for you yesterday was helpful."

"Very helpful. Thank you, Watson."

I waited for him to elaborate. He didn't. I persisted.

"Why did you prevent me from canvasing the 'Rose and Thorn'?"

"I did not want you to become known to the denizens of that establishment at that time, Watson. My own investigations had shown that the "Rose and Thorn" is the front for another, more shady business, the "As You Like It Club".

"The house of ill-repute mentioned by Thomas Tittlemouse!" I cried.

"Yes, and also mentioned by our host, Mr. Hyram Flagg. Discreet inquiries of the older men in Sir William's employment led me to believe that Donald Woods frequently visited the club. In fact, he had become a regular guest during his days off. I determined that an excursion to the place would be edifying. Our dinner at Drinkwater Hall last night extended the evening right into my timeline. I had been told the pub was closed only one night a week, last night. That would have been the best time to examine the premises and perhaps get a look at the books. We could confirm Woods' involvement and perhaps even establish the reason for his murder.

"The waitress at the "Falstaff Arms" spoke of a possible romantic interest, a woman called Honoria."

"That is a very valuable piece of information. Honoria was one of the names given as one of the soiled doves working at the club. Unfortunately, we were interrupted last night. We will have to infiltrate the place in another fashion."

"What other fashion?" I asked.

Holmes sipped his coffee and ignored my question. "Inspector O'Reilly has returned to London but will return at a moment's notice. I must send him a coded message this morning, letting him know of our adventure last night. My investigation is not yet complete so we will resume our fishing so as to throw off suspicion by the murderer."

We did just that. By the early afternoon Holmes and I were back in our vacation pose. That day and the next we spent all our time tramping up and down the stream where we had caught our first fishes. Each time we returned to the "Green Bush" our landlord greeted us warmly but I could feel him following our movements with his sharp eyes. The excitement of Donald Woods' death died down as Scotland Yard let it be known that they believed the murder was done by a passing stranger.

Thursday was the day of Donald Woods' funeral. We were picked up by the Drinkwater Hall carriage and attended with Strom as Drinkwater Hall's representatives. Afterwards we were invited back to have dinner with Sir William and his wife.

Again the meal was delicious. Afterwards Sir William suggested another tour, this time of the Drinkwater Hall library.

It was a large room, lined with oak bookcases and cabinets containing curios and rare manuscripts. The books were obviously the loving labour of generations, ranging from an ancient hand-illustrated Bible from an Irish monastery to a shelf of the latest mysteries that Lady Singer confessed she read aloud to Sir William in the evenings. There were some volumes bound in limp red Morocco leather. Others were hardbound with stamped covers and touches of gilt. Long shelves of volumes were devoted to British war histories, the law, architecture, public and domestic health, popular novels of the last century, classic plays, agriculture, and nature.

In that section there was a series of six small books with blue pasteboard covers, sized to fit in one's pocket. Sherlock Holmes picked up one and flipped the pages casually. I glimpsed the title, "Nature's Gifts, Volume II."

"Sir William, these little books seem an odd addition to this magnificent collection. Did you purchase them?"

The knight turned the pages of another of the little books. "Yes, I remember. There was a door-to-door salesman. He told me he had knocked on every door in three counties around. I examined them, found the information sound and well-written. I ordered a set, I know Strom ordered a set, and some other people in the area also ordered them."

"Do you know if Donald Woods ordered a set?"

"I do not."

"What other books have you added to this wonderful collection?"

Sir William, with prompting from his wife, proceeded to pull out books and tell Holmes little stories about their acquisitions; a bargain here, a lucky find there, a presentation copy from the author, a gift from an old shipmate. Holmes seemed to be listening closely but from long experience I could tell he was not. Instead, his mind was working on another level. Something had clicked a piece into the puzzle he was assembling, and he was endeavouring to understand its significance. Finally Sir William and Lady Singer bid us farewell and, in the carriage riding back to the Green Bush, Holmes sat quietly, his fingertips pressed together and his thick brows drawn together over his grey eyes.

Sherlock Holmes wasn't there in the morning for breakfast, having gone out an hour before I awoke. The skies outside our window were crowded with dark grey clouds. The wind had picked up and the trees were rustling loudly. It all promised a big storm. I decided to stay in our suite to wait for him rather than tramp out into the countryside. My friend came back in the middle of the morning, and paced the sitting room as I lounged in an armchair, a yellow-back novel I had brought from London in my hand.

"Today is Friday, Watson. I believe that this case could be wrapped up by tomorrow morning, just in time for us to catch our train home."

"Where did you go so early this morning, Holmes?"

"I went to Drinkwater Hall. I am sure, Watson, that you noticed my interest in that little set of books in Sir William's library. Paging through the one on trees, I saw that the relevant pages of "Nature's Gifts" matched the pages sent to Donald Woods as threats. They did not come from that book, of course. Its pages were intact. Further investigation was necessary. Thus I rose early this morning and hiked over to Sir William's. I did not remember seeing those books in Woods' house. I looked again. The set was not there and there were no signs of it ever having been there.

"I called on Strom and was invited to breakfast. I told him I was doing one last saunter around the neighbourhood before leaving tomorrow. During the meal in his sitting room I was able to examine his bookcase and determined that he did indeed have a set of the books. I found all the pages of the relevant volume were intact. His books were not involved in this murder."

"So that clue is worthless."

"I would not say that yet. I have more investigating to do. Do you have any plans for dinner, Watson?"

I was surprised by the question. Sherlock Holmes did not normally concern himself with food in the middle of a case. "Dinner? I thought we were eating here at the Green Bush."

"No. I am bored with their cuisine. I think we will eat in Shottery instead. The threatened storm is about to break. Today is a good day to stay inside with a book."

A few minutes later a cloudburst settled the question. The rain came down in sheets and coated the window panes. Holmes went into his room. I sat, irresolute, wondering if he was lured there by the small morocco case and the little bottle hidden in his valise. I could not open the door and ask him what he was doing. That would not be the action of a gentleman or a friend. Yet how could I just sit here, my mind teeming with visions of him pulling out the case, holding up the vial, adjusting the minuscule plunger....!

I was about to jump to my feet, to do what I knew not, when the door opened and Sherlock Holmes stepped out.

"Watson, this rain has made me restless. I need something to read. I was not as foresighted as you were, to bring a book or two."

I looked into his eyes and saw no sign of the demon. Holmes left to find the reading room downstairs, urging me to stay where I was. I didn't listen. I made a brief search of his valise, found his case and bottle undisturbed, and went back to my book. The muted sounds of the rain outside provided a calm background to the absorbing story I was reading.

I didn't notice how much time passed until Holmes returned, carrying a couple of books in his hand. Instead of joining me in the sitting room, he went back into his room and firmly shut the door. At lunch he came out and we took our meal in the small glassed-in porch just off the main dining room. The rain was coming down more moderately now, but the skies were dense with overcast, and all outside was wet and sloppy.

My friend had something on his mind, for he spoke little and picked at his food. After the waiter had brought our coffee and the last of the other diners had left the room, he turned to me with a wry twist to his mouth.

"I suggest, my dear Watson, that you take a nap this afternoon, for the investigation bids fair to keep us out late."

"What do you mean, Holmes?"

"We will leave here at eight o'clock tonight. We are going out for dinner. I have ordered the trap that met us at the rail station. On the way to our destination I will explain all."

That was all I could get out of him. I have mentioned Holmes' exasperating habit of never disclosing his plans beforehand, for the man loved drama and lived to astonish friend and foe alike. After several attempts to get him to talk, I gave up and followed his advice.

By eight o'clock our trap had arrived and the young lad stood outside in the slop, holding the horse's head. We came out onto the front porch. I had dressed in what passed for my best clothing and Holmes was garbed the same. The horse trotted along for a few minutes but as soon as we were well away from the Green Bush Holmes called to the driver and the trap pulled off the road and into a copse of concealing trees.

Sherlock Holmes spoke softly so the driver could not hear us.

"My search for reading material today bore welcomed fruit. I checked the Green Bush reading room for a set of "Nature's Gifts" and found it." He pulled volume two out of his pocket and opened it. "See here. Three pages have been ripped from the relevant chapter. Note the ragged edges of the missing pages between the leaves."

"What does it mean, Holmes?"

"It means our host is involved in some fashion with the blackmail of Donald Woods. As for the murder, we must have more information. But I cannot discover that information, my dear Watson, without your help."

"I am always happy to serve, Holmes."

"Excellent! I knew you would not falter. Tonight you will visit the 'As You Like It Club' as a customer."

I sat silently. What was there to say? I found the task

distasteful, but if it were necessary to solving the case then my duty was clear. Holmes briefly explained what he required of me and told the driver to continue on.

The trap dropped Holmes off two blocks away from the "Rose and Thorn." I was delivered in solitary grandeur to the front door. As I entered the public house I was surprised by the décor. Somehow I had anticipated something lush and vaguely erotic. Instead I saw the ordinary walls and seatings of an old English pub. There were few patrons. Dim yellow bulbs glowed overhead. Scuffed furniture, plastered surroundings, a soot-blackened stone fireplace and a small curved bar guarding a rack of brandies and wine faced me. Behind the bar a door with a frosted glass window interrupted the row of bottles. The owner, a tall whipcord of a man sporting a twisted nose, stood behind the bar. He ran a cloth over the surface and asked me what I would have.

I ordered a beer. He bent down to draw it from a cask beneath the bar top. As he placed it before me I leaned forward and said the phrase Holmes had given me: "I see this drink is just as I like it."

He gave me a wink from his heavy-lidded eye. He removed the glass of beer. Then he came out from behind the bar and led me gently by the elbow to a door on the right of the fireplace. He nodded to one of the loungers sitting by the bar and the man nodded back. When he opened the door I saw stairs going down into darkness. I hesitated, but he urged me forward. Together we stumbled down the steps and along a black corridor. In a few minutes we were mounting another set of steps. When the handle of the door at the top was turned and the gap widened it was as if a jewel box had been opened.

The large room was brightly lit by electric lamps. Overhead were two elaborate chandeliers, hung with crystals and glowing with white bulbs. The ceiling and the walls were draped in red velvet. Scattered over the parquet floor were lavender overstuffed chairs, little tables, blue chaise lounges, chintz sofas, and many, many thick soft cushions. In one corner was a gilded iron spiral staircase that led to the upper floor and in another was a fully-equipped bar. Next to that was a player piano. Everywhere were flashes of gold and silver. The air was thick with incense. Yet all that paled before the other feature that came into focus as my eyes adjusted from the darkness of the passageway.

There were women there. Thomas Tittlemouse had referred to them as "hostesses," but these were like no other hostesses I had ever met. They were wearing very little clothing. Their bare arms and legs gleamed soft pink in the overhead lights. I counted at least three of them, draped over the furniture and standing in provocative poses by the bar. I saw feathers and flashes of white satin and black or red lace. There was no safe place to look. I stood stock still, trying to hide my discomfort. One of the women, younger than I but heavily painted, detached herself from the others and approached me.

"Hello," she said brightly. "My name is Muriel. What's yours?"

"J...J...John," I stammered. She was very close to me and her breath was sweet. A soft hand tugged on my sleeve and I found myself sitting in one of the armchairs with Muriel on my lap. She was blonde and wearing what appeared to be a short black-lace satin shift and pink feathered mules. The neckline was cut very low and I could see her rounded breasts through the thin material. She giggled and wriggled, and asked me if I didn't want to buy her a drink.

My purpose there was to divert the inhabitants and buy Sherlock Holmes time. I motioned to the tall man and asked Muriel what she would like.

"I only drink champagne, love," she said, stroking my cheek with a manicured nail. The owner stepped behind the bar and produced a bottle and two glasses.

I felt something was expected of me so I took her hand and squeezed it. She responded with another giggle and snuggled into my arms. Then she straightened up and accepted the glasses. She barely sipped at her own but insisted on feeding me the entire contents of mine. It was refilled and the bottle was left on a convenient table by the chair.

I must admit that all her moving around in the chair was having an effect on me. Desperately I tried to think of some way to get her off of my lap. Unfortunately she mistook my efforts as eagerness on my part and began to whisper in my ear of all the delights I could find up the spiral stairs as she fiddled with my tie and ruffled my hair.

I was given more champagne. The bottle was drained and another one ordered. Finally she slid off my lap and I was drawn to my feet. Before I could understand what was happening my foot was on the lowest step of the stair and she was guiding me upwards.

I couldn't resist or make a disturbance because the owner was watching me. I fumbled my way up a few more steps, Muriel delightfully encouraging me, and then salvation came with the distant cry of "Fire!"

The door by which the owner and I had entered burst open and the man who had been sitting by the bar popped in, his face a mask of urgency. "Frank! There's a fire in the bar!" As if to prove his words a thick wisp of smoke swirled past him into the room from the passageway behind.

Instantly the others in the room, including the owner and the stranger, ran for a tapestry hung behind the piano. I followed. Shoving the instrument aside and tearing down the wall hanging revealed a door. The owner flung it open and we all tumbled out into a dirty alley. We had been in one of the seemingly abandoned warehouses situated in the street behind the "Rose and Thorn."

To my amazement two other women ran out behind me, followed by two men. One was a beardless youth who took to his heels down the street and vanished into the night. The other man was fat and came out pulling on a coat, his tie flung over his shoulder. He was shoeless and his trouser braces were swinging around his hips. When he turned away from the rather overweight woman who came out with him I saw his face.

At that instant my arm was seized in an official grip. Everyone who had escaped from the building except for the beardless young man found themselves in the unyielding custody of the local constabulary. Inspector O'Reilly, his sergeant and one of his constables were there, too, so Scotland Yard was well-represented.

"The fire! My bar!" cried the owner, as he struggled to escape the law's clutches.

"Do not worry," said a familiar voice. "A small fire in the office in a metal wastebasket and a couple added smoke bombs create a very effective illusion. The important papers, like the double set of books and the daily work journals, are quite safe.

"Easy, Officer, if you please! That is Doctor Watson and despite his untidy hair and disorderly appearance, he is on our side. Are you all right, old man?" At my nod Sherlock Holmes turned to the last man out the door.

"I thought I would find you here, Mr. Flagg!"

Indeed, it was our host of the Green Bush. He was hastily rearranging his clothing while glaring at Holmes and the police officers. He looked almost comical, with his shirt half-tucked into his pants and his bare toes digging into the sloppy dirt of the alley cobblestones. But his black eyes were mean and the scowl on his face twisted his round red cheeks into a caricature of his normal smiling face.

The woman who had come out with him was trying to keep her flimsy robe on her shoulders. Even under the lights of the police's torches clear evidence of multiple bruises and scratches on her smooth pink skin, especially her neck and arms, were visible.

"Your name is Honoria," declared Holmes.

"That's right, ducky," she said. "And who are you?"

"My name is Sherlock Holmes," he responded. "As you see, your co-workers and your...ah...employer are about to be put up on charges relating to this house. Everything about it will become known. If you and these other ladies will answer our questions, I will use my influence with the local authorities, and Scotland Yard to lessen charges raised against you. Rest assured, however, that Mr. Potter here and his lackey are not included in this offer."

Honoria gave Holmes a shrewd look. She looked to the other women, who all looked frightened, and then to the tall man called Potter. He gave her a fierce scowl and shook his head. She glanced at Hyram Flagg who had balled up both fists. He tried to take a step toward her but was yanked back by the big Scotland Yard sergeant who held his arms. The formerly affable host of the Green Bush now looked as if he could tear her apart like a sheet of paper.

She spat at both men. "You shouldn't have tried to cheat me, Frank. I know you've been pocketing the girls' tips and skimming off the top." The tall man turned white. "I've got plenty on Mr. Frank Potter and I'll be glad to tell it to the coppers, Mr. Holmes. That pal of his there, was assigned to keep us in line and not go to the authorities. He had some pretty crude methods to insure our obedience.

"As for you, Hyram Flagg, if all is to become known, then I will get my revenge. He beat me every time, Mr. Holmes, and never listened to my cries for mercy. Frank let him do it because he paid so well. Donald Woods was one of my regulars. When that poor, sweet, lonely man found out, objected and said he would tell his wife, Flagg attacked him with a tree branch. He bragged about it to me three days ago and said he would do the same to me if I ever gassed."

Flagg called her a filthy name and broke away from the policeman. He lunged at her, his fingers clawing at her throat, yelling he would kill her. It took three of us to bring him to the cobblestones and two policemen to put shackles on him. Honoria screamed that she would tell all and encouraged the other women to do the same. Holmes stood over him when he was finally secured and held the blue-backed volume two of "Nature's Gifts" aloft triumphantly.

"You left a wide trail, Mr. Flagg, and tonight has supplied the final bits of information I needed. Inspector O'Reilly, I think this is now your concern. I am satisfied, however, that the person accused, Thomas Tittlemouse, had nothing to do with Donald Woods' murder."

At that we heard a whoop and looked up to see the scarecrow figure of Thomas Tittlemouse waving at us from a rooftop across the alley. Obviously he had heard his vindication from Sherlock Holmes and was waving enthusiastically. I saw him take a step backwards and with a final happy shout he disappeared.

O'Reilly stepped forward and gave Hyram Flagg the usual cautions. The Scotland Yard sergeant and the constable hustled him away. The women were taken away to get their statements, Muriel already giving great indications of Thomas Tittlemouse's prediction for talking. Frank Potter and his pal were arrested and left to the tender mercies of the local police. The local fire brigade arrived and as they tended to the dosing of the fire the inspector turned to my friend.

"That was a good night's work, if you ask me." he said. "When I got your wire, Mr. Holmes, I dropped everything to catch the next train. Sir William put us up when I was here before and he offered me a room anytime I needed it. Even though it is late, Strom will let us in."

Strom did let us in. He ushered us to Sir William's sitting room. O'Reilly requested a drop of brandy as a nightcap, and as Strom poured out the portions, the doors opened and Sir William rolled in, clad in pajamas and his robe, a maid pushing the Bath chair and his hastily dressed wife behind him.

"I couldn't miss all the excitement!" said our client. Strom got them settled and gave them their share of the refreshments. I just toyed with mine for I was still feeling the effects of all the champagne I had been forced to drink earlier. Sherlock Holmes stood in his favourite pose before the fireplace, filled his pipe with Lady Singer's permission, and when he had it drawing properly, began his report.

"When we were called in to this case, I saw at once that it was not going to be easy to solve. I had no equipment here, I didn't know the local scene, and Donald Woods seemed to be a man so devoted to his work as to have little or no private life. I did determine that the murderer had to be strong in order to be able to rip that branch off the living tree.

"In an examination of Woods' home I found three printed pages hidden in Woods' desk. With Watson's help I recovered the coded messages Woods had been receiving. He had been ready to give someone special knowledge that would injure the miscreant. The miscreant offered to pay him off during a meeting on Sunday night. Instead Woods was murdered, struck down by a desperate man.

"We had a visitor in our rooms that night. It was Thomas Tittlemouse, local poacher, who had been accused of the crime. He protested his innocence and I believed him."

"Why, Mr. Holmes?" asked Sir William.

"Because he was armed with a hunting knife and your gamekeeper was killed by a tree branch. Who would disdain such a handy weapon as a knife for a crude tree branch that had to be broken off a nearby tree? I sent Watson out the next day to discover what Woods did during his days off. He came back with one important fact. Donald Woods had mentioned a woman's name, Honoria, as his 'lady friend.'

"While Watson was doing that, I tracked down Thomas Tittlemouse. He had mentioned something that intrigued me. He had spoken of the 'As You Like It Club.' As a patron of the 'Rose and Thorn,' he was well-aware of its existence. He gave me all the particulars he knew. There had been similar cases in San Francisco in '58 and Lyons in '64. When Inspector O'Reilly and I had questioned the Drinkwater servants earlier, two of the older men had acknowledged that they knew of the club, although they denied ever having visited it. I planned out my next move and stopped Watson from knocking on the door of the public house.

"That night I tried to pick the lock of the 'Rose and Thorn,' but was interrupted. I sent Inspector O'Reilly regular reports of what was happening, holding him ready at a moment's notice to return to Stratford-upon-Avon as needed.

"In an effort to disarm the murderer's fears of discovery, whoever he was, Watson and I renewed our vacation. Scotland Yard assisted by declaring that they believed the attack had been random and the attacker had left the area. Then, Sir William, you invited us to visit your library.

"In your magnificent collection of books, I found the series of little blue-backed volumes of 'Nature's Gifts.' The printing of three consecutive pages of the second book in the series matched the information given on the threatening notes sent to your gamekeeper. I immediately vowed to find the volume from which were torn the pages sent to Donald Woods.

"The salesman had told you he had knocked on every door in three counties. I didn't have time for that, so I concentrated on Stratford-upon-Avon and Shottery and the people who were closest to Donald Woods. Time was running out as I methodically eliminated everyone I had on my list of suspects."

Sherlock Holmes glanced at the mantel clock, which was just chiming midnight. "Then yesterday it rained. The storm was too violent to allow fishing. Watson, clever man, had brought reading material from London but I had not. I decided to check out the Green Bush reading room.

"There it was! A complete set of 'Nature's Gifts.' The books were tucked on a lower shelf in a corner. I examined the second volume and the relevant pages had been removed. Here, just as I found it."

Holmes brought forth the blue-backed book opened to the correct chapter. Sir William and Inspector O'Reilly passed it back and forth with exclamations of wonder and surprise. His audience waited eagerly to hear the rest of Holmes' story.

Holmes cleaned and filled his pipe again and held a match to it. "The rest was simple. I had merely to establish motive and to seek witnesses. A casual mention by Mrs. Flagg of her husband's plan to be absent that evening made me decide to put my plan into practice at once. Accordingly, I told her we would eat out, informed Watson what he needed to do, and put the plan into effect.

"Watson left me a few blocks away and entered the 'Rose and Thorn' alone. When he did not quickly return I waited a few minutes. Then I managed to enter the bar through the window in the office behind the bar. No one in the pub suspected a thing.

"I searched the desk and bookshelves of the office. I found the first and second set of financial records and the day-to-day journals. It was obvious at a glance that there was enough skulduggery there that Inland Revenue, if not other agencies, were going to bring the owner, Frank Potter, to the dock. I couldn't be sure how long Watson could hold out against a bevy of eager females, so I set a small fire in the metal wastebasket and tossed a couple of plumber's rockets in after I crawled out the window.

"One of Potter's friends raised the alarm. I gathered up Inspector O'Reilly and his army of police, whom I had arranged to have outside the pub waiting for my signal.

"All went according to plan, the miscreants were arrested, Mr. Flagg tipped his hand, and I understand the women involved are very willing to give evidence about the entire enterprise. Mr. Flagg will greet no more guests at the door of the 'Green Bush.'"

The next morning, as our bags were loaded onto the same carriage that had brought us to the guest house from the station, I saw Holmes pull aside the young lad who had carried our luggage when we first arrived. They conversed briefly and Holmes pressed a sum of money into his hand.

Soon after that Sherlock Holmes and I mounted the steps to the train from Stratford-upon-Avon back to London. As the train pulled out of the town and gathered speed I caught a glimpse of the fanciful outline of the Green Bush roof line over the fields.

There had been much disarray at the guest house that morning when Holmes and I paid our bill and left. Mrs. Flagg had sat behind the desk in the lobby, alternately crying and calmly toting up bills and collecting money. As we took one last look at the "Steamboat Gothic" building, I said something about her changing moods to my friend and Holmes shook his head.

"Undoubtedly she knew of his predilections, Watson, but I am certain she knew nothing of the murder. It was fear that she would divorce him if she learned about his connection to the 'As You Like It Club' that motivated Hyram Flagg's actions. She has been badly used and I pity her. Flagg, a known ne'er-do-well, married her because she inherited the 'Green Bush' from her first husband and he saw an easy living. He enjoyed playing mine host at a successful guest house, and he also enjoyed the dubious entertainments he could indulge in at the 'As You Like It Club.' Remember, Watson, no man is a hero to his valet...or, in this case, his errand boy."

The Case of the Refurbished Room

"You see the problem, Jeeves?"

"I do, sir."

"Do you have any thoughts?"

"The problem appears quite insoluble, sir."

"Yet you agree that something must be done?"

"Yes, sir."

"I have been thinking about it since breakfast, Jeeves, and I think I have a solution."

"Indeed, sir?"

"Since we can't count on co-operation from Aunt Agatha, I think we need a detective."

"A detective, sir?"

"Yes. One of those chappies so good with disguises and spotting suspicious characters lurking about the butler's pantry with one eye on the silver and the other on Milady's jewels. A detective could sort this whole thing out. Do you know any detectives, Jeeves?"

"As a matter of fact I do, sir. An experienced man."

"Is he any good?"

"He has been called so by others."

"What is his name?"

"Mr. Sherlock Holmes, sir."

"What, the bloke in the stories in that magazine?"

"Yes, sir."

"I thought he was just a fictional construct."

"He is as real as you or I, sir."

"How well do you know him?"

"Well, sir, as a matter of fact, he is my uncle."

"Your uncle?"

"Strictly speaking, he is my great-uncle."

I stared at Jeeves in surprise. Somehow I had never thought much about his relatives. He brought them up now and then in conversation, but the impressions left were fleeting. If I had thought about his origins at all, I had rather believed he had sprung full grown, like Minerva, from the wainscoting just before I had opened my apartment door that first day and found him standing in the hall.

"Didn't one of those stories say he was going to retire?"

"Yes, sir, and in fact he is currently residing in a cottage on the South Downs. But he still does a little work for old friends and family members."

"And you are a family member."

"Yes, sir."

"Well, that would explain a few things. Would you call him up, apprise him of our problem and get him up here?"

"I will do so at once, sir."

Jeeves shimmered away and left me sitting on the sofa in the library of Woollam Chersey, my Aunt Agatha's estate in Hertfordshire. I had carefully chosen the library for my rendezvous with Jeeves because with Agatha's husband, Spencer Gregson, away to Sumatra looking out for his rubber stock interests, the room was guaranteed to be as deserted as Death Valley at high noon during a heat wave.

I was at Aunt Agatha's digs for my health. That is, after a little practical joke aimed at Tuppy Glossop had misfired at the Drones and left the entire place awash knee-deep with Sunlight Soap suds, I had decided that a little holiday away from London might be beneficial for my well-being. I had accordingly wrangled an invitation to Woollam Chersey without disclosing to my formidable aunt the true reason why. I admit that Aunt Agatha is not the most sympathetic of relatives, but Aunt Delia was spending the summer in Monte Carlo spending some of the proceeds of the sale of her magazine *Milady's Boudoir* so my options were limited. Besides, Anatole, Aunt Delia's unsurpassed chef, was at Woollam Chersey.

I arrived late with no dinner. Jeeves managed to scrounge up a tray for my room. It held pretty poor pickings, and I began to wonder if Anatole had lost his touch. After a cigarette and a couple of chapters of "Death at the Lawn Party," a real thriller I had picked up at a Boots just before I left London, I went straight to bed. During breakfast the next morning the supply of bacon and ham seemed to have run out before I came down, and I was confronted with a choice of scrambled eggs, raw fruits, nuts, little brown crackers and herbal tea. There was an odd group of four women in lavender overalls already at the table. They ate in silence, giving me strange looks all the while despite my charming greeting and efforts at bantering small talk. Then they disappeared like pale lilac puffs of smoke into another part of the house. Aunt Agatha sat down beside me with a plate of fruit and crackers and sniffed when I asked as to the availability of meat.

"Meat clogs your inner self. It weighs down your blood and impedes its passage through the brain. You can't afford to eat meat, Bertie. Your brain needs all the blood it can get."

"Don't tell me Anatole is ill!"

"There is nothing wrong with Anatole. After he arrived I told him there would be no need for his services. He immediately took a room at the local inn, the "Bread and Cheese," and is reported to spend all his time reading cookbooks in the public library."

"Why in the world weren't his services required?"

"That is none of your business, young Wooster. Cook has stretched her abilities and has proven adept at preparing these healthy meals. Once you understand how things are arranged around here you will no longer complain. If you can't sustain yourself on what I supply, you can go back to London."

Since all the bubbles hadn't popped in the foyer of the Drones yet, I decided to shut up. Instead I consulted Jeeves. He had bad news from downstairs. We put our heads together and the above conversation took place.

Jeeves brought home the bacon to the library only a few minutes later. He reported to me that Sherlock Holmes had agreed during a phone call to journey up to Hertfordshire that morning to the nearby town of Grantham, where Jeeves had booked him a room at the "Mary and Matthew."

At three o'clock I hopped into the two-seater and buzzed off to Grantham. I found Sherlock Holmes waiting in the lobby. His long, lanky limbs, clothed in an ancient grey tweed suit, were folded into an armchair. He had a profile that could slice cheese with a nose sharp enough to pick up the Munster and slap it on bread. The entire visage was coated in wrinkles like ribbons on a fashionable chapeau. The whole ensemble was topped off with a head of white hair and a generous serving of eyebrows. He raised one as I approached.

"Mr. Wooster."

"Yes. How could you know?"

"Your sophisticated London air is evident. You wear a bespoke suit from Savile Row with tasteful Argyle socks and your spats are handcrafted by Anson of Bond Street. Your hat is from Bodmin's and your profile is well-known in certain social circles. You smell of laundry soap suds."

"That is amazing!"

"It is nothing. Jeeves mentioned the red carnation in your buttonhole. However, this place is too public. Come up to my room and you can tell me your problem there."

In his room he sat me in a chair and took the one opposite, leaning back and placing his fingers tip to tip as he listened to my concern. I decided that there was no need to burden him with an account of why I was at Woollam Chersey, but plunged into the situation I had found on my arrival.

"My Aunt Agatha is preparing for a big shindig at her estate in order to benefit the Distressed Daughters of the Clergy, one of her pet charities. She decided to hold a banquet and invited all her high-tone friends. She is counting on their deep pockets to raise a boatload of money for the Daughters, who, according to her, are forced to live in tiny brick flats located in desolate spots like Lime Regis and Wallingford. The bash is to happen in a few days. Three weeks ago she roped off the large banquet hall in the East Wing as the parade ground. It needed some work, so she ordered up a firm from London to pull everything together. They're called the Four Violettes, an all-female bunch, and she liked the idea of hiring women to do a job normally reserved for men.

"When I came down for breakfast this morning she explained that Anatole, her sister's chef who was staying here a few weeks while my Aunt Delia is out of the country, wasn't doing any of the cooking. You must understand that Anatole is an artist. His gifts are highly prized by anyone who tastes his dishes, and his skills are not to be cast aside lightly. Titans of industry and international financiers had shoved their knees under Aunt Delia's mahogany in order to slurp up Anatole's dinners. In short, only a screwball would deny him access to the kitchen. Instead, Aunt Agatha has entrusted food preparation for the banquet to these same four women.

"Jeeves called me aside and told me some troubling news from below stairs, where the help spoke with one voice. The problem began with the Four Violettes.

"The arrangements called for them to totally re-do the banquet room in question. They were given carte-blanche. To get it done in time, they insisted on shutting off the party site to casual visitors. Over the weeks they have let only Aunt Agatha in. According to Aunt Agatha's personal maid, who put together remarks from Aunt Agatha's own mouth, the room reportedly has been transformed into an exotic wonderland of fabrics and colours. During meals the Four Violettes talk of nothing else but their decorating methods. Aunt Agatha appears to have fallen under their influence to a remarkable degree. She raves about the decorators and repeatedly declares that this banquet will be memorable.

"The four were also given bedrooms on the floor above. The women roam the place freely, 'gathering vibrations' and 'consulting the estate's aura.' A series of crates and barrels are delivered to the construction site every week which are taken inside by the women. There is a lot of pounding and noise. Aunt Agatha has been signing checks like John D. Rockefeller with a twitch. The women come for dinner each night and have managed to convert Aunt Agatha to some kind of vegetarianism. The whole place has existed on raw foods and multi-grain crackers for weeks. The servants' hall is in near revolt.

"All the Four Violettes gab about at meals are their theories of design. Aunt Agatha hangs on every syllable."

"What are their theories of design?"

"Jeeves tried his best to repeat what the servants told him, but I admit I didn't understand much. If the furniture doesn't impede my path to the drinks cabinet and the floor covering doesn't make me trip over the piano, I'm generally satisfied with my surroundings. According to what the butler told Jeeves, the leader, Miss Mauve, expounds a lot on 'sincerity of vision' and 'domestic design expressing the inner truth of the individual.' It all seems a lot of moonshine to me. But when I found out Aunt Agatha had dismissed Anatole, I realized the situation was spinning out of control. Dismissing Anatole was beyond my powers to understand. I consulted Jeeves about hiring a detective, and he suggested we add you to the mix."

Sherlock Holmes shot me a penetrating look from under those bushy brows. "You suspect the Four Violettes are up to no good, Mr. Wooster?"

"Yes, Mr. Holmes. I can't put my finger on it, but the servants' talk, the Four Violettes' sole topic of conversation, the banishment of Anatole from the cooking pots and my aunt's odd fondness for handing money to these women worries me."

Holmes pulled a battered old pipe out of his pocket and slowly filled it from his tobacco pouch. He struck a match from a folded matchbook with a dark letter V on the cover and held it to the bowl until smoke rose lazily toward the ceiling. I sought out one of my own gaspers, and we puffed in silence for quite a while. I realized that he was engaging that mighty brain of his, setting the cogs in motion and grinding down the available information into flour fit to form into a palatable loaf of answers, each slice leading to the final one, the heel, the perpetrator. In his own way he was as fine a chef with mysteries as was Anatole with entrees. I had fumbled for my cigarette case twice before Holmes suddenly rose and knocked out the ashes from his pipe into the fireplace.

"Do the Four Violettes have access to a vehicle?"

"Their deliveries are made in a big white van with a picture of a bunch of violets tied with a ribbon painted on the side. One of them drives it to London each week and returns with supplies. Otherwise it's parked down by the stables."

Holmes thrust his pipe back in his pocket.

"I need more facts, Mr. Wooster. I need to get into the mansion to observe the circumstances. Can you arrange that?"

"Uh, you mean as a guest?"

"Yes, and I don't think I should go in as Sherlock Holmes. My name is too well-known in some quarters to allow that. I think this case calls for subterfuge. After all, it may take some time to solve, and it would be better if I were presented as just a harmless house guest."

I eyed Holmes doubtfully. It was at times like this that I wished Jeeves had not stayed back at Woollam Chersey. A mere glance would bring him to my side ready to suggest all types of disguises and scenarios that would explain the sudden addition of a superannuated old geezer Aunt Agatha had never heard of into her home by invitation from her least favourite nephew. However, we Woosters are not accustomed to failing in our family duties. If Sherlock Holmes needed a sneaky plan in order to get into Woollam Chersey to save Aunt Agatha from herself, and Bertram Wooster was the one called upon to devise it, then said Bertie would be as devious as possible.

"Well, you could fall off a bicycle in front of the gates and be carried in as a stranger who needs to stay until his injuries heal."

"No, that one has been done already."

"How about as a plumber who's come to check the drains? It's a big house."

"That idea has whiskers on it."

"You could knock on the door and ask directions, then faint as you leave the doorstep."

"No, that one is only good for a short observational period. At best, that would get me a brief stay on the drawing room sofa."

I was stymied. I had come out with my best brainwork and Holmes had shot me down at every turn. A silly thought struck me and I chuckled.

"Well, you could come as my old professor, Dr. Gillflower. He bored us boys to tears at Eton talking about his research into the habits and habitats of the brown British shrew. It was his life's work. He always said he was going to write a book about the little beggars."

"That's perfect!"

"What?" I had never received that reaction from any suggestion I had ever made in my life. I looked at Sherlock Holmes suspiciously. Maybe his great mental powers had been exaggerated by the popular press. Or maybe his brain was slipping due to old age. How old was he by now, anyhow? Could I find out by counting the wrinkles on his face, like reading the interior rings of a stump in order to tell the age of an ancient tree?

"I will go back with you now," he said. "You will introduce me as your old tutor on a walking tour, whom you met at the local pub. You shall tell your aunt that I have finished my research and only need a quiet place to write out the manuscript."

The detective shoved a few things into an old carpet bag and snapped it shut. "You said yourself that it was a big house. Let's go."

I had no choice. All the way back from Grantham to Woollam Chersey, I racked my brain to come up with details for a plausible story that would gull Aunt Agatha into allowing the old boy into staying at the house in the middle of hectic preparations for the Daughters of the Distressed Clergy's banquet.

I needn't have worried. Sherlock Holmes sailed past the butler right into the small morning room where Aunt Agatha was going over the menu for the big night and right into her good graces.

I never realized that detectives had attendance at a charm school in their training curriculum, but Holmes must have graduated summa cum suave. Within five minutes Aunt Agatha, who had started out handing him an icy handshake and a glance designed to make him drip away down the front steps like water from a shaken umbrella, had thawed to the point of offering him a bedroom and insisting that he sit with her after dinner and spill all my schoolboy secrets.

"I will consider it an honour, Dr. Gillflower."

"I am most grateful, Mrs. Gregson. My publisher demands that I have a useable manuscript ready as soon as possible. I just need a little space in which to write while my rooms at Eton are being cleaned over vacation."

"Well, space is one thing we have to spare. I don't think we've discovered all the bedrooms yet, and we've had the place for years. Let's see, Miss Mauve is in the Burma Room, and Miss Heliotrope is in the Siamese one adjoining. Miss Puce and Miss Orchid share the India Room. You will do fine in the Chinese Room at the end of the East Hall.

"The ladies spend much of their time working on a project on the floor below, so the Chinese Room will be nice and quiet for you. I'll have a servant place a ream of paper and a supply of ink in it at once."

"I must send to Eton for my notes. They are too bulky to carry on a walking tour. They should arrive in a week. Have you any other guests, Mrs. Gregson?"

"Well, I have my nephew, Bertie, here. You may have remarked how much he resembles a gob-smacked frog, but I'm sure his appearance hasn't changed that much since his days at Eton. One of these afternoons you and I must sit down and you can tell me detailed stories of his activities at school. He sleeps in the Egyptian Room.

"And there's old Mr. Cole. I put him in the Monarch Room. He's so reserved most of the time I forget he is staying here. He showed up on my doorstep two weeks ago with a letter from my husband, asking that Mr. Cole stay here for a while. He's an old friend of Spenser's and needs a bit of a rest cure. The man hasn't said fifty words since he arrived. He seems rather feeble and spends most of his time sitting on a bench in the Peacock Garden. That's on the east side of the house and was laid out by Capability Brown.

"Dinner is to be served at eight. The gong will sound at seven-thirty. I'm so glad you will be staying with us, Dr. Gillflower. I am really looking forward to anything you can tell me about dear Bertram's school days. His letters were always so infrequent and grubby; one never knew just what he was up to."

Jeeves led Sherlock Holmes to his room and later I saw them taking a tour of the grounds. At the appropriate time, the second gong sounded and we gathered at the dining table.

As the first course was dispensed by the liveried servants, I took a fresh gander at the Four Violettes. On Aunt Agatha's right was Miss Mauve, a tall lath of a woman age about fifty wearing lavender? She inspected the spoons with a critical eye. Miss Orchid, who looked like the old witch in a storybook, dressed in a dark plum evening gown, sat on Aunt Agatha's left. Dr. Gillflower, i.e. Sherlock Holmes, sat between Miss Mauve and Miss Puce, who was wearing a gauzy gown in her namesake colour at least fifteen years too young for her. Mr. Cole, of medium height and portly appearance, sat beside Miss Orchid, silently dipping bread into the thin cucumber broth. He frequently ducked to avoid the wrinkled flying elbow of Miss Heliotrope, decked out in grape and adorned with more necklaces and bracelets than had the Hebrews fleeing Egypt, as she attacked the consommé as though she hadn't eaten in four days. I knew that couldn't be true, since I distinctly remember seeing her at breakfast just that morning.

Aunt Agatha had seated me at the table's foot, for want of a better relative.

As we dug into the fish, I heard Holmes asking Miss Mauve about her philosophy of decorating. Her refined yet commanding voice easily carried the length of the table and overrode any other conversations.

"There are two kinds of people in the world, Dr. Gillflower; the ones who glory in tasteless furnishings replete with fuss and feathers and those whose surroundings reflect their natural natures. Mrs. Gregson has a beautiful inner soul."

I nearly choked on a fishbone.

"Tell him about my aura, Miss Mauve," cooed Aunt Agatha.

I narrowly escaped another tussle with the fish.

"Why are you gasping and wheezing down there, Bertram? Drink some water and don't disturb us."

"Yes, Aunt Agatha." I emptied my water goblet and frantically signalled for a refill.

"You must understand, Dr. Gillflower, that such an aura such as Mrs. Gregson's is rare," Miss Mauve said. "Her shimmering pinks and magentas are interwoven with rich threads of gold and silver. These colours denote high levels of spirituality. Such a one as dear Mrs. Gregson is closer to the ultimate ideal of human evolution than are other base mortals."

The ultimate ideal of human evolution forked up flounder with gusto.

Miss Heliotrope took up the pitch. "She has a great deal of attitudinal healing power. When her psychic energy is surrounded by the correct environment, she will be able to channel her advanced meditative state into visualizations that will benefit all mankind for the better. Our aim is to create such an environment for her to exercise her great powers in peace and harmony."

The fish slices were carted off and the main entrée, nut cutlets with mushrooms, was set before us. I noticed that all Four Violettes put aside their own spirituality long enough to wolf their portions down before the servants got a chance to switch plates again.

"What must one do to create such a place of peace and harmony?" asked Holmes.

This time it was Miss Orchid's turn. "The furnishings must be of the purest natural materials, yet infused with the good vibrations of the original owners. Self-sacrificing woods, silkworms fully informed of their true, ultimate fate within the world's great natural circle of life, fabrics woven by innocents of Nature, preferably found in primitive lands where the bonds between the Earth and its children are not tainted by industrialization."

"Only such things can be used to bring into existence a place worthy enough for the inner soul of Agatha Gregson," murmured Miss Puce. "It is our life's work to nurture such an essence for the betterment of all mankind."

Sherlock Holmes appeared to be lapping up this applesauce like a dehydrated poodle. Aunt Agatha was silent, but there lingered around her mouth a little smile, as if all her personal opinions of herself had finally found sanctuary with those who understood, those who would champion her cause past any number of dragons and trolls determined to rain on her parade.

"I would be interested to see your work," said Holmes.

Miss Mauve frowned as she swallowed the last bit of cutlet.

"I am sorry to tell you, Dr. Gillflower, that only those who share an elevated inner soul, such as Mrs. Gregson, can appreciate the elements with which we work. The crass population who are unworthy of the positions they hold in life or who have not the intelligence to grasp the principles of this universal philosophy are unable to understand the cosmic importance of our labours. All they would see would be as smoke and mirrors, insubstantial and fleeting. Only those of higher understanding, the true chosen ones, would find themselves in a place of unsurpassed beauty, awash in Mother Nature's clean light, where every item around them would fulfil its cosmic purpose with grace and loveliness and where tranquillity and unity would fill the very air that sustains life. Fortunately, dear Mrs. Gregson assures us that she has surrounded herself with a household of elevated souls, each worthy of the faith and trust required in performing the duties assigned to them by Life so that she is left free to fulfil her own important destiny."

"Have you seen this project, Mr. Wooster?" asked Holmes.

"No," I mumbled through a mushroom.

Miss Mauve sniffed. "I am an excellent judge of character, Dr. Gillflower, and my assessment of Mr. Wooster decided me against allowing him to see our work. He would never appreciate it. Unfortunately, many men fall into that category."

Old Mr. Cole stared at his plate.

There didn't seem much reason to talk after that. Dessert, a serving of carob cake with organic sultanas, was consumed in silence and the party dispersed. The last I saw of Sherlock Holmes he was headed for the library with Aunt Agatha in hot pursuit. She was babbling about "young Bertie's school days." I jumped into the two-seater and headed for the nearest decent restaurant.

There's not much to tell about the next couple of days. Dr. Gillflower couldn't start writing until his notes arrived, so Holmes spent most of his time roaming the grounds and house. I saw him sitting with old Mr. Cole in the Peacock Garden. The two men, one clad in grey tweed and the other in faded blue, sat puffing on their pipes, gazing at the aged bricks covered with ragged ivy on the walls before them. Around them the gay colours of the garden tossed in a light breeze, almost mocking with their youthful dance the advanced years of the quiet pair.

I spent most of my time reading in the hammock under the trees at the edge of the Peacock Garden. "Death at the Lawn Party" was a real gripper. I thrilled as bodies dropped like soufflés at Old Brantley Manor and the bewildered Lord Smitty-Smitty and his beautiful assistant, Lady Angelica Cumberline, stalked the killer. I had just gotten to the exciting part where Smitty-Smitty and Lady Angelica had followed a mysterious figure to the old mill at midnight and were huddled in the bushes outside when I heard a loud sneeze. I dropped the book and jumped out of the hammock in surprise. I searched the surrounding bushes but found nothing.

Aunt Agatha spent most of her time closeted in her office, fielding phone calls from the invited. All of them, she reported to us at dinner, were very excited about the event.

I was still trying to get used to the cuisine, a hopeless task, and found the menu unusually foul the next evening. A meatless curry masqueraded as the entrée, and the final cheese plate was heavily stocked with Limburger and runny Gorgonzola. Feeling a bit queasy I retired to bed with a hot water bottle pressed to my middle. Jeeves admitted before he closed the door to my room that his tummy felt a bit afflicted also but assured me he would be back in form by morning.

The weak sunlight of a barely born day was still below the horizon and the light had to fight its way through the spreading morning mists when I heard screams and shouts and opened my eyes. I blinked twice before I made out the figure of Jeeves standing by my bed.

"Jeeves?"

"Yes, sir."

"Is someone screaming?"

"Yes, sir. I believe it is the first housemaid."

"Any particular reason why the first housemaid is screaming?"

"Yes, sir. I think it is connected to the fact Mrs. Gregson requests your presence in the main hall downstairs at once."

"Does she realize I haven't yet had my morning cup of tea?"

"Yes, sir. In fact, no one has had their morning cup of tea. Mrs. Gregson assured me she wishes to see you at once, and you must not stand upon ceremony for her sake."

"My God. As bad as that?"

"Yes, sir. In fact, I would strongly suggest haste."

That tore it. If housemaids were screaming and Aunt Agatha was anxious to see me in my 'jammies, all hell had broken out at Woollam Chersey, and I needed to rally 'round. I threw off the covers, slithered into my robe and slippers and hotfooted it down to the main hall. On the way I asked if Sherlock Holmes had been alerted, and Jeeves assured me he had.

The noise grew louder the closer I got and when I arrived at the bottom of the staircase, I could see that the first housemaid had been joined at the chorus by the second housemaid and the tweeny. The other servants, some in their uniforms and some still in nightdresses, were attempting to comfort them as Aunt Agatha glared at them all. She stood next to a glass display case stripped clean of its contents that held pride of place by the library door.

Clad in this early hour in his grey tweed, Holmes stood by a front window, peering out across the gravel drive toward the mist that obscured the estate's main gate nearly a half-mile away. Aunt Agatha saw me and took a deep breath.

"That is enough, Scrubbish. Neeton and Trotter, you will be quiet. There is no danger now. The thieves are long gone, and they will not return."

"Oh, 'lor, ma'am, we might have all been killed in our beds!" choked the housemaid.

"Well, you weren't and there's no reason to go to pieces now that it's all over. Cook, take them all downstairs and make some tea. Wilberforce, ring up the police. Tell them there has been a robbery at Woollam Chersey and to come at once."

"There is no need for that, Mrs. Gregson," said Holmes. He left the front window and joined us. "Mr. Cole is actually Chief Detective Inspector Newcastle Cole, Scotland Yard. He was sent down here on the trail of the Purple Gang, swindlers and thieves, better known to you as the Four Violettes. He's gone down to meet his colleagues at the roadblock at the end of the drive. Scotland Yard has everything well in hand."

The housemaid looked like she was swelling up for a second verse at mention of Scotland Yard, but the others managed to hustle her and the other upset women downstairs before she could give voice again.

Aunt Agatha fixed a cold eye on Holmes and, for some reason, on me.

"Bertram, I demand an explanation. Who is this man you have brought into my home?"

Without my morning cup of tea, I was at a distinct

disadvantage. I blinked and swallowed.

"Ah, well, you see, Aunt Agatha, I was only trying to help..."

"Speak up, Bertram! You're dithering!"

Holmes stepped forward.

"You mustn't blame Mr. Wooster, Mrs. Gregson. He has been most helpful. I am not Dr. Gillflower. I apologize for the deception. My name is Sherlock Holmes."

"Sherlock Holmes?"

"Yes, ma'am."

"The man from the stories?"

"Yes."

"I thought you were a literary construct."

"That is a common misconception. As you see, I am real enough for practical purposes. I have known about the activities of the Purple Gang for some time. In fact the Gang had played a part in masterminding the Grosvenor Square furniture van case I worked on years ago. After I arrived, I suspected they might be involved in nefarious doings here at Woollam Chersey. I recognized Inspector Cole the first night we met. In consultation the next day in the Peacock Garden we agreed to keep up the charade of being strangers.

"Since the women had been invited into your home, they had not broken any laws. Inspector Cole and I knew it was only a matter of time, however, until a crime was committed. The inspector had men stationed at every road leading away from here nightly for the past few days. We had agreed to take turns keeping watch over the

Four Violettes each night, but fell into the trap of the choral hydrate drops slipped into the curry last night at dinner, as did you all. In the dark of night the women loaded up the furnishings from the banquet room plus anything else they could carry and fled the premises. However, the roadblock was in place. They all were captured and the van's contents secured."

"What was taken?" I asked.

Aunt Agatha, who made a striking figure in a magenta brocade dressing gown and a head full of pink curlers, nearly wrung her hands. "This case contained every one of Spencer's antique silver snuffboxes, even the one with the emerald on the lid, along with the eighteenth century silver chocolate serving set, the gold inkwell that belonged to Spencer's great-great grandfather, the silver letterbox I inherited from my grand-aunt Amelia and the matched set of dueling pistols handed down from Uncle Albert, who always claimed he got them from a member of the Hellfire Club when he was a boy."

"Quite a haul," I whistled. "Was this case the only one broken into?"

Aunt Agatha gasped and stared at me like last night's landed flounder. She took off. We followed. A hasty tour of the downstairs disclosed that three other rooms had been ransacked. Silver plate, old Chinese vases and numerous jewelled bibelots that normally took up space on the table tops and mantelpieces of the state rooms were missing. Aunt Agatha stopped short in Uncle Spenser's study and stared down at his desk where a golden statue of Ganesh had once resided.

Her voice was low and defeated. "How could I have been such a fool? I welcomed those women into my home, fed and housed them for three weeks, even gave them gainful employment. See how they repaid me! Perfidious, scheming, deceitful hussies!"

"Speaking of gainful employment, what do you think they did to the banquet room?" I asked. Aunt Agatha shot me a look that could have fried bacon on my forehead if we had any in the larder.

That question resulted in another parade as Aunt Agatha, Sherlock Holmes and I, trailed by the faithful Jeeves, hurried to the room in question. The doors were locked but Sherlock Holmes knelt before them and brought out a black leather case from his coat pocket. He produced a set of picklocks and set to work, soon having the doors open. Aunt Agatha's agitation about the robbery and being kept in the dark about the origins of two of her houseguests was quickly forgotten in the shock of the sight that greeted us all inside the banquet room. Holmes pulled out a little battery-powered torch and clicked it on.

It was dark inside the room, an Egyptian blackness that seemed to swallow up the light from Holmes' little torch with a gulp, like a hungry whale crossing the path of a solitary anchovy. I groped for the electric switch by the door and when I found it, clicked on the lights.

We blinked in amazement. It was still dark. Slowly I realized that the entire room, every inch of the walls, ceiling and even the floor, had been painted flat matte ebony. The chandeliers were nearly useless, wrapped in swaths of black fabric, half their light bulbs missing. I took a couple of steps forward and stumbled into something hard.

"What in blazes...?" I rubbed a tender part of my anatomy. Sherlock Holmes stepped inside and ran his light over the room's contents.

"Don't move," he warned. "Every piece of furniture in this room has been painted the same black as the walls and ceilings."

"What about the windows? Open the curtains, Jeeves and let's get some light in here," snapped Aunt Agatha.

Jeeves carefully made his way to the nearest window and felt along the jamb. An instant later he pulled back the floor to ceiling curtains (thick black light-absorbing cloth, I noticed) and let in the weak light of the rising sun as it struggled through the drifting swaths of mist surrounding the estate.

"Covering the windows with black curtains ensured that no natural light would be able to penetrate into this room," said Holmes.

"Excuse me, sir," said Jeeves. "But I feel I must mention that I see no sign of the self-sacrificing woods, the fully informed silk or the fabrics woven by Nature's children untainted by modern civilization in this room. In fact, the chairs and tables, what I can see of them, resemble the original furniture I saw during a previous visit last year."

"That's right," said I. I ran my hands over the surface in front of me. "I can feel the gouge I put into the centre of this table top with a bottle of Uncle Spencer's best during a little dispute I had with Tuppy Glossop over a trump, no trump last summer."

"Stay where you are," commanded Holmes. Carrying his tiny spot of light he picked his way the length of the room, examining the painted chairs and tables that filled the area. I shivered. With his head of white hair and his shabby grey tweed suit, he glimmered like a ghost in the faint light cast by the one uncovered window as he moved in a wavering path to the far wall.

He came back and turned off the light in his hand. "There are no signs of the crates and barrels of materials the women had delivered here. I fancy the containers of self-sacrificing woods and other choice furnishings are in the back of the lorry the police stopped, along with items taken from the house. Let's check their bedrooms."

Well, it was a painful sight to see. Each bedroom occupied by the Purple Gang had been stripped of every valuable artefact which represented years of acquisition by a team of dedicated materialists. Aunt Agatha was the closest I had ever seen to tears.

"Don't feel so bad, Aunt Agatha," I said. "According to Mr. Holmes, the police have stopped the van and recovered all your stuff. You should have it back in a few days."

"A few days! A few days! What good will recovering my property do me in a few days? The banquet is tonight!"

I could see her point. In fourteen hours her invited guests, loaded with compassion and cash for the Distressed Daughters of the Clergy, would be pounding at the door, eager to congratulate themselves for their selflessness by stuffing their faces with fine cuisine in an atmosphere of peace and harmony. Instead they would be faced with small brown crackers served in the Black Hole of Calcutta.

Detective Inspector Cole came up the stairs. "I am happy to report, Mrs. Gregson, that we have detained the Four Violettes and their loot. Sergeant Fidler and Constable Boular spent the last three nights camped out just outside your gates but the wait was worth it. We found crates and barrels of rich materials in the van along with many items obviously taken from the house. Miss Mauve declared it "a fair cop" and they put up no resistance."

"What about getting my things back?" demanded Aunt Agatha.

"We'll have to keep the van's contents for several days in order to inventory everything. It's necessary for the prosecution chappies."

"In the meanwhile, what am I to do about the banquet? The Four Violettes were going to fix the food. Now I have no chef!"

I squared my shoulders. Never let it be said that Bertie Wooster doesn't stand by his friends, even in the teeth of an aunt's fury. "You are the one who threw Anatole out of the house, Aunt Agatha," I reminded her. "It's because of you that he has been languishing at the "Bread and Cheese," wasting his time among cookbooks instead of whipping up marvels for our delectation. If you apologize hard enough and offer enough compensation, he might agree to come back and cook your banquet. Heaven knows what's in the larder, but I for one think that whatever's there, Anatole stands the best chance of making it palatable for your high-toned friends."

Aunt Agatha's better qualities came to the fore. She knew petty differences between Anatole and herself must be set aside for the benefit of the greater good, the Distressed Daughters of the Clergy. For the second time in three days my advice made sense, which was definitely some sort of record. Besides, her back was to the wall. She could hear in her mind the comments her guests would make when confronted with nothing but raw fruits and carrot batons with unsigned checks in their pockets. She squared her shoulders.

"I'll go get Anatole at once. It won't be easy, but for the Distressed Daughters I will humble myself, as long as no one but Anatole sees me do it. When we get back, I'll think about something to do with the banquet hall. It's unfortunate that there is no other room in the house big enough to accommodate everyone."

She swept out of the corridor toward her room to dress. Jeeves and I retreated to my bedroom, leaving Holmes and Inspector Cole to go to the local police station where the Purple Gang was being held.

"Rum doings, eh, Jeeves?"

"Quite, sir. I suggest the light green heather tweed, sir, with the Lincoln green tie."

"All right. How's the weather?"

"The day promises to be fine, sir."

"Too bad about that room being painted black. It will take months to restore it."

"Yes, sir. A regrettable occurrence."

"Here, Jeeves, Aunt Agatha is in a real pickle. Even if she can get Anatole back to cook the food, where will she serve it? Half the rooms downstairs are missing their component parts, just the little things her friends would notice and ask her about. The ladies might have second thoughts about trusting their cash to a woman who invites thieves into her home. It could cut into the take for the Distressed Daughters something fierce, not to mention making public Aunt Agatha's embarrassment and lapse of judgment. She will never be able to hold up her head in Mayfair again. Do you have any ideas?"

He was silent as between us we got the body draped and shod. Finally, as he gathered up the shaving things he coughed gently.

"Speak, Jeeves."

"I cannot help but notice your present reading material on the bedside table, sir. I was wondering, as the day is so fine, and the Peacock Garden very lovely at this time of year, if perhaps…"

I grasped the concept at once. "Jeeves, you've done it again! An outdoor banquet! An evening lawn party! What a wonderful idea! We can get the black tables and chairs moved out to the greensward, drape them in white linen and fill every candlestick available. We'll get those Japanese lanterns out of storage and hang them in the trees. With the rose bushes and the blooming flower beds, it will be a sensation!"

And so it was. Aunt Agatha, returning a little battered from her negotiations with Anatole, wearily agreed to everything, and soon all the servants were trotting back and forth setting things up. Thankfully the best china and glassware, along with the state silver, had been safely locked up in the butler's room, away from the clutches of the Four Violettes.

I was holding the back door open for the men carrying the chairs out to the garden when Anatole arrived. He nodded to me with the air of a conqueror as he paused to survey his kingdom, the kitchen.

"Mrs. Gregson, she comes to me on her hands and knees, Mr. Wooster," he said. "She pleads for the help of the one and only Anatole to save her important banquet, to make it magnifique! Of course, I say that in life one must take the smooths with the rough. She offers me plenty of smooth and so I am here, as you say, to save her bacon!"

"Good luck on finding the bacon," I said as he began to work.

Anatole ransacked the larders and, muttering expressively in French, created delicious miracles out of nearly nothing. Upon arrival the guests were diverted from the important rooms of the house where the gaps among the decorations stood out so blatantly. As a result no one suspected that half of Aunt Agatha's valued possessions were currently in the hands of the police.

Later that evening, after the revels had ended and the many checks collected had been secreted in a locked box under Aunt Agatha's bed, Sherlock Holmes and I took a final stroll around the Peacock Garden while the servants cleared the tables.

"Did you suspect the Four Violettes were really the Purple Gang when we met at Grantham?" I asked.

"No. Jeeves had given me only the sketchiest outline of the problem here. But I recognized Spencer Gregson's name and that was what intrigued me. Many years ago Dr. Watson and I investigated a case involving the Giant Rat of Sumatra, a story for which the world is not yet prepared. Mr. Gregson happened to give us a small bit of information during that investigation that ultimately saved our lives. I was glad to repay the debt, no matter in how indirect a fashion."

I sank down on a garden bench. "I admit I'm confused. Just what was going on around here?"

Holmes pulled out his pipe. Out of the gloaming Jeeves appeared with a lighted match. When the tobacco was burning to his satisfaction, Holmes leaned against a tree and addressed us.

"The swindling began a long time ago, when the Purple Gang first formed in London. It was made up of a clever group of crooks who specialized in burglaries and confidence tricks. The leader was a young woman, known to you as Miss Mauve, who was connected to an old adversary of mine called the Professor. He taught her a great deal before he…well… dropped out of sight, and although she was young, she put her knowledge to use.

"Scotland Yard has an extensive file of unsolved thefts and daylight burglaries that goes back at least thirty years. Detective Inspector Newcastle Cole was assigned to follow the cases about five years ago. He determined that most were perpetrated by the Purple Gang. He caught word of their whereabouts last month and managed to get an invitation to Woollam Chersey from an unsuspecting Spencer Gregson before Gregson left for the Far East. Cole has been here watching the women ever since. By the time I arrived no crime had been committed yet, so he couldn't arrest them. He wanted the evidence to be iron-clad this time. Scotland Yard decided at the outset that neither Mr. nor Mrs. Gregson would be told about the decorators' backgrounds for fear something might be said in passing that might spook them. The villains may have abandoned the scheme then and there and slipped through the inspector's fingers as they have done before.

"Inspector Cole and I joined forces. He organized squads of men to blockade the exits while he and I watched the women. I even climbed into that large tree that supports one end of the garden hammock to peer into the banquet room's windows."

"That must have been the sneeze I heard!" I exclaimed.

"No doubt. Perhaps the women heard it too and grew suspicious or it was just the right time to load up the van and disappear. Neither of us expected the drugged curry. I blame myself for that. It's an old trick I should have anticipated. There is nothing new under the sun. It has all been done before. Anyway, the entire household was drugged and the Four Violettes packed up everything valuable they could fit into the lorry and left. They were quite surprised to find the Hertfordshire Constabulary waiting for them outside the gates."

"I'm glad they were caught, Mr. Holmes, and I thank you for your help," I said. "Aunt Agatha would never have recovered from the embarrassment and humiliation of being exposed as a woman foolish enough to entertain crooks. Not to mention her buying all that piffle about her being the ultimate ideal of human evolution and decorating with self-sacrificing woods. Now she can merely say she was co-operating with the forces of law and order in bringing a nefarious band of criminals to justice. She comes out as quite the heroine, and I am the fair-haired boy."

"Not exactly, sir," murmured Jeeves. "I have come out to the garden to find and warn you. During the banquet Mrs. Gregson had a long talk with Lady Keyestone, Mr. Glossop's mother's best friend. Lady Keyestone told her all about Mr. Glossop's unfortunate adventure at the Drones just before you arrived here. Your aunt has taken it into her head that you are responsible for the deluge of soap suds that washed young Glossop down the main stairs and nearly out into the street. The last time I saw her she was stalking the halls in search of you and she did not look pleased."

On certain occasions there is no one like Bertie Wooster when it comes to rising to an emergency. Instantly I was on my feet, my brain a-buzz with plans.

"Where is the two-seater, Jeeves?"

"I took the liberty of pulling it around to the tradesmen's entrance, sir."

"My suitcase?"

"Packed and in the back, sir."

"We had better not go straight to London right away. Too easy to trace me there. Also, Tuppy Glossop may be waiting. Vengeful family, the Glossops. Such a sad character trait. Where would you suggest, Jeeves?"

"I understand that the weather is very fine on the French Riviera this time of year, sir."

"Then the French Riviera it is. Thank you again, Mr. Holmes. Let's go, Jeeves. I think I see Aunt Agatha pushing her way through the rose bushes toward us and the thorns don't seem to be slowing her down at all!"

Bringing Holmes the Bacon At Last!

Call them hogs, porkers, boars, gilts, piglets, sows, barrows, feeder pigs, shoats, swine, the "other white meat" or pigs, the useful animals that give us ham, bacon, chitterlings, pork chops, baby back ribs, roasts, suckling pig and all the ingredients for Spam surround us. It is not a surprise that they show up within popular culture. Literature has a long and proud history of pigs within its pages. Just a brief glance back would reveal universal giants such as The Empress of Blandings by P. G. Wodehouse, Napoleon by George Orwell, Wilber by E. B. White and Winnie the Pooh's little friend, Piglet, by A. A. Milne. Remember the pig so necessary to the plot of "The Lord of the Flies" by William Golding? Modern children's books such as *Olivia* by Ian Falconer and *Mercy Watson* by Kate DiCamillo continue to gather new fans.

We learn of pigs at our mother's hock…er, knee. Who as a child hadn't counted his toes to "This Little Piggy" and thrilled to the story of "The Three Little Pigs"?

Television and movies glorify the pig. Arnold Ziffel starred in the 1965-1971 sitcom "Green Acres" with Eva Gabor. Miss Piggy carried Kermit the Frog for years on "The Muppet Show" and subsequent movies. "Babe" and its sequel "Babe in the City" entertained millions of fans in theatres. Various pig-like beings appeared in the adventures of Doctor Who. In the Mel Gibson movie "Mad Max: Beyond Thunderdome" methane-producing pigs housed in the cellars produced "green" energy to power Tina Turner's cage-match edifice, the Thunderdome.

I am happy to report that Dr. Watson has also contributed to this branch of letters. The Canon contains, by my count, 21 mentions of pigs and references related to pigs.

In the adventures of "The Engineer's Thumb", "The Sign of

Four" and "The Naval Treaty" ham or bacon was served at breakfast.

In "The Redheaded League" Jabez Wilson copied the entire section of the Encyclopedia Britannica covering information under the letter A, starting with the word aardvark. Aardvark is a Dutch word meaning "earth pig.

Watson mentions an unwritten Holmes mystery, "the Contents of the Ancient British Barrow" in "The Golden Prince-Nez," Among its several definitions a barrow is a castrated male pig. What could Holmes have been searching for?

In "The Missing Three-Quarter", Cyril Overton was the captain of the Cambridge Rugby team, worried over the disappearance of his teammate Godfrey Staunton. Rugby is a very physical game that developed in England as a contest to propel an inflated pig's bladder from one village to the next. By the time Watson played rugby for Blackheath and Overton played for Cambridge the bladder had been replaced by a ball made of pigskin.

Watson also spoke of his rugby prowess in the "Sussex Vampire"

Bacon was mentioned in an American slang phrase Holmes used in his character of Altamont the spy in "His Last Bow." Waving the naval signal papers over his head, he cried triumphantly to Von Bork, "You can give me the glad hand tonight, mister. I'm bringing home the bacon at last." Little did Von Bork realize that it was actually goose and his was cooked.

In "The Illustrious Client" discouraging reports of the state of Holmes' health were circulated in the press after a murderous attack upon him. They included mention of erysipelas, which is a skin infection that can spread throughout the body and attack the brain. It is also found in hogs and requires vaccination.

In "The Valley of Fear" Holmes received a coded message that he deciphered. Holmes and Watson consulted Whitaker's Almanack and turned up the word "pigs'-bristles." There was an active market for pig by-products including pigs'-bristles in Victorian England. These hairs from pigs' bodies were used to make toothbrushes until the late 1930s. The bristles also went into hairbrushes. The pig hooves were boiled down to create glue and their fats were used for soap and candles. The leather was used for shoes, belts, handbags and balls for sport, like rugby.

During the early stages of the case of the murder at Birlstone Manor, Scotland Yard's Inspector McDonald and White Mason of the Sussex Constabulary sent out a nationwide call for information about the elusive bicyclist seen near the Manor. In an excess of citizenly vigor, reports came in about sightings as far apart as Liverpool, Leicester and East Ham, near London.

The body of Brunton, the butler of "The Musgrave Ritual," was found smothered in a hidden cellar, crouched on his hams.

The Sepoy Mutiny in India was mentioned in both "The Sign of Four" and "The Crooked Man." The conflict between the British Army and their Indian soldiers began in 1857 when a rumour swept through the country that the new ammunition issued by the British that needed to be bit open before loading was packed in beef tallow and hog lard. Both Muslims and Hindus found that repugnant and mutiny resulted. It was during the conflict that Jonathan Small and his friends found the Agra treasure, and Henry Wood found himself captured by the rebels.

In "The Sign of Four" Sherlock Holmes engaged the services of Toby, the best tracking nose in London, to find the murderers of Bartholomew Sholto. Put upon a scent of creosote, Toby first leads Holmes and Watson to a barrel of it by the docks. The size is not specified, but it could have been a hogshead.

The murderous little Tonga was described as an Andaman Islander and a cannibal. It was only his affection for Jonathan Small that kept the one-legged man from Tonga's menu. A South Seas polyglot word for human meat was longpig.

In "The Adventure of Black Peter" Holmes surprised Watson before breakfast one July morning by strolling in with a barb-headed spear tucked under one arm. He had spent time down at Allardyce's butcher shop, attempting to transfix with a single blow a pig carcass swung from a hook in the ceiling. Being an incompetent harpoonist, he failed and realized that only one with special skill could have committed the murder.

Several questions arise as regards to that pig. What kind of pig was it? Did Allardyce let Holmes poke at the thing all morning for free? What became of the meat?

It was not a guinea pig. A native of South America, guinea pigs were known more as pets than food in England. One would not have been available at the butcher's. A typical guinea pig's body weighed between 1.5 to 2.5 pounds. It would have been frail enough to let the barb of the harpoon go through easily. That was what Holmes found he could not do.

Nor was it a peccary, a relative of the pig, from the southern United States deserts south to Patagonia. Holmes was looking for something that would equal the size and bulk of an adult human male. The average peccary, depending on the breed, weighed between 37 and 88 pounds on the hoof.

Was it a wild boar? Wild boars were extinct in the British Isles by the 1300s, despite repeated efforts, particularly by James I in 1610, to restock them, although wild boars lived in Germany until 1910, and thrive today in France and parts of Eastern Europe. Was it a gift from the King of Bohemia?

Wild boars were found in India, where a sport known as "pig-sticking" was enjoyed by the British inhabitants and their hosts, the Rajas. No one recorded how the pigs felt. Did Watson get a CARE package from an old friend in the 66th Berkshires? Once you have eliminated the impossible, take a hard look at the improbable. The fact Watson was assigned to the Berkshires was suggestive.

A Tamworth or Landrace pig produced the finest bacon, but would not have carried the bulk needed for Holmes's experiment. A lard hog, such as a Berkshire, was closer, but usually didn't reach the size Holmes would have been looking for. Another lard hog, the Yorkshire, fulfilled all requirements as to weight, length, breadth and depth of body. I believe it was a Yorkshire pig, country grown, that Holmes selected to experiment upon. A country grown pig would have been fatter due to the skim milk it was fed by the farmer. Years of drink in a fifty-year-old man would have likely turned some of his body to fat.

No Victorian businessman would have let even the great Sherlock Holmes spoil a nice pork carcass beyond salable limits. I believe Holmes had to pay cash money for that pig. Having bought it and being in his own words "a poor man," as he said in "The Priory School," no doubt he had the shredded, ripped remains delivered to Mrs. Hudson. He probably chose a carcass close to the size and weight of Black Peter's torso. Peter Carey was described as having "a broad breast." That would be about 100 to 130 pounds of dressed pork dumped on Mrs. Hudson's kitchen table.

What did she do with all that meat? Remember, it was a hot July day. Refrigeration was in its infancy and people still relied on the ice man who delivered great chunks of lake or river ice to their homes and businesses every day in the summer months. Imagine the scurry and the bustle, not to mention the unspoken thoughts, as Mrs. Hudson and the maid and even the little boy in buttons flew about bringing out tubs, getting extra ice, chopping the carcass into manageable chunks and trying to decide what to do with such an inconvenient windfall.

Some chops and a loin roast could be cut out for immediate use. The front and rear legs, along with part of the sides, could be sent back to the butcher's to be cured into hams and bacon. The rest of the meat would have been ground into sausage in order to save it. That is, if the carcass were female. If it were a male all the meat would be turned into sausage, due to the stronger taste of the boar.

Mrs. Hudson may have had her own family recipe for sausage. Such recipes were part of the dowry of a young woman in Victorian times. Grinding all that meat after separating it from the bones, adding the special herbs and spices, then boiling the links so they would keep until used must have taken the rest of the day and into the night. Mrs. Hudson deserved the sausage she surely reserved for her own breakfast the next morning.

In "The Hound of the Baskervilles" the Hall was reached through "the lodge-gates, a maze of fantastic tracery in wrought iron, with weather-bitten pillars on either side, blotched with lichens, and surmounted with the boars' heads of the Baskervilles."

The phrase "the boars' heads of the Baskervilles" would indicate that the same heads appeared on the Baskervilles' coat of arms. The coat of arms would have appeared on the stationary Watson used to make his reports to Holmes.

During Watson's visit, the local countryside was terrorized by the escape of Seldon, the Notting Hill murderer, from Dartmoor Prison. Notting Hill, a handsome quarter of the Royal Borough of Kensington, at the time of the Baskerville adventure "was notorious for its pig-keepers, brickfields and attendant public health nuisances with rubbish and effluent standing in holes where the clay for brick making was dug."

In "The Veiled Lodger" Watson presented us with a different

kind of pig. This was in repeated references to Ronder, the owner of a famous traveling circus. The entertainment's chief attraction was a very fine North African lion named Sahara King. Ronder and his wife performed a featured act in the lion's cage. His wife described Ronder as a man of many enemies. In his cups, he was horrible. It was because of his drinking that the fortunes of the circus declined. A huge bully of a man, he cursed and slashed at everyone who came in his way. All the best performers left. Mrs. Ronder called him a monster.

Ronder deserted his wife for others. He tied her down and beat her with a riding whip. He was terrible at all times and murderous when drunk. He was had up for assault, and for cruelty to the beasts. A coward as well as bully, he found out about his wife's lover and tortured her more than ever.

Holmes showed Watson a newspaper photograph of Ronder, his wife and the lion Sahara King. Holmes described him as "a porcine person." Later in the story, after Watson saw a picture of him that Mrs. Ronder had kept, he wrote that it was "a dreadful face – a human pig, or rather a human wild boar, for it was formidable in its bestiality. One could imagine that vile mouth champing and foaming in its rage, and one could conceive those small vicious eyes darting pure malignancy as they looked forth upon the world. Ruffian, bully, beast – it was all written on that heavy-jowled face."

I feel it is necessary here to say a few words in defense of the pig. It is true that many people view the domesticated pig as dirty, stupid and ugly. The Bible and the Koran warn against the consumption of pork. The smell of its waste is very pungent. A pig glories in mud baths. It has a solid barrel-like body with short legs perched on tippy-toe hooves and a strange-looking snout it uses to dig in the dirt.

Pigs are seen as dangerous. Wild feral pigs attacked the boy in the movie "Old Yeller." In the novel "Peyton Place," one of the characters disposed of her stepfather's body by giving it to the pigs in the barnyard to devour.

They even named a strain of flu after it.

That is only one side of the story. Various breeds of pig have been used in medical research for decades. When not kept in confinement, the pig will not soil where it sleeps. It is a prolific and good mother, and will build its litter of newborns a nest out of straw or grass in which to shelter. As a herd animal, the pig will forage for its own food in a family group. Since it has no sweat glands, the pig uses mud baths to keep cool. Left to itself, the pig will never dangerously overeat when given access to unlimited food. This is in contrast to the dog, the horse, or the human.

The pig is more intelligent than the dog and can be taught similar tricks. There have been documented cases where pigs have saved their owners' lives. A pig named Priscilla saved a young boy from drowning; one named Spammy led firefighters to a burning shed to save her calf friend Spot; and a porker named Lulu found help for her human companion who had collapsed from a heart attack.

Let us admit that even the lowly pig has given service to the Master. In its own way, it has demonstrated the best quality of a good Sherlockian. That was expressed best on a poster I once saw; "For breakfast, remember, the hen is involved, but the pig is committed."

The History of the Criterion Restaurant in London

One of the major charms of the Sherlock Holmes stories is its blend of factual and disguised information. The disguised information was necessary to conceal the identities' of Sherlock Holmes' confidential clients. Watson changed points of fact that could have revealed places, times and names in the stories. Without such "doctoring" of the facts, Holmes would not have allowed the tales to be published. Watson agreed to the restrictions in order that the stories could be made available. He believed, and rightly so, that the deceptions were well worth the trouble, in order to bring to the public the skills and actions of such an amazing detective as his friend.

Watson did not carry Holmes' adventures solely into the realms of imagination. After all, Holmes' methods were founded on logic. At the centre of each case was a solid core of facts, and deductions made from those facts. Watson displayed great skill as a story-teller in weaving his variations in and among the hard truths that were in each tale.

Many Canonical adventures show their factual bones by the real places that are mentioned in them. Great Britain is real and London is real, and I think the nicest part of "The Grand Game" is to search out and walk the grounds of the actual places where Holmes and Watson trod.

The Criterion Restaurant, the subject of this paper, is real.

In the early 1870s the area of London that was Piccadilly Circus was reconstructed after the demolition of the popular coaching inn "The White Bear." Thomas Verity, who had just designed the Royal Albert Hall, was hired to design the Criterion Restaurant. The grand frontage was constructed on the south side of Piccadilly using Portland stone in a French Renaissance style. The Restaurant opened in 1873, and in 1874 the Criterion Theatre was completed. By 1890 the building held under one roof the Criterion Theatre, the Criterion Restaurant, reading rooms, a cigar divan, billiard rooms, a picture gallery, hairdressing rooms, a concert-hall and a ballroom, all designed by the same architect. Over time many improvements were made, including an elaborate air-conditioning system and a suite of Masonic rooms.

Thomas Verity was famous for his magnificent interiors, extensively decorated with intricate mosaics and tile-work.

The final cost of the entire project was calculated at 80,000 pounds, about $8,000,000 in today's money. It was rated the finest work of Thomas Verity's career. It was not until 1893 that the statue of Eros was erected in Piccadilly Circus. Repositioned at least once, it now stands on a raised plinth just west of the restaurant's entrance. To the east of the entrance is the Underground Piccadilly stop with its ornate ironwork

A curved marquee with leaded stained glass bearing the legend "Criterion Restaurant Est. 1874" guards the entrance to the present Criterion Restaurant. The restaurant is noted for its line of burnished golden neo-Byzantine arched ceilings with coffered corners which run from the front of the bar and the restaurant for the entire length of the room until they end at the terrace at the back of the block. Upon entering from Piccadilly one is given the impression of one long, large, airy space. Numerous Arabian arches line the length of both walls with marble inlays, ornate mosaics and glittering mirrors between them. A raised area beyond the bar houses the restaurant. A fine marble fireplace and a spot in which to address diners are two of the restaurant's features. The bar has two large lamps with white shades along its length and a large vase near the doors filled with flowers. Small round tables fill the floor between the entrance doors and the restaurant area. Larger round tables set with snowy napery and gleaming silver, china and crystal are placed in the raised eating area in back and its adjoining terrace.

Over the years since its creation the restaurant space had a variety of uses, all involving food. At the beginning of World War II the beautiful walls and ceilings were covered in sheets of Formica to protect them from the results of possible German bombs. After the war the space was utilized as a twenty-four hour a day Boots chemist shop. Not until 1984 was the Formica removed and the amazing decorations rediscovered. They had been hidden for over forty years. The Criterion Restaurant was restored to its former glory when both the restaurant and the theatre were closed for refurbishment in 1989, not to be opened again until 1992. Another refurbishing led to a grand relaunch of the restaurant in 2009.

In the beginning of "A Study in Scarlet," in 1881, Dr. Watson is found at the "Long Bar" at the Criterion bemoaning his financial troubles. How he came by them is understandable when one learns that at that time at the Criterion Bar bottled Bass, an English beer, cost four pence, and Scotch and Irish whiskies went for four pence a glass, albeit of generous measure.

At the "Pavilion," just across the Circus, bottled Bass went for three pence, whiskies were three pence, and a bottle of Guinness stout cost two and one-half pence.

Figuring a shilling as $5.00 in buying power of that day, and a penny as twenty-five cents, a glass of beer cost $1.00, while just across the road the same beer could be had for seventy-five cents, a saving of 25 cents. No wonder Holmes later had to lock up Watson's check book!

Watson was met there by young Stamford, his former dresser at Bart's, who persuaded him to return to the famous London hospital for an introduction to Mr. Sherlock Holmes. A plaque honouring that historic meeting is installed on the wall across from the present bar. It reads: HERE, NEW YEARS DAY, 1881 AT THE CRITERION

LONG BAR STAMFORD, DRESSER AT BARTS, MET DR. JOHN H. WATSON AND LED HIM TO IMMORTALITY AND SHERLOCK HOLMES. The Sherlock Holmes Society of London and the Baker Street Irregulars—1981—By the Inverness Capers of Akron, Ohio.

Watson and Stamford in 1881 was not the only famous meeting in the history of the Criterion Restaurant. In the early 1900s the English Suffragettes, working to get women the vote, held their monthly organizational meetings at the restaurant. Winston Churchill and Prime Minister David Lloyd George met there in 1906 to discuss the liberal policies they wanted to implement in the new Labour Government.

In 1908 H. G. Wells hosted the inaugural Dinner of the Royal College of Science's Old Students there. In 1923 the Criterion Restaurant was the scene for a series of luncheon clubs which were frequented by such future literary and intellectual heavyweights as Sir Hugo Walpole, G. K. Chesterton, Bertram Russell and Edgar Wallace.

But there were meetings at the Criterion Restaurant when it first opened that drew quite a different kind of patronage. It was popular from its opening and attracted both sporting men and the elite of society. Adam Worth, an English citizen who had begun his criminal career during the Civil War in America, had gained experience after the war by illegal activities in New York. Robbing the Boylston National Bank of Boston after the war earned him a large stake. He had rented a shop next door and had tunnelled into the vault unseen.

But by then he had gained the interest of not only the local police departments involved in New England but also of the Pinkerton Detective Agency. Founded by Allan Pinkerton, the Agency grew as the United States developed after the War Between the States. Pinkertons were often hired to track down the nefarious individuals who robbed banks and freight companies.

After being personally questioned about the Boylston Bank Robbery by Allan's son, William Pinkerton, Worth decided to return to Europe in the early 1870s. There he established a criminal empire, first in France and then in England. He even took a well-appointed apartment, 198 Piccadilly, near the Criterion, as a sort of headquarters. It cost 600 pounds a year. It is currently the Bradford and Bingley Building Society – just the sort of establishment Worth would have cheerfully robbed during his heyday. The Criterion Restaurant became one of his favourite hangouts.

During his lifetime he stole between $2 and $3 million worth of goods and jewellery. He became the model for Professor James Moriarty, and in his lifetime was called "The Napoleon of Crime." He was pursued by the private detective, William Pinkerton, and had a mortal enemy in Detective Inspector John Shore of Scotland Yard.

The Pinkerton Detective Agency considered Adam Worth "the most remarkable, most successful and most dangerous professional criminal known in modern times." For years he perpetuated every form of theft—check-forging, swindling, larceny, safe cracking, diamond robbery, mail robbery, hold-ups on the road, every degree of burglary, and bank robbery—with perfect immunity. He led operations in Great Britain, on the Continent and in the United States. He prided himself on never using violence.

William Pinkerton had followed Worth for years, but the master criminal knew that neither the private detective nor Scotland Yard had enough evidence to take him in. In 1875 the two men met at the popular Criterion Restaurant, at the bar. Worth felt confident enough, surrounded by his felonious companions, to offer Pinkerton a compliment, while damning his English counterpart, Inspector John Shore.

Shore, he declared, "could thank God Almighty the Pinkertons were his friends or he would never had gotten above an ordinary street pickpocket detective,"

"What he said was true," William Pinkerton wrote later in the official history of the Pinkertons. "Outside of our agency, Shore would never have amounted to anything."

Adam Worth made his mark on the art world in 1876 by stealing the famous Gainsborough painting "The Duchess of Devonshire" from a London art dealer. An unforeseen consequence of that action was that Worth fell in love with the painting and could never bring himself to sell it. Instead, he kept it for the next twenty-five years. He had two confederates in the theft, and naturally, they expected their share of its worth.

Junka Phillips was one of them. He was an enormous man, over six feet, four inches tall, and pressured Worth, who stood five feet, four inches, to pay up. When the money didn't appear, Phillips peached to the Yard. The detectives still had no proof for the courts, but concocted a plan to get a confession. Inspector Shore promised Phillips leniency and a monetary award to help trap Worth at the Criterion. Phillips called for a meeting at the restaurant to talk over the situation. Worth suspected his confederate and took up a hidden position before the appointed time.

He saw Junka Phillips enter the bar with two known detectives from Scotland Yard. Naturally the Napoleon of Crime didn't appear and neither did the painting. But Adam Worth knew he had been betrayed.

He vowed revenge. He set up another meeting with Phillips the next day at the Criterion Bar. Phillips showed up in a belligerent mood with another thug well-known for his skill at fisticuffs. Worth recognized a heavily disguised Inspector Greenham sitting at the bar, ready to overhear and make note of everything said between the two men. Obviously, Phillips was trying to get Worth to make an incriminating admission in front of a witness.

Phillips began by accusing Worth of stealing the Gainsborough. Worth said nothing. Phillips expanded his accusations, but Worth refused to respond. Frustrated, Phillips, a great unthinking hulk, reverted to type. He took a swing at Worth.

Adam Worth had a professional policy of non-violence, but this time he broke it. He reached up and punched Phillips in the eye. When the big man fell, Worth kicked him in the head four or five times, right in the middle of the bar.

The sight of the shorter man striking down the giant stunned Phillips' backup man into immobility. Inspector Greenham had to pull Worth off his erstwhile cohort. Realizing that Worth knew who he was, the Scotland Yard man denounced him for "striking an old man like that." Worth retorted that it "looked to him that Phillips had Greenham there to get him into trouble." With that, Adam Worth dusted off his jacket and left the bar. Like the celebrated Roaring Jack Woodley, Junka Phillips went home in a cart.

The original Napoleon of Crime had an active career well into the 1890s but after a jewel robbery he was arrested and suffered prolonged imprisonment on the Continent. His health shattered, he arranged to give up "The Duchess of Devonshire" to the Pinkertons. He accepted $25,000 as a reward for handing it over and moved to the United States where he retired on the money. He died in 1902.

The Criterion Restaurant has been the location of scenes from films like "Batman, the Dark Knight" and ITV television programs like "William and Mary." Many notable people, such as Winston Churchill, David Lloyd George, H. G. Wells, Helen Mirren, and Russell Crowe have graced its glittering interior. We can justly claim a bit of its fame, as Sherlockians, for Dr. Watson and young Stamford are among the most famous of its patrons.

Watson had to disguise many of the locations in the Canon, leading us a merry chase to find the true site of Baskerville Hall and Musgrave Manor. But he did us all a great service by giving us the Criterion Bar in "A Study in Scarlet." It's a real place in which to bend a real elbow and raise a real glass. The Criterion Bar and Restaurant will exist, on and off the page, as long as Sherlock Holmes and Dr. Watson exist.

At the end of every Seder meal, Jews say "Next year in Jerusalem!" It is a call to remember their history, to work to reach their personal goals, and to express their yearning for their spiritual home. This is the 40th celebration of the founding of the Criterion Bar in Chicago. That is a very notable anniversary for a Sherlockian group and worthy of celebration. Please allow me to say, "Next year at the Criterion!"

'The Jewels of the Agra Treasure, or Honestly, Officer, the Box Was Empty When I Opened It'

In "The Sign of Four" a box filled with jewels was sought by almost every major character in the novel. The Agra treasure consisted of 143 Diamonds, nearly 300 pearls, 97 emeralds, 170 rubies, 40 carbuncles, 210 sapphires, 61 agates, and beryls, onyxes, cat's eyes, turquoises, and an unnumbered amount of other stones. They were probably all cut gems, except for the pearls.

The treasure was kept in a chest of Indian workmanship and of considerable weight. It had no key when the police recovered it from Jonathan Small. Dr. Watson had served in India during the Second Afghanistan War. He identified it as an example of Benares metal-work. Benares is a city in India, situated on the holy river of the Ganges in the north-central part of the sub-continent. The chest had a thick and broad hasp, wrought in the image of a sitting Buddha. The box was massive, well-made and solid, clearly constructed to carry things of great price.

The walls, floor and lid of the container were two-third of an inch thick and made of iron. The actual size of the chest was not given. It was small enough that, while very heavy, Watson could carry it by himself.

This paper gives a short description of the four most valuable kinds of gems described by Small as being part of the Agra treasure contained in the box.

The "Great Mogul" diamond mentioned in the story actually existed. It was found in India in 1650 as a 787 carat rough stone. It was cut and described in 1665 as a high-crowned rose-cut stone. Its owner, Nadar Shah, King of Persia, was assassinated in 1747 and the stone disappeared. Some experts believe it may have been re-cut into either the Orlov Diamond of the Romanov Imperial Jewels or into the Koh-in-noor, now a part of the British Crown Jewels.

Diamonds were said in ancient times to assist the wearer's stomach and brain. They were thought to strengthen the memory. Diamonds supposedly promoted purity, life, joy, innocence, repentance and honesty. The finest diamonds are a clear blue-white colour but they can come in other hues, like yellow or pink.

Diamonds come from Africa, India, Russia, South America and even the United States.

Emeralds are a grass-green variety of beryl. They can be cut in rectangular, round, oval or square shapes. Some are shaped into cabochons. It is the birthstone of Taurus the Bull, April 20 to May 20. They are the gemstones of the 20th, 35th and 55th year of marriage. Ancient emeralds were found in Upper Egypt in 2000 B.C. They were highly prized by Alexander the Great and Cleopatra.

The Moguls, or rulers, of India inscribed sacred texts on large emeralds and wore them as talismans. For their size, emeralds can be more valuable than diamonds.

Emeralds supposedly had many virtues. They were used as antidotes to poison in the Middle Ages. The wearer of an emerald was said to gain wisdom, success in love and constancy of mind. Worn as an amulet, emeralds were thought to give good fortune, and symbolize rebirth and youth.

The Agra treasure emeralds could have come from the Urals, Africa or India itself.

Pearls come from mollusks like freshwater clams or saltwater oysters. They are formed by the mollusk coating a tiny bit of irritant like a grain of sand within the shell with mother-of-pearl, the substance the inner shell is made of. Irregularly-shaped pearls are called baroque pearls. Freshwater pearls have been found in the Mississippi River as well as various inland creeks. Over a short period of time in the late 1800s, three pearls were found in clams in Evansville, WI. Cultured freshwater pearls have been grown in the streams of Bavaria, Australia and the United States.

Man-made or cultured pearls have been made in China for over a thousand years. In the 1890s the Japanese began producing an improved cultured pearl.

Saltwater pearls are called Oriental pearls. They can be cultured or natural pearls. Natural pearls have been found in the Persian Gulf, the waters between India and Sri Lanka, Indonesia and the South Pacific. They have also been found in the ocean off Western Mexico.

Pearls can be cream-colored but also black, rose, grey, blue, yellow, lavender, green and mauve. Pearls are the birthstones of Gemini, May 21 to June 21. A pearl is said to symbolize love, success, and happiness. They are the gemstone for the 1st, 12th and 30th year of marriage.

Rubies are made of corundum, which produces both rubies and sapphires. Large, fine-quality rubies are rare and valuable. They may be cut into mixed-cut ovals or antique cushions if they are lighter-coloured stones. Dark red rubies are made into cabochons or into beads. Only diamonds are harder gemstones.

The name ruby comes from the Latin "ruber" which means red. The best rubies are a deep, pure, vivid red. Gemologists must carefully tell the difference between pinkish, purplish or orangey red rubies and pink, purple or orange sapphires

Rubies are the birthstone for Aries, March 21 to April 19. They supposedly signify primal energy, self-assertiveness, daring, initiative, enterprise and adventure.

During the Middle Ages, a ruby worn on the left hand was thought to bring its owner lands and titles, to bestow virtue and protect against seduction. They were thought to guarantee health, wealth, wisdom and success in love. Some people of India believed possessing a ruby would enable them to live in peace with their enemies.

Rubies are found in Afghanistan, Kenya, Madagascar, Burma, Sri Lanka and Thailand.

The Agra treasure box once held well over a thousand precious jewels. Yet it was more valuable when Dr. Watson and Mary Morstan discovered it was empty. With the gems gone the honest Doctor felt himself free of the taint of fortune hunting and allowed his love for Mary to express itself. Proverbs 31:10 says "Who can find a virtuous woman? For her price is far above rubies." Watson agreed. After his declaration of devotion to the woman he loved was accepted, Watson wrote "Whoever had lost a treasure, I knew that night that I had gained one."

It's a Small Sherlockian World, After All

Many people know the game called "Six Degrees of Kevin Bacon." The purpose of the exercise is to link anyone in Hollywood to the actor Kevin Bacon in as few steps as possible. Since Kevin has appeared in a lot of movies with many other actors, the results usually come in well under six steps.

The game is also known as "Six Degrees of Separation" and can be extended to many other situations involving famous people, including people one knows in real life. For example, I once had a dentist whose cousin married Bill Murray. Bill Murray, on "Saturday Night Live" appeared as Inspector Lestrade in a 1970s skit with Michael Palin as Holmes and Dan Aykroyd as Watson. Gildna Radnor played the client. She married the talented actor Gene Wilder. Gene Wilder worked with Douglas Wilmer in the film "Sherlock Holmes's Smarter Brother." There are only five steps between me and BBC's 1964 Sherlock Holmes.

I set myself an exercise to connect William Gillette, the famous actor and co-author of the stage play "Sherlock Holmes" which was first performed in 1899, to the latest incarnation of the Great Detective in the 2012 television series "Elementary." The game rules were changed to include as many steps as possible and cover as many actors as could be squeezed in. It ended up going something like this (with apologies to Kevin Bacon)....

William Gillette first performed Sherlock Holmes in 1899 in the stage melodrama "Sherlock Holmes" he wrote himself in collaboration with Arthur Conan Doyle. Later an English tour of the play starred H. A. Saintsbury in 1903. Saintsbury later performed in "The Speckled Band," which was written by Doyle, in 1905. In 1916 Gillette put his stage performance on film for Essanay Studios. He became a radio Sherlock Holmes when he voiced Holmes in the 1930 "Speckled Band."

As a one-act curtain-raiser during a later tour of another of his plays Gillette wrote "The Painful Predicament of Sherlock Holmes." As "Billy" Gillette had the services of a young Charles Chaplin, who went on to perform in Hollywood and did very well. Ethel Barrymore appeared as Gwendolyn Cobb in the first performance of "Painful" in 1905. She was the sister of actor John Barrymore, who played Holmes in the 1922 silent film "Sherlock Holmes" based on the Gillette play.

Barrymore's Watson was Roland Young. He later played Uriah Heep in the 1935 MGM movie "David Copperfield." Basil Rathbone played Mr. Murdstone, David's stepfather, in that film. Rathbone played Holmes in the 1939 "Hound of the Baskervilles" which featured Richard Green as Sir Henry.

Green starred in the British television series "The Adventures of Robin Hood," which ran from 1955 to 1959. Also in the cast for most of the 143 episodes was Archie Duncan as Little John, who had played Inspector Lestrade in the 1954-55 TV series "Sherlock Holmes" with Ronald Howard as Holmes. Howard was a guest star on "Robin Hood." Also in the Robin Hood cast was the Sheriff of Nottingham, played by Alan Wheatley, who was given his own Sherlock Holmes series in 1960 by the BBC.

Ronald Howard was backed up by H. Marion Crawford as his Watson. Crawford played Dr. Petrie in the "Brides of Fu Manchu" in 1966 and in "The Vengeance of Fu Manchu" in 1967.with Douglas Wilmer as Nayland Smith.

Douglas Wilmer played Sherlock Holmes in the 1964 BBC television series. He also had a successful film career which included a part in "Anthony and Cleopatra" in 1972 with Eric Porter, who later played Moriarty opposite Jeremy Brett's Holmes in the Granada series episode of "The Final Problem." Wilmer also appeared in "Patton" in 1970 with George C. Scott. Scott later portrayed a man who thought he was Sherlock Holmes in "They Might Be Giants."

Ian Hunter was a frequent guest star in BBC's "The Adventures of Robin Hood." He appeared as Watson in "The Sign of Four" with Arthur Wontner as Holmes in 1932. He was chosen to be Watson for that film because his acting was considered "more romantic" and the plot concerned Watson falling in love with Mary Morstan.

Wontner's regular Watson who appeared in the other four Holmes films between 1931 and 1937 was the actor Ian Fleming. He was Watson in "Murder at the Baskervilles" in 1935 and "The Triumph of Sherlock Holmes" in 1937, both of which starred Lyn Harding as Professor Moriarty.

Arthur Wontner also played Holmes on British Radio in 1943 with Carleton Hobbs as his Watson. Hobbs later played Holmes in another British Radio series during the 1950s and '60s.

Lyn Harding played Dr. Roylott in "Sherlock Holmes and the Speckled Band" with Raymond Massey in 1931. Massey's son, Daniel, appeared as Neil Gibson in the Granada episode of "Thor Bridge" in 1991. He was also the former brother-in-law of star Jeremy Brett, who was married and divorced from his sister Anna years before.

After the Holmes films Arthur Wontner was in the cast of "Thunder in the City" in 1937 along with Nigel Bruce and Ralph Richardson. Richardson later played Watson to John Gielgud's Holmes on BBC Radio's Light Programme in 1954. In the last episode, Orson Welles played Moriarty. Orson Welles had adapted William Gillette's "Sherlock Holmes" to radio in 1938. Gielgud played the Prime Minister in the 1978 "Murder by Decree" with Christopher Plummer as Holmes.

Christopher Plummer played Holmes with Thorley Waters as his Watson in a BBC Television broadcast in 1977. The story reenacted was "Silver Blaze." In 1983 Waters played Major Sholto in Ian Richardson's TV "Sign of Four." Waters played Watson in the 1974 "Sherlock Holmes' Smarter Brother". Lord Redcliff of that film was played by John Le Mesuier who was Barrymore in the 1959 "Hound of the Baskervilles" with Peter Cushing as Holmes.

David Hemmings played Inspector Foxborough in "Murder by Decree" with Plummer as Holmes. Hemmings also played the part of Nigel in "A League of Extraordinary Gentlemen." Richard Roxburgh portrayed Moriarty in "Gentlemen" and later played Sherlock Holmes in the 2002 "Hound of the Baskervilles." His Watson was Ian Hart who performed as Watson in the 2004 TV movie "The Adventure of the Silk Stocking" with Rupert Everett as Holmes.

Roxburgh's "Hound" had Stapleton played by Richard E. Grant, who in 2002 was Mycroft in "Sherlock: Case of Evil." He also played Holmes in the 1992 film "The Other Side" with Frank Finlay as Sir Arthur Conan Doyle.

"Murder by Decree" had Frank Finlay as Lestrade. He appeared as Professor Coram in the Granada series episode "The Golden Pince-Nez" in 1994. His son Daniel played the Russian Vladimir. That episode also had Charles Grey guest-starring as Mycroft Holmes.

Charles Grey played Mycroft Holmes in four Granada/Jeremy Brett episodes. They were "The Greek Interpreter," "The Bruce-Partington Plans," "The Golden Pince-Nez," and "The Mazarin Stone." He appeared first as Mycroft in the film "The Seven-Percent Solution" with Nicol Williamson in 1976. Laurence Olivier, a friend of Douglas Wilmer, was Moriarty in that film. Grey was the villain Blofeld in "Diamonds Are Forever" with Roger Moore.

Moore played Holmes in "Sherlock Holmes in New York" in 1976 with Patrick Macnee as his Watson. In that TV film Moriarty was played by John Huston, whose father Walter was reputed to be the Holmes in the 30-second 1900 silent movie "Sherlock Holmes Baffled," the Great Detective's first appearance on film.

In the Granada/Jeremy Brett series Colin Jeavons portrayed Inspector Lestrade six times. Jeavons played Moriarty in the 1983 BBC TV series "Baker Street Boys," a series centered on the Baker Street Irregulars, Holmes' "unofficial police force." Dr. Watson in that series was played by Hubert Rees who was Lestrade in Tom Baker's TV "Hound of the Baskervilles" in 1982.

Between 1939 and 1946 Basil Rathbone made a total of fourteen Sherlock Holmes with Nigel Bruce as Watson and they did over 200 Holmes/Watson radio plays. A short audio clip from one of his radio plays, "The Adventure of the Red-Headed League," was inserted into Disney's 1986 "Great Mouse Detective" as the voice of Sherlock Holmes.

In one Rathbone/Bruce movie, the 1946 "Terror by Night", the actor Alan Mowbray was cast as Watson's old friend Duncan Bleek. Mowbray portrayed Holmes's friend Inspector King-Gore in the 1932 "Sherlock Holmes" with Clive Brook. Brook's Watson, Reginald Denny, portrayed Holmes in the 1933 "Study in Scarlet." Billy Bevan had a part in that movie and later appeared in the Basil Rathbone/Nigel Bruce film "Terror by Night" in 1946.

In the Rathbone/Bruce film "Sherlock Holmes Faces Death," Peter Lawford played a British sailor in a pub. He later played Sherlock Holmes in an episode of "Fantasy Island", which ran on television from 1978 to 1984.

The second son of an English baronet, Nigel Bruce was popular in Hollywood, where he lived for many years. One of his friends was the actor Cedric Hardwicke who played Holmes in a radio play based on "The Speckled Band" and broadcast from Liverpool in 1945. During the '30s and '40s Hardwicke often entertained Nigel Bruce at his Hollywood home, where Bruce met Edward Hardwicke, Cedric's son.

Edward Hardwicke played Sir Arthur Conan Doyle in the film "Photographing Fairies" in 1997. He was the second Dr. Watson for eight years in the Jeremy Brett/Granada series. In 1994 he portrayed Dr. Watson in the episode "The Dying Detective" with Susannah Harker who played Mrs. Savage. In 1979 Susannah Harker played Irene St. Clair in the film "Crucifer of Blood" with Charleton Heston as Holmes.

Also in the cast of "Crucifer of Blood" was Simon Callow as Lestrade. He was Holmes on radio in 1993 in the series "The Unopened Casebook of Sherlock Holmes" in Britain.

In "Crucifer of Blood" the part of Major Alistair Ross was played by Edward Fox, who played Dr. Watson in "Dr. Watson and the Darkwater Hall Mystery" in 1974.

"The Crucifer of Blood" started as a play on Broadway in 1978. In that production Dwight Schultz portrayed Major Alistair Ross. In 1980-81 the "Crucifer of Blood" was put on in Los Angeles and had Heston as Holmes, Brett as Watson and Schultz again as Major Ross.

Charleton Heston played "Chinese" Gordon in "Khartoum" in 1966 with Douglas Wilmer. Gordon was an actual person who was mentioned in one of the stories from the Sherlock Holmes Canon. Heston played the title role in the film "Antony and Cleopatra" in 1959 which also featured Andre Morell. Morell was Dr. Watson to Peter Cushing's Sherlock Holmes in the 1959 Hammer "Hound of the Baskervilles." Cushing played Holmes in the BBC 1968 TV series "Sherlock Holmes." His Watson was Nigel Stock, who had also played Watson in the 1965 series with Douglas Wilmer. Stock performed in "Young Sherlock Holmes" as the inventor Professor Waxflatter. He was Holmes in the 1983-84 play "221B" that was recorded for BBC Radio in 1986.

Freddie Jones also appeared in the film "Antony and Cleopatra." He later played parts in the Granada/Jeremy Brett series episodes "Wisteria Lodge" in 1987 and "The Last Vampyre" in 1993.

Douglas Wilmer, who also had a part in "Antony and Cleopatra," played Sherlock Holmes in the 1964-65 BBC Television series. The episode "The Illustrious Client" featured Peter Wyngarde as Baron Gruner. Wyngarde was Langdale Pike in "The Three Gables" in the Granada/Jeremy Brett series. The same Wilmer series featured David Burke as Sir George Burnwell in "The Beryl Coronet."

David Burke was the first Dr. Watson in the Granada series with Jeremy Brett. His real-life wife, Anna Calder-Marshall appeared in "The Eligible Bachelor" of that series in the part of Agnes Northcote/Lady Helene.

The Granada "Sherlock Holmes" ran from 1984 to 1994 with Jeremy Brett as Holmes for the entire series. Jeremy Brett and Edward Hardwicke played Holmes and Watson on the stage in "The Secret of Sherlock Holmes" which ran for a year in London in 1988.

In 1994 Jeremy Brett was Holmes in "Shoscombe Old Place" with Jude Law playing Joe Barnes. Law was Watson to Robert Downey, Jr.'s Holmes in the 2009 and 2011 "Sherlock Holmes" movies. In 2009 David Burke played The Gravedigger to Jude Law's Hamlet on stage in London.

Robert Downey Jr. had played Charlie Chaplin in a 1992 film biography of the young actor who had been hired by William Gillette to play Billy in the London production of the stage play "Sherlock Holmes." Also in the cast was John Thaw as Fred Karno. Thaw portrayed Jonathan Small in the Granada/Jeremy Brett episode of "The Sign of Four".

In 1993 Heather Chasen portrayed the Honorable Amelia St.

Simon in the Sherlock Holmes/Granada series episode "The Eligible Bachelor" with Brett as Holmes. She had previously portrayed Aunt Rachel, the unpleasant relative of Guy Henry's Sherlock Holmes in the 1982 TV production "Young Sherlock, The Mystery of the Manor House".

Jonathan Pryce played Culverton Smith in the Granada/Jeremy Brett episode "The Dying Detective." He later portrayed Sherlock Holmes in the BBC TV program "Sherlock Holmes and the Baker Street Irregulars" in 2007.

William Gillette's play "Sherlock Holmes" was revived in 1976 by The Royal Shakespeare Company. When it came to the United States and appeared in New York Holmes was played by (among others) John Neville, who in 1965 portrayed Holmes in the movie "A Study in Terror." Frank Finlay played Lestrade for the first time and Anthony Quayle played Dr. Murray. Quayle was Sir Charles Warren in the 1979 film "Murder by Decree".

Robert Stephens was also Holmes in the RSC New York "Sherlock Holmes." In 1970 he played Holmes in Billy Wilder's "The Private Life of Sherlock Holmes." Irene Handl played Mrs. Hudson in that film and later was Mrs. Barrymore in Peter Cook's "Hound of the Baskervilles." Christopher Lee appeared as Mycroft in the film "The Private Life of Sherlock Holmes."

Christopher Lee was Holmes in the 1991 TV series "Sherlock Holmes: The Golden Years" which included "The Incident at Victoria Falls" with Patrick Macnee as Watson. Joss Ackland played the King in that and portrayed Jephro Rucastle in Granada's "The Copper Beeches." Natasha Richardson played Violet Hunter in "The Copper Beeches" episode. Her mother, Vanessa Redgrave, portrayed Lola Deveraux in the movie "The Seven Percent Solution" with Nicol Williamson in 1976.

Patrick Macnee appeared on a fourth-season "Magnum, P.I."

episode in the 1980s as an old friend of Jonathon Quayle Higgins. He believed he was Holmes and Higgins (John Hillerman) was Watson. In 1991 John Hillerman later appeared as Watson with Edward Woodward's Holmes in "Hands of a Murderer." Macnee also played Holmes in the TV film "Hound of London" in 1993.

"Sherlock Holmes and the Deadly Necklace" was the title of Christopher Lee's first Sherlock Holmes movie, released in 1962. Thorley Waters was his Watson. Lee also appeared in Peter Cushing's 1959 "Hound of the Baskervilles" as Sir Henry Baskerville.

Douglas Wilmer and Thorley Waters appeared in "Sherlock Holmes' Smarter Brother." Leo McKern played Moriarty in that movie. Later on McKern had his own television series "Rumpole of the Bailey". Several of his featured cast members also appeared on the Granada "Sherlock Holmes" series. Those included Julian Curry as Dr. Schlessenger, Patricia Hodges as Lady Hilda Trelawney Hope, and Dennis Lill as Inspector Bradstreet. Lill played Watson in the 1979 London stage production of "Crucifer of Blood."

"Sherlock Holmes' Smarter Brother" had Roy Kinnear as Sigerson's housekeeper. Kinnear portrayed Ethel Selden in Peter Cook's 1976 "Hound of the Baskervilles."

Thorley Walters played Major Sholto in the 1983 BBC TV film "Sign of Four" with Ian Richardson as Holmes. Richardson also helped expand the Sherlockian universe in 2000-2001 by appearing as Dr. Joseph Bell in the series "Murder Rooms."

Richardson played "The Priest" in "Man of La Mancha" with Peter O'Toole. O'Toole voiced Holmes in four cartoon depictions of the Sherlock Holmes novels in 1984 for Pacific Arts of Australia.

Richardson also played Hamlet in the Gravedigger scene in an episode of the 1969 "Kenneth Clark's Civilization" TV program. Horatio was played by Patrick Stewart who later appeared as Captain

Jean-Luc Picard in the TV series "Star Trek: The Next Generation." His co-star Brent Spiner portrayed the advanced android Data who played Sherlock Holmes on the Holodeck during two episodes of the science fiction show.

The Royal Shakespeare Company's revival of William Gillette's "Sherlock Holmes" toured the United States during the late 1970s. Two of the actors playing Holmes were Frank Langella and Leonard Nimoy. In 1981 Langella made an HBO movie of the play. Dwight Schultz played Bassick and Susan Clark was Marge Larrabee. She later appeared as Annie Chapman in "Murder by Decree".

Leonard Nimoy was a veteran of the original "Star Trek" TV series from 1966 to 1968 and portrayed Mr. Spock in the 1991 Star Trek motion picture "The Undiscovered Country." In one scene he mentioned that "an ancestor of mine" had remarked that "Once you have eliminated the impossible, whatever remained, however improbable, must be the truth."

Ian Richardson's version of "The Hound of the Baskervilles" had Denholm Elliot as Dr. Mortimer. Elliot also portrayed Stapleton in Peter Cook's 1978 "Hound of the Baskervilles" with Cook as Holmes. In 1988 Peter Cook played Norman Greenhough, publisher of the magazine "The Strand" in "Without a Clue" with Michael Caine portraying the Sherlock Holmes character. Ben Kingsley, who played Dr. Watson in "Without a Clue," played Reverend Templeton in "Photographing Fairies" with Edward Hardwicke as Conan Doyle.

Richardson's "Hound of the Baskervilles" had Connie Booth as Laura Lyons. She played Mrs. Hudson/Moriarty with John Cleese as Holmes in the 1977 TV film "The End of Civilization as We Know It." John also played Holmes in "Elementary, My Dear Watson" during an episode of the Comedy Playhouse in 1973.

Ronald Howard's 1954-55 Sherlock Holmes TV series was

produced by Sheldon Reynolds. Reynolds also produced "Sherlock Holmes and Doctor Watson," a similar series filmed in 1979-80 in Poland and starring Geoffrey Whitehead as Holmes. "The same name was taken as the first title of a TV series produced by the Russian studio Lenfilm from 1979 to 1986. It starred Vasily Livanov as Sherlock Holmes and Vitaly Solomin as Doctor Watson.

BBC Radio 4 has broadcast a series called "The Further Adventures of Sherlock Holmes" since 2002. Geoffrey Whitehead played Col. Upwood in one of the episodes and Roy Hudd played James Phillimore in another. Hudd had appeared as John Gedgrave in the Granada series "The Dying Detective".

John Wood portrayed Holmes in the Royal Shakespeare Company's "Sherlock Holmes" New York production. He was in the 1971 film "Nicholas and Alexander" with Rasputin played by Tom Baker. Baker played Dr. Who on the BBC from 1974 to 1981. He played a Holmes-like Dr. Who in the 1977 "Talons of Wei-Chiang." In 1982 Baker portrayed Sherlock Holmes in the TV series "Hound of the Baskervilles." In 1985 he appeared in the stage play "Masks of Moriarty." Baker later appeared as Collington Smith on radio in an episode of "The Further Adventures of Sherlock Holmes."

The Dr. Who franchise produced a later Dr. Who companion, Captain Jack Harkness, played by John Barrowman. In 2006 he headed up a Dr. Who spin-off program, "Torchwood." One of the members of the cast of "Torchwood" for the first three years was Gareth David-Lloyd. He played Doctor Watson in The Asylum production of "Sir Arthur Conan Doyle's Sherlock Holmes" in 2010. Yes, it's the one with the dinosaur. It really isn't that bad.

"The Further Adventures of Sherlock Holmes" radio show also starred actor/writer Mark Gatiss as Bert Stevens. He was an experienced writer for Dr. Who. He appeared as Mycroft Holmes in the 2010 BBC TV series "Sherlock". He also wrote and co-produced this "new Holmes for the 21st century" series with Steven Moffatt and helped to cast Benedict Cumberbatch and Martin Freeman as Sherlock Holmes and Doctor Watson. During the second season of "Sherlock," Douglas Wilmer, who appeared in the BBC 1964 "Adventures of Sherlock Holmes" TV program, appeared as a Diogenes' Club member horrified by Watson's talking out loud in the club during "The Reichenbach Fall." That series continues on PBS's Masterpiece Mystery series.

The Robert Downey Jr. movie series "Sherlock Holmes" with Jude Law as Dr. Watson also continues with the film "Sherlock Holmes: A Game of Shadows." The Columbia Broadcast System broadcast a 2012 American series called "Elementary" starring Jonny Lee Miller as Holmes. Early in his career Miller formed a film and theatre production company with Jude Law and others. In the summer of 2011, he alternated in the roles of Dr. Frankenstein and the Creature with Benedict Cumberbatch of "Sherlock" on the London stage.

The saga of the movies, stage plays, radio plays, video games, television episodes, YouTube films and podcasts of the Great Detective has a long and varied history and a vibrant and interesting future. Over the coming years and decades (might we think centuries?) more manifestations of Holmes and Watson will appear, based loosely or firmly on the original stories of the Canon. This exercise of linking many actors to his service is admittedly incomplete. Everyone is invited to add their own information to the "Six Degrees" game. May the final piece never be placed into position.

References
The Television Sherlock Holmes by Peter Haining (Virgin Books, third revised edition 1994)
Starring Sherlock Holmes by David Stuart Davies (Titan

Books, revised edition 2007)

Stage Whispers by Douglas Wilmer (Porter Press International 2009)

IMDb on the Internet

How Much Is That Hound Dog In The Window?

Set: A counter (table, lectern) positioned perpendicular to the audience in the center of a small stage. A sign reading "Sherman's Pet Shop" is taped to the end facing the audience. The background is neutral. A bell is on the counter. CHLOE has an emery board.

Actors: One man and one woman. He is JACK STAPLETON, dressed in an overcoat and soft-brimmed hat. He is determined to make this purchase. The woman is CHLOE, casually dressed in a teen-age fashion. Her hair is piled on her head in an untidy bunch and she is chewing gum. She is bored and wishes she were anywhere else.

The scene opens with CHLOE standing behind the counter stage right and filing her nails with an emery board. STAPLETON enters stage left and walks up to the counter.

STAPLETON : Hello, miss. I want to buy a dog.

CHLOE ignores him.

STAPLETON: (Louder) Hello, miss, I want to buy a dog. (No response) Miss, I want to buy a dog!

CHLOE motions to bell. STAPLETON stares at her then rings the bell.

CHLOE puts down the emery board and takes a deep breath, as if preparing for an ordeal. She speaks in a bored nasal voice. Throughout the skit, she never gets excited.

CHLOE: (In a monotone and by rote) Hello-sir-Welcome-to-Sherman's-Pet-Shop-located-in-Pinchen-Lane-London-My-name-is-Chloe-How-may-I-serve-you?

STAPLETON: Like I said three times, I want to buy a dog.

CHLOE: What sort of dog, Mr....?

STAPLETON: Stapleton, Jack Stapleton. I want a hound. It's got to be a hound. I want one that can track a man across the moors.

CHLOE: The moors, sir? Where are these moors?

STAPLETON: In Devonshire. The hound needs to sure-footed and able to run fast.

CHLOE: We've got a lot of hounds in the back room, sir. Marty can bring out whatever you choose. Perhaps what you want is a greyhound. They run fast.

STAPLETON: No, not a greyhound. I want something that will hunt.

CHLOE: A pack of twenty foxhounds could track a man across the moors. I could give you a quantity discount. Twenty animals, complete with collars, a month's supply of dog food and all their shots, for the price of seventeen. You would have to arrange transportation.

STAPLETON: No, no! That's not what I want. I want a hound!

CHLOE: A basset hound? They are very intelligent and sooo cute. There is one in the back called Pickles.

STAPLETON: Miss, please listen to me. I have come here all the way from Devonshire to buy a hound. I have only a few hours. I have to catch the train at Victoria Station later to get back home before I'm missed by my wi—sister. What other hounds do you have in the back?

CHLOE: There is a bloodhound, sir.

STAPLETON: No bloodhound. There can't be any mention of blood. It's supposed to look like natural causes.

CHLOE: What?

STAPLETON: Never mind. No bloodhound. What else do you have?

CHLOE: There is a basenji from Africa. They are known as very fast runners.

STAPLETON: Basenjis don't bark, do they?

CHLOE: No.

STAPLETON: That won't do. I need something that can send long, haunting, scary howls echoing across the moor in the dark of night to terrify the peasants and worry the people of the Manor. I'd like it to be the size of a large calf.

CHLOE: (Misunderstands) The size of a large cat? I've got just the thing. A dachshund named Pierre. I'll have Marty bring it out.

STAPLETON: No, no, no! (Takes a deep breath. This is harder than he expected.) Miss, I want a dog that will strike horror into the hearts of everyone who sees it.

CHLOE: Then you want a Chinese Crested dog. Believe me, those things are ugly. It's enough to give a person nightmares.

STAPLETON: I want a Hound!

CHLOE: All right, sir. Here at Sherman's Pet Shop we pride

ourselves on satisfying our customers. Now, let me think. (She thinks, screwing up her face and putting her hand to her forehead while staring out into the audience. She continues to chew her gum.)

STAPLETON (Waits, and waits and waits. He is tense, almost ready to explode in frustration. Finally…) Miss, perhaps I should look somewhere else.

CHLOE (snaps out of her trance.) Oh, no, sir, I'm sure we have what you want here at Sherman's Pet Shop. How about an Afghan hound?

STAPLETON: No, no. For once, there are no Afghans in this story.

CHLOE: If you want a big dog, I have an Irish Wolfhound.

STAPLETON: That's more like it.

CHLOE: There is only one problem. It only hunts Irish wolves. And they're extinct. How about an Otterhound? Oh, it has the same problem.

STAPLETON: It only hunts Irish wolves?

CHLOE: No, sir, what a silly idea. It only hunts otters. You don't have an otter problem on the moor, do you?

STAPLETON: Otter than trying to get my hound, no.

CHLOE: We do have a Norwegian Elkhound. But…(Her voice trails off.)

STAPLETON: Let me guess. It only hunts elk.

CHLOE: Norwegian elk. (Eagerly) But it's very good at it.

STAPLETON (Finally cracks.) Look, lady, all I want is the fiercest, nastiest, loudest and most dangerous beast you can give me!

CHLOE (Perks up.) Well, why didn't you say so? (Turns and calls to the back room) Marty, bring out the Pekingese!

STAPLETON (Throws up his hands, grips his hat and pulls it further down over his head, and quickly exits stage left.)

CHLOE: (Again, in a monotone and by rote) Thank-you-sir-for-visiting-Sherman's-Pet-Shop-where-all-your-pet-needs-can-be-met-please-come-again-good-day. (She goes back to her emery board and nails.)

My Correspondence with Vincent Starrett

In 1966 I was just a baby Sherlockian, 16 years old, living on a farm in northern Illinois. I had received a copy of the one-volume "Complete Sherlock Holmes" from some friends for Christmas in December, 1965. By the New Year I was converted. I developed a keen eye for anything Holmes-related. The pickings were pretty thin, since no one around me was in the least interested in the Great Detective.

Every Sunday my father would pick us up from Sunday school and get a copy of the Chicago Tribune newspaper at the local drug store in Hebron. Suddenly, I noticed that in the Arts and Leisure Section a column would run occasionally that mentioned Sherlock Holmes. It was called "Books Alive" and was written by a man called Vincent Starrett.

I started a scrapbook and clipped out the columns. In the course of the year I collected five articles. An undated column of "Books Alive" spoke of Chris Redmond's editing of the Baker Street Pageboys magazine and of the New York City Baker Street Irregular Birthday Dinner. In March of 1966 the column was a review of the Sherlock Holmes vs. Jack the Ripper movie "A Study in Terror." In April there was a review of the parody stories collected in Robert L. Fish's "The Incredible Schlock Homes."

July brought comments about Christopher Isherwood and his book "Exhumations." Isherwood had written a new introduction to the Sherlock Holmes story "The Speckled Band." Isherwood referred to Holmes as "a comic character" and Starrett summed up Isherwood as "talking through his hat."

In November Vincent Starrett gave a review of Katherine Greenleaf Pedley's brochure titled "Moriarty in the Stacks", about the book forger Thomas J. Wise. The man practiced his nefarious skills during the 1880s and '90s, the same time as Sherlock Holmes was available to investigate the case.

I wrote to Vincent Starrett in care of the Chicago Tribune. I didn't keep copies of my letters, but I kept his replies. The first letter I wrote mentioned that I wanted to start a group called "The Baker Street Collection." I also asked about the Baker Street Irregulars and asked for a copy of his poem "221-b." The reply came on a hand-written plain postcard with my farm address on the front under a 4-cent Abraham Lincoln stamp.

3749 N. Fremont St---
Chicago, Ill. 60613

Dear Gayle---
You are now
a member of the B.S.I.
I have just made you
one of us. Good wishes!
I like the name you
have selected for your
group. I'll be glad
to send you a copy
of 221b; just give
me a few days! I'll
pass your letter on to
the head of our Chicago
group.
   My best to you all!
Vincent Starrett

One odd thing I noticed about his writing was that he circled every period at the end of sentences but not the periods in the B.S.I. reference. Every period was double-struck, like this – ..

The letter I received later was typewritten and double spaced on a plain sheet of white paper and must have arrived in a large manila envelope because there is no sign that it was ever folded.

3749 North Fremont Street

Chicago, Ill. 60613

4August 1966

Dear Gayle:

Delighted to welcome the BAKER STREET COLLECTION to the Baker

Street Irregulars. You are now one of us! I do this by fiat, with the

approval of the organization. To register your group, write a letter

to Julian Wolff, M.D., editor of the Baker Street Journal, 33 Riverside

Drive, New York, N.Y., 10023, telling him about your club, and about

our correspondence—yours and mine. There are no dues that I know

anything about; but Dr. Wolff may ask you to subscribe to the Journal,

which is a quarterly magazine of Sherlockiana that you would enjoy.

I don't know the statistics of our organization now; but the membership is larger than your brother thinks; or so I believe.

I am glad to send you a printed copy of my sonnet 221-B that

I happen to have on hand. I sign it for you with pleasure. It was

printed, you will note, for one of our Oklahoma members.

Let me know how you come out with the good Dr. Wolff! And thank

you for your letter.

Canonically yours

(signature)

Vincent Starrett

Gayle Lange, B.S.I.
11301 Lange Rd.
Hebron, Illinois

Sorry about the delay in answering your letter!

The "Oklahoma member" was John Bennett Shaw.

I have no other correspondence from Vincent Starrett but I did send him an invitation to my high school graduation in 1967.

The Toast to the Master

We gather together to honor the Master.
We come from afar just to congregate here.
We come here by aeroplane, by taxicab and boat train
To salute him with a toast for another great year.

He says he's retired now and yet we still need him.
We think of him often, yes, he and his friend.
Those two men as a beacon, our faith will never weaken,
For they both are forever
World without end.

Also from Gayle Puhl

Sherlock Holmes The Folk Tale Mysteries – Volume 1

Jewel thefts, missing persons, even murder are all elements in the world of the great detective Sherlock Holmes. What connects the stories in this book is that the cases he and his biographer Dr. John H. Watson investigate are based on adventures beloved of childhood. In a novel twist to the usual Holmes pastiches, Mrs. Puhl has based her plots involving Mr. Sherlock Holmes on folk tales, nursery rhymes and other snippets of children's literature. She has brought them into the Victorian era and kept them true to the expectations for Holmesian stories. But these are not children's tales. There are no talking rabbits, no flying carpets or magic wands. There is not always a happy ending. They are all grounded in the logical world of Holmes and Watson.

Also from Gayle Puhl

Sherlock Holmes The Folk Tale Mysteries – Volume 2

A home invasion results in property damage. Children disappear and a disgruntled ex-employee is suspected. Girl visits relative, walks in on scene of carnage. A man searches for days, seeking his lost love. A young woman accuses her father's wife of attempted murder. Dramatic news from CNN? Stories ripped from today's headlines? No, they are cases investigated by Mr. Sherlock Holmes and his intrepid companion and biographer, Dr. John H. Watson. Drawn into the dark underbelly of folk tale reality, Holmes and Watson travel the streets of London and into the far English countryside to discover the truth about some of the most famous accounts found in childhood literature.

Also from Gayle Puhl

Gayle's story, The Case of The Cursed Clock, is one of thirteen to appear in the 4th 'Art of Sherlock Holmes' book, with an amazing piece of art created from the story by American artist Diego Perez.

The piece is also available as an authenticated print from The Conan Doyle Estate Shop.

https://shop.conandoyleestate.com/products/46-the-case-of-the-cursed-clock

MX Publishing

MX Publishing brings the best in new Sherlock Holmes novels, biographies, graphic novels and short story collections every month. With over 400 books it's the largest catalogue of new Sherlock Holmes books in the world.

We have over one hundred and fifty Holmes authors. The majority of our authors write new Holmes fiction - in all genres from very traditional pastiches through to modern novels, fantasy, crossover, children's books and humour.

In Holmes biography we have award winning historians including Alistair Duncan, Paul R Spiring, and Brian W Pugh

MX Publishing also has one of the largest communities of Holmes fans on Facebook and Twitter under @mxpublishing.

www.mxpublishing.com

Also from MX Publishing

Our bestselling books are our short story collections;

'Lost Stories of Sherlock Holmes' , 'The Outstanding Mysteries of Sherlock Holmes', The Papers of Sherlock Holmes Volume 1 and 2, 'Untold Adventures of Sherlock Holmes' (and the sequel 'Studies in Legacy) and 'Sherlock Holmes in Pursuit', 'The Cotswold Werewolf and Other Stories of Sherlock Holmes' – and many more……

www.mxpublishing.com

Also from MX Publishing

"Phil Growick's, 'The Secret Journal of Dr Watson', is an adventure which takes place in the latter part of Holmes and Watson's lives. They are entrusted by HM Government (although not officially) and the King no less to undertake a rescue mission to save the Romanovs, Russia's Royal family from a grisly end at the hand of the Bolsheviks. There is a wealth of detail in the story but not so much as would detract us from the enjoyment of the story. Espionage, counter-espionage, the ace of spies himself, double-agents, double-crossers...all these flit across the pages in a realistic and exciting way. All the characters are extremely well-drawn and Mr Growick, most importantly, does not falter with a very good ear for Holmesian dialogue indeed. Highly recommended. A five-star effort."

The Baker Street Society

www.mxpublishing.com

Also from MX Publishing

The Missing Authors Series

Sherlock Holmes and The Adventure of The Grinning Cat
Sherlock Holmes and The Nautilus Adventure
Sherlock Holmes and The Round Table Adventure

"Joseph Svec, III is brilliant in entwining two endearing and enduring classics of literature, blending the factual with the fantastical; the playful with the pensive; and the mischievous with the mysterious. We shall, all of us young and old, benefit with a cup of tea, a tranquil afternoon, and a copy of Sherlock Holmes, The Adventure of the Grinning Cat."
Amador County Holmes Hounds Sherlockian Society

www.mxpublishing.com

Also from MX Publishing

The American Literati Series

The Final Page of Baker Street
The Baron of Brede Place
Seventeen Minutes To Baker Street

"The really amazing thing about this book is the author's ability to call up the 'essence' of both the Baker Street 'digs' of Holmes and Watson as well as that of the 'mean streets' of Marlowe's Los Angeles. Although none of the action takes place in either place, Holmes and Watson share a sense of camaraderie and self-confidence in facing threats and problems that also pervades many of the later tales in the Canon. Following their conversations and banter is a return to Edwardian England and its certainties and hope for the future. This is definitely the world before The Great War."
Philip K Jones

www.mxpublishing.com